ALEX HOEFT

Who We Thought We Were

Cover design by Roderick Brydon, klrcovers.com.

First edition

ISBN: 979-8-9986059-0-1

For those who value their friendships so much it hurts.

And, of course, my favorite people, from A to Z.

Chapter 1

J osie is twelve minutes late, and if Adam were here, he wouldn't
bat an eye.

"You run about nine minutes behind, on average," he once told
her, after a month of careful calculation.

"That's nine minutes of anticipation, dude," she replied.

On her second lap around the block, Josie spots the house, hurriedly
pulling into the single driveway on a corner of Valley Street. She
eyes the two-story as she exits the car, with its bright, white-washed
walls and terracotta roof shingles, its numerous arched windows and
well-kept yard. It's the kind of residence people pass on the street and
wonder what the owners do for a living, how they're able to afford
such a spacious place in San Francisco, the city of squished and stacked
homes slanted along hilly streets.

Josie isn't wondering; she's focused on becoming the tenant.

She stalks up the front path, pulling her hair into a ponytail as she
goes. A pretentious brass knocker is centered on the sturdy slab of a
front door. Josie uses it with a smirk.

Immediately, the door is opened by a woman who gives Josie a tight
smile, tablet secured under one arm. "Josephine?"

"Call me Josie. But, yeah. Hey."

The woman doesn't say anything further, only steps back to grant
entry, dark eyes on Josie's admittedly harried appearance, which is

in high contrast to her own look: hair that's been gelled back into a ponytail at the nape of her neck and a purple pantsuit cut to embrace her femininity.

Josie takes in the entryway. Black and white marbled tiles checker the floor, leading to a staircase. On the right is a closed door, painted black, stark against the white walls. Lining the left wall of the entryway sits an emerald green velvet vanity bench and a large potted plant, its leafy foliage rippling to the steady flow of A/C. There's another door, also black, also closed. It's like the entrance to a museum, and Josie stifles the urge to whisper.

She takes another step forward, close enough to catch a hint of something flowery from the woman's perfume. "So you're my roommate? Potentially?" she asks, gaze tracing the rectangular moldings on the walls.

"No. I'm Evelyn, Ramona's assistant." A small chime sounds, and she glances at her watch. "And I need to leave by 1:30."

Josie lifts an eyebrow, but nods and follows Evelyn, now moving swiftly, diagonally clipping across the floor in black heels.

"This is the entryway, obviously. And that," Evelyn says, with a jut of her chin to the door on the right, "is Ramona's room."

Opening the door on the left, she glances back, her eyes flitting down to Josie's Converses and back up. Josie gives her a wide smile in return, cheeks aching with the falsehood. She wants this bad enough to not purposely mess it up.

The black and white tiling extends down a hallway. "Closet, bathroom, fitness room," Evelyn says. "Door at the end leads out to the garage and patio."

Josie moves past her, touching a finger lightly to the textured wall.

"If you could not," Evelyn says, voice sharp. Josie drops her hand but doesn't look back.

The fitness room is home to a stationary bike, rack of weights, and

2

treadmill. Through its window, parked in the driveway, is Adam's Subaru—Josie's borrowed steel chariot for the summer. She wanders farther down the hall and glides her hand across the tops of the washer and dryer, a sleek black pair of front-loading units; not a speck of dust. As she returns, she asks, "Utilities are included in the rent, right?"

Evelyn, scrolling on the tablet and wrist jangling numerous gold bracelets, pushes from the wall with her hip and says, "Yes. Ready to head upstairs?" She turns without waiting for a reply, clearly uninterested in small talk—which, fine. Josie wouldn't be either in any situation other than this one.

At the top of the stairs is a wide, arched entryway to the kitchen, but Evelyn moves to the right, down a hall. "Bathroom and closet," she ticks off as she passes them, "and where you would stay." She stops just to the left of an open door. Josie enters, knowing what she'll find based on the listing's photos.

The bedroom is simple, but it is everything—and more so in person. Where Josie's basement room in the Bernal Heights neighborhood is small, gray, and void of sunlight, this one is bright white, sunshine pouring through the windows framing a reading nook. The bed in Bernal, a twin she'd haggled for on Craigslist; here, a king-sized mattress she could swim in, float on, drown beneath its duvet. A desk topped with a domed golden lamp and a box for keepsakes. A plush rug across the floor. A closet she could cartwheel across.

She's already spent hours picturing living in this room—manifesting it, praying to all the gods, prepared to perform witchcraft to call this place home. She can see herself typing out a story on her laptop at the desk, or lying across the bed with a textbook in hand, highlighter between her teeth. And at the bench seat, the sprawl of Adam, nose buried in a book.

She crosses to the windows. The patio below; a collection of outdoor seating and plants fills the space.

Josie purses her lips, thinking of her current corner of the city, with its five-square-foot patch of yellow grass she and her roommate claim as a yard-slash-garbage can stash.

"Josephine?" Evelyn calls from down the hall.

"Josie," she corrects as she follows the voice to the kitchen. When she enters, she asks, "Does Ramona own this place?"

Evelyn leans against a counter and says primly, "Her father does."

"And if I wanted to stay longer than a year, is that possible?" For the price and space, Josie may want to stay forever.

She swears Evelyn almost laughs. "I seriously doubt it."

Josie forces a stiff smile in return, acts like it's funny. "Why does Ramona even need a roommate if her dad owns the house?"

But Evelyn's clearly given up on Josie, back on her tablet, with occasional pings from her watch. Josie waits for an extended moment, then turns her attention to the remaining rooms, each as grand as the rest of the house.

The fact that Josie's current abode—where she shares a room with a thirty-seven-year-old woman named Feather—and this place can exist in the same city isn't surprising. She's been covering real estate for her internship all summer, the highest of highs and lowest of lows in terms of California living. She and Adam often joke about the financial successes needed to afford a luxurious life in the Bay; "Do you think that person is regular rich or San Francisco rich?"

What *is* surprising is that this new place, while many times nicer, is half as expensive as her current rent. She's somehow tapped into the grid, beaten the simulation to find this place. She's finally stood out in the cosmic scheme of the universe.

She supposes she has Feather to thank for that. Two weeks before, Josie came home to find her roommate had cut up the pages of Josie's new textbooks to create fanned cutout displays of what Feather said was supposed to be a butterfly in one and a heart in another. She'd

4

planned to sell them, the latest craft she wanted to get good enough at to find buyers for on Etsy. That's what Feather proudly told Josie as she presented the origami from hell. Josie can still barely stand to look in the direction of her roommate, her rage not at all sated by the yelling match that followed the grand reveal.

The next morning, she'd signed up for housing notifications. The act was nothing more than an attempt to establish a light at the end of the tunnel. She hadn't expected to jump on any listings. Gas, food, a way of life were only getting more and more expensive. Even with money saved up through her summer internship, it was hard to argue with the inexpensive cost of her current apartment.

The notification popped up last Wednesday. Student-only, fully furnished private room, three hundred dollars a month, Noe Valley neighborhood, one roommate. *Scam*, Josie immediately thought as she tapped the link. The pictures showed a luxurious opportunity. Rooms decorated as if they were being featured in a magazine that Josie wasn't rich enough to do anything more than drool over. A beautiful, beautiful scam. She applied anyway.

Then she was talking to an actual property management representative who said she was a prime candidate and would she like to tour the place before signing? Measuring up was not Josie's usual MO. She jumped in head-first.

Josie returns to the entryway with Evelyn, who says, "If you're still interested, contact the management company to finalize things. I believe they're holding it for twenty-four hours for you to make a decision."

Josie can't help but expect a catch. "Can you tell me about Ramona?" she asks. "What it would be like to live with her and stuff?"

Evelyn, who has to have scrolled at least a mile on her tablet since Josie showed up, finally looks up. "'What it would be like'?" she repeats slowly.

Josie manages to not roll her eyes. "Is she nice? Funny? A baker? A good friend?"

"Ramona Taylor is not my friend, she's my boss."

"Is she a good *person*?" Josie wants some sort of identity to associate with Ramona, some proof that heading into this living situation blindly will be as wonderful as the set-up implies.

Evelyn starts to reply, but cuts herself off as the front door opens and a well-dressed, middle-aged woman enters. Evelyn stiffens, and Josie, immediately assuming the newcomer is another housing candidate, can't help but mimic her.

"Nara," Evelyn says. "I wasn't expecting you. We're wrapping up."

But the woman's gaze is only for Josie. She strides forward, arm extended, her long black hair smooth and shiny. She reaches for Josie's hand, not yet raised, and shakes it firmly. "Josephine, correct? Nara. You have no idea how grateful I am to have you living with my daughter."

"Uh," Josie says, taken aback by not only the suddenness of the situation, but also what appears to be genuine gratitude in Nara's words. She looks briefly and imploringly to Evelyn, whose face is unreadable. She wants to say she hasn't technically agreed to move in yet, but is so thrown off by Nara's eagerness that she only gets out, "You're welcome?"

This close, Josie can't see a single wrinkle, no lines around Nara's mouth as she gives a toothy grin.

"I apologize for my late arrival. I expected Ramona to be here and only just learned she wouldn't make it." There's a pointed glance in Evelyn's direction. "Evelyn gave you the tour? Any questions?"

Josie's mouth catches up to her brain. "Nope, I think I'm good," she says. "It's all really nice."

"Any way we can make this a more college-friendly space?"

Any hesitancy Josie had over Evelyn's bitchiness has completely

6

burned off. "Not unless I get my own assistant, too?" she asks, brows raised as she nods toward Evelyn.

Nara's laugh is loud; Josie tries not to smile too widely.

"Oh, you'll be perfect for Ramona. I'm sorry she's not here." To Evelyn, Nara adds with a glance to the tablet, "Is the paperwork all in order?

Evelyn flips her ponytail over her shoulder and tightens her grip. "I told Josephine to contact the property management company if she's still interested in living here."

Josie leans forward slightly and, after clearing her throat, says, "I go by Josie. And I can sign right now."

Chapter 2

The sky above Oakland is blue, the clouds are white, and Josie is a full hour late in picking Adam up.

It isn't unexpected, and Adam has made himself comfortable in the airport's passenger pickup section. He leans against his duffel bag, book propped open on his chest. As far as he's concerned, there are many, many worse situations to be in.

She'd shot him a text forty minutes ago—*uuuugh*—and a picture of standstill traffic on the Bay Bridge. He smiled, responding, *Drive safely. I'm okay.* To which she replied, *can't drive anything if I'm not moving.*

Around him, travelers wait for their own rides or wheel suitcases to the parking lot. Adam barely pays attention, eyes skimming across the pages as he reads. He turns the page, pulling the words closer. He always gets like this at the ends of books, reading so fast his eyes blur. His gaze is so intense on the page that he doesn't realize the car pulling up in his periphery is his own Subaru Forester, doesn't realize Josie is hurtling toward him, a blazing comet, until she yells his name. "Adam!"

He starts, squinting up at her, then breaks into a smile. Climax of the book or not, he hasn't seen Josie in three entire months. He stands and meets her tackling embrace. They're close in height; she has an inch on his five-seven, and her wild tangle of dirty-blonde curls bombards his senses, smelling like the same cheap strawberry conditioner she's always used. She'd deny it if he ever told her, somehow seeing it as a weakness, but Josie gives the best hugs.

She pulls back and narrows her eyes as she says, "You are *never* allowed to leave me again."

Adam's smiling the hardest he has all summer. "Never."

She laughs, an abrasive crack of her vocal cords he's come to love, and hugs him once more. Adam tucks the novel into his backpack. Trailing Josie, he assesses his car's state as she opens the hatchback. No new dents or scratches that he can see, though the back seat is strewn with clothing and food wrappers. "Yikes, Jo," he says, loading his bag.

"I know, I know. Things have been insane."

When Adam handed Josie his keys in May, he'd gone through the motions of begging her to take care of his car and to not get in any accidents. But part of him expected a two-in-the-morning call from her, profusely apologizing that she'd totaled his car because "some dick was riding me on the freeway and I brake checked him and—" So a backseat looking like she's been living in it is fairly tame.

Still, when he slides into the passenger seat, he can't help but immediately poke through the cup holders and center console, both of which are filled with Josie's mess. "Gross," he says, holding up a hardened, half-eaten cheeseburger wrapped in a napkin.

"A whole summer for me to forget how nitpicky you are," Josie grumbles.

"Says the one whose burger crust is petrifying in my car." But he's cheerful for the first time in a long while as he drops the leftover food back into the cup holder.

Josie guides the car into the slow-moving procession circling the Oakland airport. "How was the flight?"

Adam settles into his seat, clicking the seatbelt into place. "Uneventful."

"Crying children? Someone eating seafood next to you?"

"Nope."

"You had a layover in Vegas, right? Good people-watching?"

"It's . . . a really good book," he admits.

Josie *tsks*. "You're gonna get mugged one day."

He shrugs, then blinks. "Wait a minute. Why are you driving my car with me here?"

She gives him a feline smile, face as freckled as ever. "Natural order of things. How was that city council meeting last night?"

"It was okay. I don't know how politicians do it. You have to have a phenomenal poker face." He shakes his head. Three months interning for the *Salt Lake Tribune*; he'd lost count of the numerous meetings he'd had to attend. "The things people say during public comment . . ."

"I could do it," Josie says.

He feels a smile start. "Oh, Jo."

"I could!" she protests, swiping at a stray curl once, then again when it falls back into place. "Best poker face ever."

"What about that one time at the—"

"I *know* what you're going to say and that absolutely does not count. He was being a creep."

"And for that assignment with—"

"These are few and far between, dude. I could do it." She points at her face, where she's relaxed all her features into bored disinterest. "Go on, tell me something shocking."

"Um . . ." He thinks, briefly, guiltily, of Ari, then rebuilds that wall. "Jon told me he still has feelings for you?"

He watches her fight it, a pull at her mouth, a twitch of her right eye, then fail, expression settling into one of lukewarm outrage. "He'd better not."

Adam's laughing as he says, "He doesn't, promise. But thanks for proving my point."

Josie reaches over to poke him in the side. "Brat."

He leans away, then cringes as Josie speeds up to shift into the correct lane to exit for the Bay Bridge, sharply cutting in front of another car. "A whole summer for me to forget how much of a manic driver you are," he says, clutching his armrest.

"Oh, please," she scoffs. "I've heard your horror stories about the freeways in Utah. You left me your car for a reason."

Adam gives a half smile, eyes on the lanes of brake lights before them. It's true he opted for public transit while he was living with his parents over the summer, both to avoid the frenzy of commuter traffic and as a ready-made excuse to spend less time at home. Less time stumbling for a finish line he'd already fallen short of.

Even still, his mother spent the months watching him with what he used to believe was encouragement but had since learned was thinly shrouded expectation. "Promise me," she whispered years ago, a hand to his cheek, her eyes twin in color to his. He promised her, only to become a liar.

Adam hadn't FaceTimed with Josie on the worst days, when his culpability gnawed to the bone.

It's as if she can sense his train of thought now, because she says, "Hey. You did it. You lived at home all that time. I know it wasn't easy, but you did it."

He waits a beat before responding. "I don't really want to talk about it."

"Adam."

He shakes his head. "It's— Everything was fine. Is fine."

"You know it's okay to admit it wasn't, right? It's just me."

"Can we . . ." he replies. "Sorry, but can we not do this right now? Please?"

"I'm just trying to help." But there isn't much warmth in her voice.

He rakes a hand through his hair. "I just spent an entire summer d-dealing with everything. Can I be back for more than ten minutes before we have this conversation?"

Josie doesn't say anything, gripping the steering wheel as she slows. They've reached the lines of cars waiting to pass through the toll booths on the bridge.

The promise Adam made to his mom serves as the backdrop to every decision he makes. The oldest of five children, he was raised in an orthodox Mormon household. The Church of Jesus Christ of Latter-day Saints: the one true church, the only path to eternal salvation of the highest order; doctrine revolving around Christlike love and the salvation of all mankind. He lived it and loved it, succored by the unwavering faith of his parents. Luke Hughes provided a guiding hand in the home, stern and patriarchal in his principles; as by-the-rules with his parenting as his financial advising job was by the numbers. But Lois Hughes, *Mom*, took the mantle of nurturing her children more seriously than anything—everything—else.

Adam was never without the knowledge that his mother loved him dearly. Her firstborn, the beginning of her miraculous motherhood journey. School lunches packed with care; bedtime stories read to him, then alongside him when he fully inherited her love for books; a soft and comforting embrace when he needed it more and more as he grew older. The perfect disciple of Christ in the form of his mom.

So it made sense that his coming out was presented as a question to her one evening on a family walk, the two lagging behind, confidants: "What would you do if I was attracted to men?" He'd whispered it with his eyes cast down. A junior in high school, terrified of his yearnings. The first time he'd voiced a truth buried deep inside of him.

By then, Mormon leadership had transitioned away from deciding queerness was a choice and toward it being . . . well, not so much a *gift* from God, but more of an earth-bound impairment, a trial to be faced in this life but not the next. Those experiencing same-sex

12

attraction—the church-scrubbed name for what Adam felt—were to be loved regardless. But it was understood that acting on romantic or sexual feelings with anyone other than the opposite gender (and, regarding the latter, only within the sanctity of marriage) went against God's moral law. In eternity, after death, was when those worthy of salvation would be perfected, freed from disability—mental, physical, sexual. To obtain the highest reaches of heaven, Adam needed to marry a woman, either in this life or the next.

Adam's mom had stopped on the sidewalk at his question, hand falling from his forearm and a mix of emotions on her face. "I . . . will admit I don't quite know what to say to that," she said, turning slightly away. After a moment, she said, still looking elsewhere, "I'll speak with your father."

When they sat him down a few days later, their direction was clear: We love you, but you must stay pure. No romance, no lustful thoughts for another man. "Same-sex attraction is not a sin," his father said, "but acting on it is."

And then his mother's plea: "Promise me."

Adam kept his promise upon moving to San Francisco for college. Church felt different here. Same tenets, but fewer . . . demands than in Utah's sometimes oppressive culture. He arose each Sunday to attend the young single adults ward for members aged eighteen to thirty-five within the city reaches; he prayed morning and night; he taped up the scripture verse his mom hand wrote for him before he left: ". . . *it is upon the rock of our Redeemer, who is Christ, the Son of God, that ye must build your foundation; that when the devil shall send forth his mighty winds . . . when all his hail and his mighty storm shall beat upon you, it shall have no power over you . . .*"

He tried to stay faithful. He honestly tried—even after what happened freshman year.

Perhaps his foundation was fundamentally faulty, and that's why he crumpled so quickly. Maybe it was the physical distance from his family and the emotional distance his mom had adopted since he came out. Regardless, by moving to the city, Adam's true self began to stir.

Josie drives the car through the toll booth, and they pick up speed. Adam sighs. She's only ever tried to help him, in her own bold way. "Sorry."

"Forget it."

"Josie . . ."

"It's fine. I know you get weird about your family. I shouldn't have brought it up." She shakes her head like she's clearing thoughts. "I'm glad you're back. I realized that I need more friends than just you." She reaches over to grab his knee and shake it. "Especially since you're going to ditch me after this semester. You and your nerdy fast track to graduation."

"I'm not going anywhere," he says.

"You're right. I won't let you. Got any story ideas yet for Tilton's capstone?"

Adam feels a spike of panic. Both he and Josie are taking the class with a notoriously demanding professor. Rumors have floated down since Adam was a freshman about how important the semester-long final project is for the senior capstone: a news article that'll launch students into their careers, edited under the hand of an award-winning journalist. "No? Did she— Was something sent out? I was focused on the reading. What do we have to—"

"Nothing, chill. I was just wondering if you'd given it any thought."

"I haven't considered anything specific yet. Have *you*?" He can't help the surprise that slips through.

Josie smacks his shoulder. "Rude. I'm fresh off an internship too, remember? I've got all sorts of ideas to knock Tilton's socks off. This'll be the semester you're chasing *me* for the top grade."

He gives her a fond look. "I don't doubt it."

14

She narrows her eyes like she doesn't believe him, then sits up stick-straight. "Oh! By the way: I . . . found a new place to live!" She lifts her fingers from the steering wheel and wiggles them in a version of jazz hands.

They're nearing the city, its buildings growing taller the closer they drive, a welcome sight. The baseball stadium to their left, pier after pier to the right, Coit Tower's commanding presence in the distance ("It looks like a tampon," Josie once told him with a shrug).

Adam tilts his head. "You did? When? And where?"

"Okay, so you know how Feather murdered my books the other week?" She fills him in on signing up for housing notifications, the listing appearing from on high, her rental application's selection, and that day's walk-through of the space. "So, yeah. Hopefully my roommate's cool because I already paid the deposit. Locked in for a full year, baby."

"What's her name?"

"Ramona Taylor." Josie glances at him. "You haven't read about her in any of your books, right? Famous serial killer or something?"

Adam hums. "The name rings a bell, but not for any evil vibes. I'm sure you're fine. And it sounds like an incredible opportunity."

"Every once in a while karma smiles down on me," she agrees. "I have to work tomorrow, so the plan is to move in Saturday. Can I use your car?" She flutters her lashes. "And your muscle?"

He gives her a half smile. "Yes. Just keep my car until you're done. I can bike to work."

"Back to that Bay Area grind and seven-dollar gas prices!" she trills. "You ain't in Utah anymore, Hughes."

Twenty minutes later, Josie pulls up in front of Adam's place, cramped living quarters over a garage a couple miles from campus that he shares with Jon. Adam gets out of the car and unloads the trunk while Josie scrolls on her phone.

15

"Thanks for picking me up," he says, one hand atop the open passenger door as he leans over to peer inside.

She looks up, face softening at whatever she sees in his expression. "I'm sorry about everything you had to go through this summer."

Adam gives a small smile, projecting a nonchalance he doesn't feel. A warbled heartbeat of a moment passes as the weight of the San Francisco he left returns. He remembers Ari's hand around his, Ari's lips against his own; the connection they'd built in the spring, and one that Adam let his fears destroy. The thoughts still dog him.

"It's good to be back in the city," he says, but his voice is not quite steady.

Chapter 3

A tiny part of Josie was afraid the house on Valley Street wouldn't have quite the same shine when she showed up, keys in hand, officially a resident, mid-day Saturday.

She's wrong, and delightfully so.

"This is . . . you are . . . *three hundred* dollars a month?" Adam manages after a lap through the house. He's the perfect audience, with his audible gasps every time they enter a new room. Ramona isn't there, gone for the weekend, per a move-in email from Evelyn, which means Josie gets to infuse herself into every nook and cranny at her leisure.

She knows her expression is smug as she replies, "I looked it up, and the Zillow estimate for this place is almost five million."

"I guess if anyone deserves to live here, it's someone who had her books heinously massacred," Adam says, still slack-jawed. "What can I do now?"

They carry everything inside, not a particularly staggering amount of boxes, then divide and conquer: Josie shoving clothes in drawers in her room and Adam stacking cups and sorting cutlery in the kitchen.

He finishes before she does, appearing in the doorway wearing a slightly stunned expression as he takes in her room. "Um."

"I'm still unpacking," she says, pointing a finger at him. "You legally aren't allowed to judge my messiness for at least three weeks."

17

"Right, but I thought you were putting stuff *away*." He picks his way toward the window seat, stepping around piles of clothes and shoes; a stack of books he's leant her over the years—he grabs one of these as he goes, *The Hobbit*; and a mound of toiletry items.

"It's my style of organization," she says, sniffing a shirt. As he sinks into the cushioned seat, she asks, "Was Cal happy to see you yesterday?"

Adam nods. "He brought chocolate scones to celebrate. And he told me he's starting a book club."

"You two, I swear." Bookworms united, Adam and his boss. At least Adam gets an outlet somewhere, because Josie sure as hell isn't going around reading for fun. "Remind me what your book-reading goal is this year?"

Adam responds with a mumbled "just a hundred."

"I'm starting to think the little bit of socializing you claimed you did in Utah was actually just you breathing heavily down the aisles of your local library."

"You know that's not true. Remember when I FaceTimed you from a bar?"

"Always a DD, never a drunk, Adam Hughes's tagline."

He simply opens the book in reply.

Josie watches him a moment longer. He'd left in May in a flurry, oddly eager to get to Utah. Now he's paler than ever, with dark shadows under his eyes hinting at the difficulties he endured. He's perked up since the airport, though. Josie has too, like they're magnets, stronger when the distance between them shortens.

"Twenty bucks says you've already finished that book assigned for Tilton's class," Josie calls from the closet, where she's hanging up all her clean t-shirts (new house, new Josie!).

There's an extended pause, like Adam wants to finish the page or paragraph he's on. Then, "It's the Saturday before classes start." Another pause. "Have you *not*?"

Josie learned early on to not take offense at the incredulous but slightly insulting statements Adam can make, only because he's so damn earnest. She steps out of the closet and crawls onto the bed, laying on her stomach to face him. "Haven't started yet."

The small line between his eyebrows appears. "Jo, we're supposed to have a discussion about it in class on Tuesday."

She waves a hand. "I'll get it done."

"It's nearly three hundred pages."

"I'll get it done, dude. Really. Remember, I'm taking things seriously this year." She pulls out her phone. "I'm over unpacking. What time does the show start?"

Adam shifts to pull a piece of paper out of his pocket and bookmarks the novel. "Not 'til nine."

"Dinner before, on me?" She adds, because she can see the hesitation in Adam's eyes, the one that'll say she should stay home and read, "One last ride before senior year starts?"

The hesitation melts, nostalgia for their college days already a third-wheel. "One last ride," he agrees.

The Throne Room is a modest concert hall popular with San Francisco's student population. The music is good, the owner is semi-strict on ID, and the second Saturday of each month during the summer is half-off price on tickets for students and one free drink for anyone over twenty-one.

Those Second Saturdays always end with the welcome chaos of dancing alongside strangers, Josie's throat raw with scream-singing along to the lyrics she knows and cheering to songs she doesn't. There's something magical about the dark room, lit-up stage, thrumming beat, glittering bottles behind the bar, and faces of patrons who, regardless of them being strangers, are bonded to her through music.

She and Adam pick a mutual favorite taco place and, when their bellies are full, stroll arm in arm toward the venue a few blocks away. Alongside them, restaurant seating spills out onto the sidewalks, the city's residents and visitors alike out to enjoy the summer night air. They pass an Italian restaurant, a diner, and multiple bars, where the same Giants baseball game is broadcast across TVs. Josie feels like she's floating, the potential of her new home, her last school year spooling out before her.

Adam seems to read her thoughts. "I'm glad you found a new place to live," he says, eyes fixed on the city's skyline. "I really think it's the right move."

"Only variable is the roommate," Josie agrees as they pause at a crosswalk. She has to keep reminding herself that the house on Valley Street is not entirely hers to enjoy.

"You do have . . . interesting luck when it comes to who you live with." Adam, ever the diplomat.

"I'll say. Feather's DIY crafts du jour. And remember Olive? From freshman year?"

The sign chimes for them to cross. "The one with the dolls?"

"The one and only."

Adam nudges her with his shoulder. "At least Ramona's name isn't a noun?"

"Honestly, I've barely thought about her," Josie admits. "We'll need to deep-dive after the concert. You're still staying over, right?"

"One last ride," Adam repeats with a nod. "Have you . . ." His change in tone has Josie shifting into defense, ". . . told your mom about your new place?"

"No." She lets the words drop with the heaviness of a guillotine.

Adam's very steps on the sidewalk turn cautious. "It's just that you have this incredible opportunity. You don't think she'd want to know? To hear how you're doing?"

The Throne Room is in sight now. Josie considers a thousand ways to respond, from *she lost her chance ages ago* to *it's none of your business*, then chooses the one that'll hit him the hardest, because Adam should know better: "You don't think your parents would want to know about that Halloween party freshman year?"

Adam's arm tenses against hers. "Please don't."

"You started it."

Adam stops short, and when he turns to face her, his expression is pleading. "I'm sorry for asking about your mom. I only wanted—" Josie gives him a furious look and his shoulders slump. "I'm just trying to be a good friend."

"Be a good friend by not bringing up shit you know the answer to," Josie snaps. A small group of people skirts around them on the sidewalk.

Cold fingers circle her wrist. "Jo," Adam says. "It's been almost five years. I don't want you to lose your relationship with her forever. That's all." His eyes are wide and the color of whiskey. "Please, let's go have a fun night listening to music at what'll probably be our last Second Saturday."

The fight in Josie dissolves. She blinks and looks at the ground, making a feeble attempt to untangle the snarl of emotions in her head. *The house, senior year, Adam is back.* Good things.

She nods. "Sorry."

Adam squeezes her wrist, a silent understanding.

Josie rolls her shoulders back and clears her throat before pulling him along. "I don't want you pouting by the bathrooms like you did that one time."

"I wasn't *pouting*," he shoots back, levity in his voice.

She bangs her shoulder against his. "You were, but I forgive you."

Once inside the Throne Room, once the bass begins pounding a beat into their bloodstream, they fall into the natural steps they've navigated so many times before. Josie plows into the crowd of people already swaying and singing to the music, Adam grabbing the back of her shirt to keep close.

The stage is broad and yellow before them, the band already into its set and the crowd just starting to really perk up. Josie stops halfway into the mob, Adam next to her. Around them, the faces and bodies of strangers sway in tandem. Josie closes her eyes briefly, letting the music sink into her bones, welcoming the rhythm of the floorboards and the energy in the air. Adam is back in the city, and everything in front of her feels possible. As the song picks up, she's bouncing, then jumping, Adam alongside her, grinning like an idiot. Together, they are swept away, unified with a hundred unknown people before an altar of instruments, never happier.

Josie wakes to a drawn-out sigh. She's heard that sound before, and knows precisely the dramatic meaning behind it. Cracking an eye open, she says, "You did *not* just finish the book you started yesterday."

Adam startles, clutching the closed book to his chest. He's propped up on two pillows, dark red hair sleep-mussed and wearing a shirt she stole from him ages ago. Josie hadn't bothered changing out of her clothes when they got back from the concert, merely collapsing face first into bed, but Adam obviously made the time.

"It's a fast read," he says, rubbing his thumb across the back of *The Hobbit*. "And I've read it before."

Josie pushes up onto her elbows, shaking hair out of her face. The light in this room is different from her old Bernal Heights place. As in, there's actual natural sunlight. "What time is it?"

Adam reaches for the nightstand on his side, swapping the book for his phone. "Just after eleven." He snuggles deeper under the duvet. "This bed is incredible."

"Right? The thread count on these sheets must be a million." She scooches closer to him, and he lets out a sound of alarm.

"Jo, you still smell like smoke!"

She wraps her arms around his waist and buries her face into his neck as he squirms. "I'm just *so* happy my widdle bookworm is back!"

"Jo—!" But he's laughing as he tries to get away. "Don't you want to cyber stalk your new roommate?" he finally says, breathless.

That gets her attention. She sits up and begins pulling her hair into a high pony. "I forgot *again*! God, she could be a mob boss biding her time and I'm just here trying to love-bomb you."

Adam's obediently opening Instagram on his phone. "Ramona Taylor?"

Josie nods. "Here's to the calm before the storm."

He hits enter on the search bar.

Almost immediately, his eyes go wide and he angles the phone away from her.

Josie's heart begins to pound. Oh god, her new roomie really is a murderer. "What is it?" When Adam doesn't say anything, she reaches for the phone. "Adam—*what*?"

A small smile begins to curve up the edge of his mouth as he dodges her hand and sits up fully. He meets her eye, and there's glee there instead of danger, which shifts Josie's mood from majorly concerned to mildly pissed off. "Cut the shit," she says. "What did you find?"

Adam hands his phone over. He's biting his lip like he's trying not to laugh.

Josie stares at the phone, not understanding at first what the grid of photos is trying to tell her. She focuses on one: a young woman posing in what's clearly an attempt to be both an elegant and relatable sprawl across an expensive-looking white couch, head angled just so, black hair long and glossy, inviting her viewers to stare, to look but not touch.

The like count is somewhere over fifty thousand, the comments overly gushing, the woman stares at Josie through the phone with the

23

most smug expression she's ever seen.

Josie blinks and the expensive-looking white couch becomes a familiar-looking one. So too is the set of French doors in the background. The Valley house's TV room. Which must mean—

"You've got to be kidding me," she says. "I'm living with an *influencer?*"

Chapter 4

Adam gives Josie three minutes to scroll. That's usually the amount of time it takes for her to shift from a catastrophic reaction to . . . not quite as catastrophic a reaction. Though he may have misread the humor in the situation, because her scrolling has become more stab-like.

"Jo," he says.

She continues to stab-scroll.

He tries again. "Josie?"

She says without looking up, "An influencer, Adam. My new roommate is a social media influencer."

"Right . . ."

"It's like drinking from a Ramona Taylor fire hose. This chick is *obsessed* with herself!" Instead of outrage, however, Josie has a mischievous glint to her eye. "This is going to be incredible."

"Um," replies Adam, now wary. "'Incredible' as in you can't wait to make friends with someone who will add new perspectives to your worldview, or as in—"

Josie, still scrolling, interrupts with, "Are you kidding? A B-lister influencer sharing every second of her life?" She shows him a post time-stamped the previous weekend: Ramona in a revealing steampunk set, her chest, stomach, and legs draped in delicate-looking body chains. A barren desert landscape her stage; Burning Man, Adam immediately recognizes. The photo's caption: *We're all tiny grains of sand in the cosmic glitter jar.*

"I mean, yeah, sure, I low-key want to gouge my eyes out," Josie continues, "but I get to see how the sausage is made!"

"Just remember to be nice about how she chooses to live her life, okay?"

Josie, mid-presenting a post of Ramona in a strappy black dress and sporting a small, white paper bag, Charlotte Tilbury stamped across the front, lowers the phone. "My baseline is perfectly nice!"

Adam's mouth hangs open a second too long, he knows. Still, Josie lets him off the hook with a playful push to his shoulder. "Don't worry. I'll be nice to the popular girl who wants for nothing." Her attention returns to the phone. "Have to be, don't I? Since I'm living under her roof? Oh man, now we're at a whole new level of mystery! This chick is clearly San Francisco rich, even if this is her daddy's house. So, why a roommate? Why *me*?"

"Maybe it's a princess and pauper social experiment?"

Josie raises an eyebrow as she shows him a post of Ramona blowing out candles, the caption, *Everyone likes you when you're 22.*

"I hope the currency in this case is brain cells," Josie says, "otherwise that comparison offends me."

"Princess Josie, of course," Adam agrees solemnly, then holds out his hand. "Can I take a look?"

"God, yes. I'm already back in 2021." She hands the device over. "Save me from myself."

Adam scrolls back to the top. Ramona's most recent post, uploaded the night before, is a shot of her sitting at a table, resting the side of her head in her palm and staring at a hand of cards. Behind her is a cabin's exterior of wooden beams and a massive stone fireplace. *Lake Tahoe*, reads the photo's location.

Josie's across the room, gathering the empty boxes she's unpacked.

"Do you think she has a photographer follow her around constantly to take pictures? Or one of her friends? I couldn't do it. Having someone shove a camera in my face twenty-four seven? What a nightmare."

"If you want to try on some empathy, I'm happy to start taking photos of you." Adam scrolls past more individual shots and random day-in-the-life moments; cups of coffee, bouquets of flowers, partnerships with various clothing and makeup brands, and lots of Ramona. "While you're eating, or maybe while you're making out with the next random guy at the Throne Roo . . ." The word dies as he scrolls to the next picture.

"You act like I'm an exhibitionist," Josie grumbles from the doorway, piling boxes in the hall.

Adam quickly exits the app, his heart somehow existing both in his throat and dropping down to his stomach. He stands, shoving his phone into his pocket.

Josie glances over. "What's wrong?"

He hooks his overnight bag onto his arm, pulse a wild, rapid thing. "I, um, just remembered I have to, have to get something to Cal by tonight?"

She narrows her eyes like she can smell the lie. "It's Sunday."

"Oh— Right, it's actually, I need to get ready for church." He moves toward the hallway, hyper aware of the house's ambient noises. That isn't a door opening and closing downstairs, is it?

Josie follows him. "Why are you being weird?"

He doesn't respond, overwhelmed by a torrent of memories as he hurries down the stairs and across the entryway. Ari. Always Ari. Ari knows Ramona. The post had been of three of them, Ramona, Ari, and one other he hadn't even looked at. Curled up together on a couch, arms and legs flung possessively around and across one another. The date on the photo read April, back when he and Ari had been spending time together. He'd obsessed over the fall of Ari's dark hair, the warmth

27

of his smile—and there it all was in picture form.

"*Adam.*" Josie's voice is the snap of a rubber band against skin. She's tapping on the driver's window of his car. "What's going on?"

He rolls the window down halfway. "Sorry, I just need to go. I'll text you, okay?"

"Should I call Jon?"

"No, I'm fine," he says, seatbelt strap chafing against his neck as he starts the car. "Sorry." He reverses out of the driveway before she can say anything else.

They'd crossed paths many times over a couple months before speaking to one another. Adam coasting on his bike toward campus just before seven a.m. on Wednesdays and Fridays, his earliest start in the library archives. Ari, ever dedicated to the perfection of his body, was a consistent jogger along Adam's route as winter turned into spring—training for a marathon, Adam would later learn.

They often made eye contact at the same intersection, by a sushi restaurant that would be the spot for their first date. Ari became an unexpected bright spot long before Adam knew his name, giving him wordless, friendly waves. Adam took extra care not to splash Ari as he cruised through late winter's gutter puddles.

Ari was the one who took it to the next level, flashing Adam his usual grin one morning as he waited for the crosswalk light. "What's your name?" he called from the other side of the street.

Adam only stared back in return, caught off guard, as the traffic light turned green. The cars around him surged forward, and he fumbled to push off the ground and start pedaling. To his right, Ari was level with him and then passing, saying, "I'm Ari. See you Friday."

And he had. When Adam rolled up to the light at 6:47 that Friday morning, the other man was leaning against a light pole on the corner, waiting.

"Morning," Ari said, teeth brilliantly white against his golden-beige skin. A black headband pushed his hair back from his face. He was incredibly handsome, Hollywood beautiful. He wore a dark gray hoodie and tiny black running shorts, revealing long, sculpted legs. Adam swallowed.

Ari moved toward the curb with a grace that could give Josie's lioness prowl a run for its money.

"H-hi." Adam cleared his throat, glancing around the intersection, then at his watch, before gliding his bike over. "Um, Ari, right?"

Ari gave Adam a bright smile that had Adam's pulse dancing. "So you *did* hear me. I wondered if you thought I was just, like, yelling words or threatening to push you into traffic."

"Oh, no, I'm sorry. I— You just surprised me."

"All these weeks and I thought we had a thing going!" Ari's eyes were the color of fresh ink on a page as they swept over Adam, his backpack, his bike, and his surely impossible-to-miss blush.

Adam fumbled for his helmet strap. "I'm Adam?" he said, the words a question as he ran a hand through his hair and tucked the helmet under his arm. "I'm headed to campus."

"You're a student?" At Adam's nod, Ari raised a dark brow and again gave him another once-over. He looked westward. "SF State?"

"Yeah. Yes. Um—" Adam paused, wondering why he felt the need to catch his breath. He wished desperately he was cleverer on his feet, quick-thinking in conversations with strangers, like Josie was. But he wasn't, which was why his next words came out like another pathetic question: "Go Gators?"

Ari nodded, bemused, and Adam felt his face warm further. "Cool, I won't keep you," Ari said. "Glad to catch your name." He lifted his foot behind him, grabbing it to stretch his quad, then shifted to stretch the other. "See you Wednesday." With a wink, he was off. Adam stood on the corner, staring after him.

Five mornings later, Adam biked toward Ari, who was jogging in the bike lane. Ari held out a piece of paper, which Adam reached for automatically. Their fingers brushed, and then they were past one another.

The name Ari Banik and a phone number were scrawled on the paper.

Adam began using the piece of paper as a bookmark, staring at the letters and numbers of the note almost as often as what was in the books he read.

His awareness of Ari wasn't anything romantic, Adam told himself, but he couldn't say no to a potential friend. Especially since they would likely keep seeing each other during their morning routes. It'd be awkward if he didn't respond.

The text he typed out, then deleted, then typed out again and ultimately sent read, *Hi. This is Adam. The guy on the bike the other morning.* Ari didn't respond for hours, during which Adam second-guessed himself and swore off any future interactions, realizing he'd obviously misread the situation.

When he dared to look at his phone that evening, he found three missed calls and seven texts from Josie, and one from the number he hadn't yet ascribed Ari's name to: *go gators guy?? ;)*

Heart beating Morse code at the tips of his fingers, Adam gave a small but grateful laugh and texted back, *Sorry, yes.*

Ari's response was quick this time. Adam hadn't reached the end of the page in the book he was reading before his phone vibrated on the bed. *u r now entered in my phone as go gators :)* He added a screenshot as proof.

A current of something fluttered through Adam. *I deserve that*, he texted.

u do. u can put something lame in ur phone for my name if u want. like sexy runner guy

Adam grinned, momentarily forgetting his friends-only mantra. *Not sure how that's an embarrassing descriptor?*

shit ur rite

How about 'Intersection Stranger'? Adam asked.

ouch

Ari sent another picture. Atop a cream-colored bedspread lay a t-shirt with the head of an alligator emblazoned across it beneath the letters SFSU. *new shirt for my run tmrw.*

It was how easily he'd let go of himself around Ari that ultimately scared Adam off. And the steadiness Ari provided, the comfort. The certainty. The *wanting*. Adam opened up like a flower in bloom.

They began texting each other often. Ari told Adam about his modeling career, flashing cameras and runways and magazine spreads. He spoke of his parents who were supportive of their son's sexuality. And he talked about his closest friends, a mash-up of Gen Z's finest: a photographer, an influencer, and him.

Adam didn't tell him about religion and his struggles grappling with where he fit in, about the ache to keep a promise to his mom he'd already broken. He only said, fiddling with a napkin at a Mexican restaurant in the Castro District, that he was still figuring things out about his sexuality.

"My best friend knows," he continued. "Josie. Aside from my roommate and my family, she's the only one. She wants me to be happy the way I am. She doesn't expect me to . . . change things? Or to not, um, want people?"

"People?" Ari grinned.

Adam blushed to the tips of his ears. "Person."

Beneath the table, Ari's leg brushed against Adam's and settled there, and Adam balked. Friends didn't do this. Their stomachs also didn't perform a series of acrobatics at the thrill of their friend's touch. But he didn't pull away, and for one split second, didn't think about how wrong he was to want this. "I'm glad there's someone at least halfway decent in your life you've told," Ari said. "And, like, thank you. For telling me." He pressed his leg more firmly against Adam's. "So you know, we're all treading water. Anyone who makes you feel smaller because of who you are and who you love doesn't deserve to be in your life."

Then there was the movie, where Ari took Adam's hand in his, and Adam let him. After, they walked slowly toward their parked cars. Adam had turned quiet, pensive, and Ari let him, let the silence stretch into something comfortable between them.

Reaching his car, Ari murmured good night, but didn't move to get in. Adam opened his mouth, wanting to say something, but couldn't quite articulate the feeling tingling throughout his body. He dropped his gaze as he turned away, whispering his farewell. But Ari stopped him, pulled Adam close, tilted his jaw up, and kissed him.

It was nothing, nothing like the freshman year Halloween mishap.

Though Ari's entire body was honed into camera-ready muscle, his mouth moved gently against Adam's. Adam took a moment to catch up to what was happening. One of Ari's hands was in Adam's hair, the other gripping his bicep, Adam's own bracing Ari's hips. And then Adam was melting, sinking into Ari, pulling him closer, kissing him more urgently. The tingling he felt—excitement, he realized—was growing, expanding, burning delightfully in his chest. Kissing Ari couldn't be wrong, not with the way Adam was feeling, like Ari saw him for who he was.

But this was the very difference between identity and action.

Clear as a bell, as if she were hovering over Adam's shoulder, came his mother's voice: *Promise me.*

Adam's head snapped back, eyes wide as he stared at Ari. "I can't—" he choked out, staggering backward, and trying to tamp down the desire coursing through his veins. He wasn't supposed to do this, to kiss other guys—to act on his attraction. The Halloween party memories came crashing to the forefront: a college student dancing with him, the music a pulsing, alive thing around them. And then Adam was kissing him, and the guy was touching him, palming him in a way that felt like every dark fantasy come to life. They'd stumbled to an empty corner of the party, Adam letting the carnal actions he'd been taught not to act on become puppeteer. But then he was crying from the shame of it all and the stranger was gone, and Josie—until then a nameless fellow student in two of his classes—was helping him pull up his pants and guiding him away from the party. The darkness and depression that followed whispered a different kind of temptation into his head, oily and snakelike and life-taking.

And there he was again, with Ari, in a parking lot, staring down the barrel of the same gun.

He expected to read annoyance in Ari's expression, but the other man only looked disappointed and confused. He nodded, muttering an apology as he opened his car door and slid inside. He gave Adam one last lingering glance before driving away.

Adam began biking to work earlier, taking a different, longer route. There were no more dates, no more texts. Emotions warred in his brain: longing for Ari, anger with himself. And shame most of all—for what he felt for Ari, and his inability to do anything more.

A week later, he flew to Utah for the summer. He continued to use the piece of paper with Ari's number on it as a bookmark, a reminder of what might have happened if he'd let it go further. He wasn't sure what kind of punishment he was inflicting upon himself by keeping it.

Adam now knows, as he drives away from Josie's new house, that the punishment is yet to come.

Chapter 5

As quiet and gentle as Adam is to the general world, to know him is to know his flair for the dramatic, and while driving away without explaining himself isn't completely abnormal, Josie can't help her alarm.

She calls his cell. Once, twice, three times she gets his voicemail.

She then rings Jon, who answers with a delighted noise on the second ring. "Josefina!" he coos into her ear with a Latino emphasis he has no ancestry for. "I heard you got frisky with some poor fella last night."

Josie grins, her limbs loosening. "Adam wasn't supposed to tell you! He knows how jealous you get."

"He texted me as it was happening. I'll never recover." She hears the murmur of a TV on his end. "Speaking of which, you still holding my poor roommate hostage?"

"That's why I called." Josie heads back inside. "He just left here in a huff, and I have no idea why. He said he was going to church, but I don't believe him. Will you text me when he gets back? And see if he'll say anything to you about why he's wigging out?"

There's the clink of a bottle on a table. She can picture Jon at his house, wearing his preferred outfit of gym shorts and nothing else, showing off his broad shoulders and dark brown skin. She knows without asking he's watching a baseball game. "Mmmm, sure, I'll keep you posted."

"Has he been any different since he got back from Utah?"

"You'd know better than me. I've seen him for about ten minutes."

Josie nods. "Fair. Well, lemme know when he gets home."

"You got it, J."

They hang up just as Josie reaches her room. There's the pile of empty boxes outside her door, but continuing unpacking is the last thing on her mind, still frenzied by Adam's dramatic departure. She shifts into better familiarizing herself with her new home.

All but cracking her knuckles, she heads for the TV room and begins poking through the drawers of the coffee table and the shelves of various cabinets. Only blankets and board games.

The kitchen is more intriguing: locks on some of its cabinets. Josie considers the security for a moment—not unreasonable, what with her being a stranger to Ramona. Still, she can't help but bristle; she doesn't want to be Ramona's enemy. She's here for cheap housing. And maybe for the occasional open admiration from Ramona's mom. Ramona the Influencer is merely unasked for but well met entertainment.

Downstairs, the hallway with the fitness room holds nothing beyond bare bones. Exercise equipment, hallway closet completely empty, and only toilet paper and a plunger under the sink in the bathroom.

Ramona's bedroom is the same case as the kitchen cabinets: Josie is denied by a lock. She can't manage to take offense at that one.

She leans against Ramona's door to survey the entryway in all its glory, afternoon sunshine spilling from a window across the checkered floor. Despite her roommate's laughable lifestyle centered around finding the right angles for photos, Josie's looking forward to the access behind the scenes—figuratively, considering the locks. The drama of a rich girl's life! The hysterics! Josie's convinced it'll be front-row access to a reality TV show, the kind where you constantly feel really good about your mediocre-at-best life choices.

Sighing, she pulls up Ramona's Instagram profile and taps on the story update. A group of twenty-somethings piled in an outdoor hot tub, on a deck surrounded by pine trees. Josie can see Ramona amid the others, *besties!* written in cursive writing across the top.

Josie closes the app, pretending that were she the type of person with that many people who cared about her, she wouldn't brag exactly the same way.

Josie wasn't lying when she told Adam senior year is her year. Yes, okay, maybe she hasn't ever been the best student, but it's her last semester with Adam, and last year pursuing a formal education. She wants to enjoy the top of the pile. She's off to a good start—catching the right person's attention to move into the Valley house. The fondness in Nara's eyes, the sense of caring for Josie even though she'd just met her, felt downright alien. She's spent years refusing to look too closely at the mostly empty space around her, and her inability to stop the warmth in her chest over a parent-shaped presence is embarrassing.

She spends the remainder of the day in bed reading the assigned capstone book (Josie 2.0!). Plus a couple Netflix shows in the background for when her eyes go fuzzy from all the text. Jon texts her at one point late in the afternoon, but his update isn't as helpful as she'd like: *Adam just got back. Doesn't look like he went to church. He's in his room now.*

How'd he seem?

Little skittish. told him to text you.

Josie opens up her text thread with Adam, hoping to see three dots signifying that he's typing out a message to her, but there's no movement. She taps out and sends, *Do you want me to come over?*

Adam's reply is quick, causing a pinch in her chest, knowing he purposely ignored her calls earlier: *I'm okay. I'll see you tomorrow on campus.*

It's dark out by the time she rolls out of bed. Worry over Adam has combined with antsiness over Ramona's arrival. She peeks out the blinds, as if Ramona's merely been waiting in the backyard for Josie to finally notice. As it turns out—and Josie nearly jumps out of her skin—there is someone out there. Her eye trips over a faint red glow coming from one of the patio chairs below. A smoker. She flips the lock on one of the windows and sticks her head out. "Excuse me, you're on private property!"

There's movement from the chair, then a figure walks to stand beneath her window. From the nearby streetlight, she can make out dark hair and clothing, and a pale face peering upward. "You must be the new roommate," comes a male voice.

Josie doesn't falter. "Even if I am, Ramona isn't here, so it's weird that you are. Beat it, Romeo."

The young man takes a drag and, after an exhale of smoke, says, "I don't remember Juliet being so hostile."

"Consider me a modern-day version. Seriously, you need to leave."

"Shall I scale the fence or do I get to let Ramona, who I just drove here with, know about your hospitality on my way out?"

Josie scowls, then shuts the window and drops the blinds before moving to her doorway, peering down the hall. Fate is ready for her. She can hear the near-silent shifting of stairs as someone climbs them. Her heart thumps loudly; it's time to meet Ramona Taylor.

Her roommate's head appears first, then shoulders, then the rest of her as she ascends.

Josie hesitates, considers closing her door and delaying the inevitable, but the potential is too good to miss. She stalks down the hall.

The appearance of Ramona is underwhelming. She stands tall at the top of the stairs, yes, eyes instantly on Josie. But there's no flickering light, no flash of lightning through the window or rumble of thunder— nor an explosion of glitter. Ramona simply appears and the house on

Valley can finally settle. Distantly, the A/C turns on, like a sigh.

Her black hair is slicked into a top knot, lips painted a deep, bloody red, and she's wearing a vertically striped set—the top boxy with long, wide sleeves and the matching midi-length skirt both bright colors. Long, dangling gold earrings hang from her lobes.

Josie takes in the picture-perfect appearance, then says, tone gauging, "Hey, I'm Josie."

Ramona moves closer, gaze flitting, crisscrossing up and down so intently that Josie is almost self-conscious. Almost. Caring about her appearance will never be Josie's downfall. When she's a foot away, Ramona's eyes go from Josie to her bedroom down the hall and back. "You need to clean up those boxes," she says. "I'm not interested in sharing my house with a slob." There is no friendliness in her expression.

Josie's hackles rise immediately. *Remember to be nice*, reminds Adam's voice in her ear. She tells Adam the Shoulder Angel to get lost. But her retort is cut off by the arrival of two others.

The first is so stupid-handsome it should be illegal. He's well over six feet; lean and sculpted beneath a dark bomber jacket and jeans. Josie's drawn to him without shame as he reaches the second floor, followed closely by a third figure: the smoker from outside, who's around Josie's height with black, wavy hair tumbling across his brow. He wears a long-sleeved white button-up, over which is a black sweater, finely threaded. A knowing smile forms as he meets Josie's eye.

Ramona's perfectly lipsticked mouth pulls back to reveal straight, white teeth as she watches Josie take them in. "Ari," she says, hand on the first guy's arm. She tilts her head in reference to the Romeo. "And Silas."

The three are an unquestionably intimidating collection, varying degrees of beauty and menace, and Josie feels like she's shrinking, a little kid among grown-ups. Instead of showing weakness, she straightens her spine, unwilling to appear small. "Welp. Nice to meet you all." Calm and collected. "I'll be around."

She stays tall as she turns back for her room, feeling their eyes on her. For a split-second, there's the urge to return to her room in Bernal Heights, windowless hovel that it was. Anything to escape the hostility emanating from her new roommate.

"Don't forget the boxes," Ramona tosses out. Josie can hear the sneer in her voice and tries to not let it affect her. She nearly trips over the small tower of cardboard, but catches herself against the doorframe with a curse, then closes her door.

The text from Evelyn comes shortly after Josie's alarm goes off the next morning. *Please take care of the boxes in front of your door. Garbage and recycling cans are in the garage.*

Josie groans as she rubs her eyes, already sick of the micromanaging. But she plays nice, disposing of the cardboard before getting ready for the first day of classes.

She's heading for the stairs, only a little bit behind, when she's distracted. Ramona stands in the kitchen, adding ingredients to a single-serve blender. She looks over her shoulder as she stuffs a wad of kale into the appliance, scans Josie with her X-ray eyes, and returns to her task. She's wearing a matching workout set, fitted bicycle-style shorts and a crop-top the same color as the pale pink roses in a vase on the banquette table. Her hair is separated into two French braids.

Josie makes a face, knowing she'll regret this, then turns into the kitchen anyway and heads for her coffeemaker. The incongruity—a decrepit black device atop the sleek surface of the kitchen—feels like a metaphor. She begins to prepare a pot, then turns to watch Ramona pour almond milk into the blender.

"How long—" Josie starts, but her last words are cut off by Ramona blending her smoothie ingredients into a sludgy green.

"*So* sorry," Ramona says without turning when she's done. "What did you say?"

Josie exhales through her nose. "How long have you lived here?"

Ramona pours the smoothie into a glass cup and sets the empty blender container into the sink. "A while." From a drawer she plucks out a straw and plops it in the drink. She grabs her phone from the counter and holds it out in front of her, smoothie glass poised, and gives a just-pouty-enough look as a camera shutter sounds.

Josie says dryly, "What's it like being an influencer?"

Ramona is typing on her phone at the speed of light and Josie would bet her first month's rent there's about to be a new story post on her Instagram. "Great." She arches an eyebrow as she looks up at Josie in silent challenge, like this is a point she has to argue often. She crosses to the fridge and pulls out a bowl—fine China, rimmed in gold—of strawberries, halved and snipped of their stems. Phone pressed under her arm, bowl in one hand and smoothie in the other, she heads out of the kitchen, through the dining room, and into the TV room.

Josie follows. Move-in instructions via Evelyn specifically stated no food allowed in the TV room, and definitely not on the very white and very expensive couch, on which Ramona is actively perching with her bowl of juicy strawberries and a drink begging to be toppled. She's turning on the Apple TV and opening the YouTube app. Her subscriptions and recommended selections show various perfect-looking people posing, with titles like 'vegan grocery haul!' and 'my NYC adventure' and 'autumn wardrobe MUST-HAVES!'

Josie leans a hip against the edge of the dining room table and asks, "What do you like about it?"

She's rewarded with what looks like annoyed surprise that Josie's still there. "What?" Ramona asks.

"Influencing," Josie repeats, unperturbed—or maybe unrepentant is the right word. "What do you like about it?"

"Um . . . ?" Ramona says slowly. "Why?"

Josie shrugs. "Figure we should get to know one another." She could press, probably would if it was Adam being cagey, but stands down. Instead, she says, "Tell me about your friends."

Ramona leans back against the couch, curling her feet up underneath her and selecting a strawberry from her bowl. "Why?" Her voice is high, affected, but carries a flatness to it that Josie knows, based on stalking Ramona online, is not the same high and affected voice she uses for her followers.

"Ari's a model, right?" Josie performed research last night.

"Obviously."

"And the other one? Silas? He takes pictures?"

Ramona eats another strawberry. "Fashion photographer."

"Do they live pretty close?"

Ramona gives her a considering look, and Josie interprets the following words as some sort of test, maybe an olive branch. "They have a place in Monterey Heights. But they're over here literally all the time."

Test, olive branch, whatever—the opening is too perfect; Josie has to ask. "Why don't either of them live here instead of a random person like me?"

Ramona's eyes flash with some intense emotion too quickly for Josie to decipher. "Trust me," she says stiffly, returning her attention to the TV. "If I had it my way, you wouldn't have made it past the front door."

Josie's coffee beeps from the kitchen and Ramona adds with a fake-looking smile, glancing her way one last time, "By the way, Evelyn will be texting you about the rules for appliances on kitchen counters."

She presses play on a video, volume loud and drowning out anything Josie might retort.

Chapter 6

Adam calls his mom while he waits for Josie at the southeast entrance to campus. It's his last first day of school, and there's a mix of emotions inside him over the milestone.

"Adam?"

He can't help the relaxing exhale that escapes him at the sound of his mother's voice, even as his shoulders square—a confusing contrast. His mom is both a landing pad and a sinkhole. "Hi, Mom."

"Today's your first day, right? Are you ready?" He can hear the sound of a sizzle, likely frying eggs for his three youngest siblings. His other sister, Emma, the second oldest, is at college, faithfully attending the church-owned institution Brigham Young University, right down the road from his childhood home. That had been a difficult conversation with his parents, explaining that he was leaving the nest, and for San Francisco nonetheless. No serving a church mission either, not for him. Not even his scholarship soothed the look on his mom's face when he told her. But his pain over church has never been just his to bear.

"I think so," he says honestly. "I'll be really busy, but I feel good about it?"

He hears the expectation even if she doesn't mean to imply anything, feels like he's swallowed a slushie too fast as she says, "If anyone can stay focused on what's right, it's you."

"Yeah," he says, after a second's delay. "Um, how's, how's everyone doing? Is Matty glad to have his room back?"

"Oh, that boy." They're back in the safe zone of conversation topics; he relaxes. "He keeps going on about those tiny skateboards—fingerboards, I think?"

Adam smiles. "Tech Decks. Yeah, I think that new neighbor introduced him? He told me about them right before I left."

"Well, it's a full-blown obsession now. Your father nearly broke his neck on one coming down the stairs the other day."

"I can only imagine," Adam laughs.

His mom continues to chatter, telling him about the start of school for his siblings and increase in sports practices she has to shuttle kids to. The words are comforting, reminiscent of the busy days of Adam's youth. Before. Orchestra, church activities, and more—his mom always waiting outside after he was done, parked in their gray minivan.

A nudge at his shoulder tells him Josie's arrived. "Oh— Mom, sorry, I've got to get to class."

"Good luck, sweetheart! Call me later to tell me about it. I love you so much."

"Love you, too," he says, softer because Josie's listening, and hangs up.

Josie's aura is frazzled. She's late, yes, but she also looks like she's burning to launch into a tirade. She must see something on Adam's face, because she hesitates, taking him in. Managing only seconds ago, the scrutiny leaves Adam with a sudden and intense urge to cry—over Ari, over his parents, over the beginning of the end of school.

Josie is not often soft with others, but he knows she makes an effort for him. Like now, when pulls him into a hug and simply asks, "Wanna talk about it?"

"No, thank you," he says into her hair.

The world around them is loud: traffic passing by on 19th, students weaving around them, excitement for a new semester palpable. Adam still hears Josie inhale, on the cusp of saying something, and braces himself. "Whatever it was that happened yesterday," she says. "It's going to be okay."

It could be, with Josie on his side. "You're a good friend, Jo," he says softly. "Thank you."

She pulls back, hands on his shoulders and expression fierce. "I'm here for you. Whether it's over a book or your family or whatever, 'kay?"

Adam nods, ever grateful for her loyalty, even when she doesn't agree with his mindset. Freshman year, as they became closer, he asked her to help keep him from acting on any feelings he might develop for another man. No more dark corners at parties. "Please, Jo," he begged. "The church—my family, I can't lose them."

Josie argued, of course. "Adam, your church preaches love but gatekeeps what it's supposed to look like. You should leave. Embrace your identity. You're in the gayest city in the world! *Be gay!*"

Adam would stay silent, unable to put to words that when you framed everything as something to be done in belief of and sacrifice for your maker, blessings were bountiful and burdens were made light.

It was a debate never settled, the largest thorn in their friendship's side. Adam repented for his slip-up, then fell back to the patterns he was born into: church and prayer and scriptures about the enduring love of Jesus Christ and the safety net of eternal families.

For two years, he found his peace by smothering his plight. Then he met Ari, and his fortitude came crashing down. Repentance only worked if you promised not to repeat the sin, but for a few weeks, all he'd wanted was to wrap himself up in the reality of romance, to lean into his attraction and find a happily ever after.

Wading back to reality since his kiss with Ari has been difficult. He hasn't returned to church. In Utah, it was all pretend. He dressed the part and borrowed his dad's car to drive to the young single adults ward, but never made it inside the chapel. His sin sticks to his skin like a bucket of red paint to a white canvas; there's no way anyone would let him through the doors without crying foul. The two who care most about him are inviting him to opposite ends of an impossible spectrum: Josie in love and his mother in eternity.

But he won't bring any of this up. Instead, he looks for a change in topic. "Did you meet Ramona"

Josie sags dramatically, looping an arm through his and pulling him along the path with the flow of students. "Oh my *god*, dude."

"Is she your new best friend?"

Josie *pffffts* with her mouth. "She's awful." She looks delighted about it, though.

Adam frowns. "Please tell me you weren't rude."

Josie waves her hand. "She started it."

"*Josie.*"

"She did!" She gives him the play-by-play, "—and she has these two cronies, Ari and Silas—" Adam looks away too fast, but Josie keeps talking, clearly unaware, "—and Evelyn's texted me like ten times since I left the house. '*Make sure the toilet bowl remains presentable*' and '*appliances go in the cupboards*' and '*did you take the boxes down like I asked?*'" She sighs, like she's tired herself out. "I dunno, dude. I didn't know the cheap rent would come with so much micromanaging."

They've reached the humanities building, where Adam's first class of the day, news media law, is held. Josie will continue on to her environmental science class. "Could you go back to living with Feather?"

Josie gives him a look as they linger next to the doors. "I haven't done anything wrong! Ramona's mom practically begged me to move in!"

"Right, I know, I'm just—"

"This isn't my fault. Ramona told me to my face she doesn't want me there. I'm in the lion's den with her and her people, who are all just sitting there, champing at the bit to maul the sweet little lamb that's just wandered in."

"Sorry, are *you* the sweet little lamb in this scenario?"

"A wolf underneath, of course," Josie deadpans.

"I wonder . . ." Adam hesitates. "Maybe Ramona's parents made her get a roommate, considering her mom was so nice to you during the tour and her dad owns the house? Maybe Ramona's frustrated by the control."

Josie's angry expression falters, but only briefly. "Doesn't mean she gets to treat me like she has," she grumbles.

"I know." He gives her a small smile. "And I know you can handle her, but maybe consider where she's coming from."

"I'm allowed to act like a normal human who leaves a brush on the bathroom counter every so often." Adam presses his lips together, trying not to laugh. Josie lightly shoves his shoulder. "I'll need backup on this whole roommate thing. No more running off, okay?"

Adam feels his smile wilt at that, at the path laid before him. He doesn't want to stymie Josie in any way for his shortcomings. Complain about it she might, he knows Josie well enough to recognize that she's excited about the housing situation and all the potential it holds. He's not going to ruin that for her. He will spend time with Josie, he will eventually bump into Ari, he will keep quiet about his still-aching heart, and he will stay righteous the only way he has left. His mom will be proud, Josie will be none the wiser, and Adam will be bruised and battered, but only on the inside.

He manages to say with a steady voice, "I'm okay. Promise."

Adam's day passes by in a blur of syllabi and crowded walkways, then a quick three hours spent at the archives. He'd been hired the year prior, answering phones and emails, and sorting requests about the various items within the special collections and archives department. He's found himself addressing more and more questions from students and faculty and giving a few tours over the past couple days. Answering questions is fine, but Adam dreads playing guide. He's not good at it, even a year into the position, and public speaking is one of his worst nightmares.

As far as being ready for his last semester, everything is buttoned up for an early graduation. Adam breezed through the book for Tilton's class, as well as one for his lit class. It'll be a slog, this semester: taking fifteen credits, working twenty-five hours a week, and keeping his grades up throughout, but Adam's ready to embrace it.

He's settled behind the front desk when Cal approaches. His boss is a thin and balding white man, a widower of ten years. "How'd that three-o'clock tour go?" Cal speaks in a perpetual whisper.

Adam straightens and stops tapping a pen against the arm of his chair.

On his first day at work, he discovered a picture on Cal's desk showing a young Cal and his wife on their wedding day in front of a familiar building, the same temple where Adam's parents were married. That Cal is or was a member of the Mormon church has always felt like a trap, like Cal's a spy that Adam's parents sent over to keep an eye on him. It's not fair—Cal's only ever been kind to him, but Adam can't help feeling like anything he says to Cal will be relayed back to his parents.

When he isn't tottering around the stacks, Cal enjoys baking sweets, and has a tradition of bringing in his latest experiments. Today there were a dozen lemon-blueberry muffins.

"Oh, hi, it was good?" Adam says. "They wanted to know about that historical children's book collection." He clears his throat. "I finished that backlog of requests so everything's up to date."

"We really have been in a sorry state without you." Cal's blue eyes are merry behind round glasses. "I suppose, though you're on the precipice of graduation, I can't tempt you to switch your degree to history or library education? Stay working here forever?"

"Does forever include tours?" Adam asks.

"Ah, well, unfortunately for you, yes. Better you than me, after all." He winks. "Now . . ." He rotates, patting his pockets. "I have a dentist appointment I must get to. Are you comfortable closing up?"

"Yes, sir."

Cal thanks him again and leaves, still patting his pockets.

Only after he's off the clock, unlocking his bike from the rack in front of the library, does Adam pull his phone out of his pocket. Numerous missed texts from Josie, asking him to come to her place after his shift so they can discuss the book for Tilton's class tomorrow. Adam's used to summarizing class assignments for her, and hasn't ever been bothered by it, but he's intrigued by her determination to be an all-star student this semester. Any way he can support her is fine by him.

As for him spending time at the Valley house . . . Well, it'll be his first test of grinning and bearing it.

At least Ramona isn't home, based on the mostly dark windows, Adam thinks as he finally nabs a parking spot near Josie's house that evening. And if she's not there, Ari won't be either. It doesn't stop him from staying fully tense as he knocks on the front door.

The porch light flicks on as Josie opens the door with a flourish, hair practically crackling as she grins. "Just finished the book for tomorrow!"

Adam's eyes widen. "Wow, you read that faster than I did."

She's deservedly puffed up as she guides him to her room. She's cleaned the space a bit since he left yesterday; he can see the floor now.

There are also random Josie personality pieces: a framed picture of them on her desk, a Shins poster that clashes horribly with the calming whites and blues of the room, and a pile of clothes already gathering on the window seat. It's all very Josie.

They get comfortable on Josie's bed, trading notes about the assigned capstone reading. Well, Adam keeps trying to start discussions and Josie plays along for a few minutes before being distracted over something topic-adjacent. She's still Josie, even in her all-star student form.

He can't help but stay on edge throughout, listening for the sound of car doors slamming, loud chatter up the front walkway. By nine o'clock, he's really starting to sweat. Ramona will end up coming home to sleep. What's the likelihood she'll have Ari in tow?

Josie's scrolling on her phone when Adam reaches his limit. "I should probably take off."

He ignores Josie's narrowed eyes as he heads for the door. "Drive safe," she says slowly as he pulls the bedroom door open and peeks out. "Text me when you're home."

Adam waves goodbye, then practically sprints down the hall, skin itching. He's almost in the clear, will live another day. But when he reaches the bottom of the stairs, the door to his right opens and a pair of people appear, mid-conversation. His freedom is lost. Adam slips, clutching the handrail and wondering how in the world such a pivotal moment could take place after a normal action like studying with Josie or descending the stairs. Or breathing, which he doesn't seem to be doing now.

This is his new normal, he recognizes, though it hurts. Because standing not three feet from him is Ari.

He knew it would happen. Knew he both wanted and didn't want it to happen. Knew he wanted to see if Ari had changed, wanted to ask if he'd run the marathon he was training for, wanted to touch him and see if his skin was still warm and smelled like something spicy and mulled. He knows these things, recognizes his want of them in a split second.

For a moment, Adam forgets that to Ari and his companion, he is completely unexpected. The look on Ari's face, the only thing Adam focuses on, is pure shock. He's actively speaking when he locks eyes with Adam, the smile dying on his lips and surprise splashing across his features. His hair is a little shorter than it had been, but everything else is the exact same—including the uneven beating of Adam's heart at the sight of him.

"Adam?" The shock in Ari's voice is clear. He moves closer, hand rising, palm up in question. Or maybe he's reaching out. "What're you—? Are you . . . ?" He looks around, bewildered, then back. "Are you here for me?"

Adam is trapped in quicksand of his own making, lost to the details of Ari. How had he ever turned away from him? Denied himself a relationship with this man? Even in the emergency of the situation, he can feel himself responding to Ari's warmth; there's a sense of peace at the center of his storm. "I . . . I, um." He looks back up the stairs, then to the woman next to Ari—Ramona, he recognizes—who's watching him with wariness. "I was— I was with Josie?" He manages a few steps toward the front door. "Sorry, I'll go."

The confusion on Ari's face hasn't lessened. He doesn't look like he's taken in anything Adam has said. His dark, shapely brows are pinched together, and Adam knows if he moves closer, he'll be able to see the tiny freckle under Ari's right eye. He's daydreamed about that freckle.

Turning with an internal pleading to *stop it*, Adam quickly crosses to the door and yanks it open. The cool night air greets him. He shivers against the temperature.

"Wait."

A murmur of voices; Adam hears footsteps across the entry.

Then Ari is gripping the door, inches away from Adam's hand on the doorknob. Adam forgot how tall Ari was, but not the way Ari's body had felt against his own when they'd kissed. It might be subconscious hope, but when Adam meets Ari's gaze again, it looks as if memories are crashing back to the forefront of his mind, too. Good memories. "How are you? How was your summer?" Ari asks dazedly.

"It, it was good." Adam's voice is higher than normal. "Look, I didn't mean t-to interrupt. I was studying with Josie, and . . . and . . ." He trails off as Ari's mouth curls upward.

"Almost forgot how nervous you get." The words are spoken affectionately.

Adam feels a tug within his sternum, invisible hands yanking him toward Ari. But he's made his decision: with Ari he will suffer in silence. And so, instead of doing something stupid, Adam steps outside.

Ari calls out to him as he descends the walkway. "Would you want to catch up sometime? Maybe over dinner or something?"

The invisible hands pulling at the rope knotted to his sternum try to turn him back around to face Ari, but he maintains composure. He doesn't respond, and it's that decision that feels like the stupidest choice yet.

Chapter 7

A tapping sound distracts Josie from following Adam out to his car—he looked seriously spooked the entire night. When she peers out onto the dark backyard, Ramona's pal Silas is tossing up a second pebble against the glass.

She snorts and pushes open her window. "You're really leaning into this Romeo thing, huh?" she calls down.

Tonight, he's in a loose, black-and-white striped top tucked into dark, slim-fit slacks. His teeth shine beneath the dark of night as he grins up at her. "Saw your light and couldn't resist. What were you up to tonight?"

Josie drops her chin into her hand, fingers drumming against her cheek. "Studying with a friend."

Between the glow of the streetlight and faint gold cast from her bedroom window, Silas is part shadow, part pale, stone statue as he perches on the arm of an outdoor sofa. He pulls something from his pants pocket and a rectangular pack from his shirt. There's a glint of metal, flash of flame, and he's inhaling on a cigarette, the red glow adding a layer of wickedness to his features. He sends a trail of smoke upward, then asks, "How're you liking living here so far?"

She shrugs. "Fancy place."

"Aren't you supposed to be a reporter? Is that really the best description you can give?"

"Journalism is about succinctness." She shifts her weight, sitting cross-legged now on the window seat. "How do you know that? About my major?"

"I may have poked through some of the applications sent in to live here. I believe it was between you and a med student at UCSF."

Josie considers this. "First time I've ever beat out a future doctor. What was my selling point?"

"You were tails in the coin toss."

"My mom will be thrilled," she says with an eye roll. "What's your deal? Photographer, right? How'd that happen?"

"Because I'm good at it. How's that for succinctness?"

"Is that code for nepotism?"

Silas smiles. "I'm a proud product of public schools, so, no."

"But you're pals with Ramona? Somehow I don't see her dallying with the common folk."

"We met a couple years ago through Ari. *They've* been pals for ages, private schools and all." He twirls the hand holding the cigarette. "But what about you, my dear Juliet? What brought you to Ramona's doorstep?"

Josie reaches for a jacket on her floor and shrugs it on. "A shitty apartment in Bernal Heights. This was too sweet a place to pass up before I finish school." She remembers Adam's theory from earlier, that Ramona was possibly under duress to have someone here. Assuming he's right, and he usually is, she wonders why Ramona would be forced in the first place.

"When do you graduate?" Silas asks.

"In the spring. Hey, Ramona's lived here for a while, right? In this house?"

Silas blows out smoke and nods. "Few years."

"Then why—"

The door from the garage squeaks as it's opened. Ramona leans out.

"Si, I need you." She catches his attention and glances up to where Josie perches. Her expression darkens. "Now," she tells Silas.

Josie can't help a laugh at the sheer entitlement.

But Silas doesn't seem phased. "'Course," he says easily, walking to set his cigarette in an ashtray on the outdoor table. He nods at Josie in farewell. She raises her eyebrows, but dips her chin and closes the window as he joins Ramona.

Professor Tilton's not there when Josie arrives to class the next morning—on time thanks to setting her alarm thirty minutes earlier than usual.

A handful of fellow seniors are already seated, including Adam, who's seated next to Miu and—Josie does not fully stifle her groan—Elliot.

Miu greets Josie with a nervous-sounding hello as she plops into the seat behind Adam. Elliot gets the same puffed-up look he had last spring when she had to partner with him for an assignment. Josie gives them both a bared-teeth smile, then Adam a pointed look for choosing to sit next to them. He appears washed-out this morning. Josie assumes another guilt-tripping phone call with his mom.

"I was just telling Adam it feels like it's been ages," Miu says, breathless as usual around Adam. "How are you guys? Ready for the start of the semester?"

Adam's sliding his phone back into his pocket after a brief glance at it, momentarily delayed in his reply. "Oh, you know, yes and no . . . How was your summer?"

Miu nods like she's a bobble head. "Really fun! I interned for the *San Francisco Chronicle*, covering education. Turns out there's a lot of stuff that happens when school is out!" She giggles, and Josie rolls her eyes. "And Elliot went home to L.A. to work for an environmental magazine. You were in Utah, right? Did you have fun?"

Adam recaps his summer while Miu looks on like she's his biggest fangirl and Elliot sits there like the brown-nosing know-it-all he is. Josie ignores all of them, pulling up Ramona's TikTok account to watch outfit-of-the-day and get-ready-with-me videos, volume low. She only looks up when Adam says her name: "—and Josie covered real estate for the *Business Chronicle*. Jo, tell them about that one planning commission meeting—"

Elliot chimes in, "Well, I got to backpack the first hundred miles of the Pacific Crest Trail with a group raising awareness about bear safety in the Western U.S. At one point, some hunters from Nevada confronted us and one guy drew a gun. It was . . ." He inflates his chest even more and his voice grows louder, ". . . intense, to say the least. My article got more views than any other story in the history of the magazine. My editor says I have a job right out of school if I want it."

It's such an obvious attempt at one-upping her that Josie shouldn't react, but readies herself anyway. Elliot is saved, however, by Tilton's arrival; the room goes quiet.

"Morning everyone," Tilton says, standing tall at the front of the classroom. She's a thin Black woman, stylishly clad, and younger than her expertise implies; early forties, by Josie's guess. Tilton has worked as an award-winning reporter for some powerhouse newspapers: *Boston Globe, The Atlantic, Washington Post*. She's known for expecting the best, and only when students give it their absolute all does Tilton bless them with a 'good job.'

"I believe I've only worked with one of you before," Tilton says. A nod at Miu. "The rest, I look forward to being impressed by the latest batch of seniors."

Josie sits up straighter, and doesn't miss Elliot doing the same.

"The senior seminar is the pinnacle of journalism at this school. At this point, the wheat has been separated from the chaff. You are here, I hope, because you believe in an informed population, and that *you* can serve as a fair informant. That is my highest expectation of you in this class: You can be a damn good writer, but if you don't present information from all sides of a story in a balanced way, the article does not do its job and your attempt is void. I will help you seek that path of ethical balance during this class, and each of your efforts will culminate in a capstone project—a semester-long assignment.

"But before we review those details, I'd like brief introductions from each of you." Tilton rolls a chair out from the desk at the front of the classroom and sits center stage, crossing her legs and surveying the group. She hasn't yet smiled, but she doesn't seem cruel either; 'badass' is what Josie goes with.

"Name, minor, where you see your career going after graduation, and what you hope to take away from this class." Her eyes land on Adam, and Josie watches as the back of his neck goes red. "Please."

Adam clears his throat. "Um, I'm Ad—"

"Please stand."

He stands up so fast that his legs careen the flimsy desk forward and his notebook and pen slide to the floor. Josie catches Miu giving him an encouraging smile as he picks up the materials with shaking hands and steps away from the desk. Clearing his throat again, he says, "I'm Adam Hughes, my minor is in literature, uh, literature in English, that is. After I graduate, I'd like t-to focus on feature writing. I mean, individual feature writing—*profile* writing, is what I mean. And the, uh, takeaway from this class, I . . . um, I'd like to hear from you about that style, I guess? Profile writing. How it can be fair while also staying true to the individual."

He sits, slouching, and Tilton looks to Josie expectantly.

Josie stands, shoulders back, and launches into her spiel. "Josie Hicks, minor in business administration. What I hope to get from this class is an article that will make newsrooms want to hire me. And," she adds, "a letter of recommendation from you, Professor."

Next to her, Elliot scoffs.

One by one, the remaining students introduce themselves, sharing their passions and where they hope the field of journalism might send them—into sports writing, or the world of politics, or tech reporting, or even law school. When they've each shared, Tilton rolls her chair back to the desk. A Mac desktop hums to life at the wiggle of her hand on a mouse, and the projector screen centered on the wall behind her flickers on.

"Your final project will be a comprehensive media production of a story," she says, pulling up a PowerPoint presentation. "I want not only an in-depth written piece, but accessories, too." The presentation lists bullet-pointed expectations: a three-thousand-word story in AP style, five usable photos, a three-minute audio preview, and a sidebar or infographic.

"You're nearly graduated journalists now, and in the new world, you're expected to do a lot more than simply write a story. This is a demanding project, but the program has prepared you for this." Tilton's eyes meet each of their own. "You've likely heard that I ask quite a bit from my students. That is true. What each of you will produce will be an article any newspaper would be happy to run, assuming the topic is appropriate. In addition to these requirements," Tilton gestures at the screen, "you will pitch your story to an outlet."

Josie reads through the slide again, aware of her growing urge to get started now, to find a Pulitzer Prize-winning topic. How amazing would it be to have outlets knocking down her door, begging her to work for them? This is her time to shine.

Tilton continues speaking, shifting the students' focus to an in-class assignment that calls on the reading homework and will need to be performed with lightning-quick speed to get done in time. "This'll be individual work," she tells them. "Please begin."

Josie exhales long and hard as everyone pulls out their laptops. The semester is indeed off to a demanding pace.

For the last few minutes of class, after everyone has stumbled their way through the assignment, Tilton pulls up more details about their final project and Thursday's homework, then shares a series of previous semesters' successful stories.

"This assignment isn't due until the beginning of December," Tilton says. "But I expect you to have topics identified sooner. Next class, I'd like three ideas from each of you about possible options. Include what your story focus will be, and at least three people you can interview for each idea."

She glances at the clock. "As you can see, an hour-fifteen passes by quickly here. The semester will, too. Do not delay getting these stories going." Tilton punctuates her monologue by sitting once more, apparently oblivious to the current of panic spreading through the room.

Adam looks shell-shocked as he and Josie leave. The expression is familiar; he tends to panic on every first day of class.

"I quit," he croaks. "That was . . ."

"No wonder they save her for level six-hundred classes," Josie agrees. "Everybody would leave before now."

Adam pushes a hand through his hair. "I thought— This semester— I should've gone easier on myself. Day two and I'm already drowning."

Josie links an arm through his, leading him down the stairs. "Listen, the first week always sucks because every professor likes to wax poetic about the entire semester instead of looking at things class by class. It'll settle. Take it one day at a time."

They exit the building, heading toward the quad's expanse of greenery—their favorite spot to decompress. "It's my worst nightmare that she calls on us at random," Adam says. "There's no way you can be off your game in that class." Glancing at Josie, he asks, "How are you so calm?"

"You're distracting me from my own anxieties, thank you very much." But the same yearning that sparked to life while Tilton was talking is still there. "Speaking of distraction . . ." She raises her eyebrows at him. "I'm sure Miu would lick the soles of your feet if you let her."

That breaks Adam out of his downward spiral; he looks aghast. "*What?*"

She grins. Sweet, oblivious Adam. "How about I find someone you're actually attracted to to go out with this weekend? I think it's long overdue that you go on a date. It could help you relax."

A flicker of something in his eyes as he looks away. "No, thank you."

"Adam, you can't keep yourself this unsoiled virgin who wrings his hands over being gay forever. You need a release."

His face reddens. "No, thank you."

They find a spot on the grass beneath a tree and lounge in the shade, using their bags as pillows. Adam pulls out his phone while Josie stares up at the sky, thinking of everything she wants to accomplish.

She's taking twelve credits this semester, including the capstone. Between classes, she'll work as a data entry assistant—a glorified quality check to A.I., but hey, it pays the bills. She begins that job next week. Loans and leftover money from her internship help smooth the other edges of living in San Francisco as a student.

They lie in silence, letting the noise of passing students fill the place of conversation. Eventually, Adam says, clearly calm enough to talk sense about their capstone, "Um, for Tilton's class— I think writing a profile will go a long way, since she's written a bunch that've received awards and is known for that skill. Plus, most of those examples she showed us were features about individual people."

Josie nods, looking over. "I figured you'd go that route. Let me guess, you already have fifty thousand ideas?"

He shakes his head, sitting up. "No. I was just thinking, since you want to really prove yourself to Tilton, maybe you should, too? Write a profile, I mean?"

Josie eyes him. "I'm more into investigative stuff." Investigative reporting is the peak of journalism, and she intends to scale it.

"Do you have any ideas?"

Josie shakes her head. "Nothing formulated yet." Because it's Adam, she allows a bit of insecurity to bleed into her next words. "I really want this story to be amazing."

And because it's Adam, whose faith in her has never been shaken, his confidence is clear even as his smile is soft. "It will be."

When she arrives home from campus, Ramona is heading out. Josie literally bumps into her when she pushes open the door.

Ramona's not alone, either. "Whoa there, cowgirl," comes a male voice as Josie catches the door from ruining Ramona's nose job. "No need to come in so hot and heavy. It's only Tuesday."

He looks to be in his late-thirties, forgettably handsome with a smarmy smile Josie immediately hates. His proximity to Ramona tells Josie they're likely romantically involved, but when Josie meets Ramona's gaze with a raised eyebrow and an *are-you-really-dating-someone-fifteen-years-older* expression, her roommate looks ready for a different kind of scolding.

"Are you and Adam dating?" she asks bluntly.

Time suspends only briefly. Josie doesn't burst out laughing, but it's a close thing. "Dude, *no*. We're friends." Then, as the question registers, she narrows her eyes. Adam hadn't mentioned meeting Ramona. "What's it to you?"

The twist of her Ramona's mouth shows how much she despises having this conversation. "I'm not exactly thrilled to be hearing his name again."

Josie must've missed the mark somewhere, because she has no idea what Ramona's implying. She looks between her roommate and the man, who's turned away to answer his phone ("Buddy. Got your email. You sure that's an accurate count?").

"'Again'?" Josie asks. "What is that supposed to mean?"

Ramona stares at her like she's the world's biggest idiot. "It means that after everything earlier this year, I hoped he was gone for good."

Annoyance stabs behind Josie's right eye. "What are you even talking about?"

An odd look dawns across Ramona's face. The ruffled offense softens to surprise before delight takes over. She uncrosses her arms. The poison in her growing smile has Josie's scalp itching. "Huh. Not that good of friends after all," she says.

Josie receives the statement like a slap. "*Ramona.*"

But her weakness is too acute; Ramona's taking the victory and running with it. She brushes a hand against the man's back. Together, they bypass Josie's blockade of the front door. As she steps outside, Ramona says, like it's an afterthought, "By the way, my parents would like you to join us for dinner on Friday."

Josie's head is spinning as is. She manages, mouth cottony, "What?"

"Dinner," Ramona repeats, pulling sunglasses from her purse and perching them on her nose. "With my parents. Ev will text you the details." She gives a wave of her fingers and heads for a Cybertruck parked at the curb, smarmy fellow dutifully holding the passenger door open wide.

Chapter 8

The pair of students exchange smiles as they turn to leave, and Adam flushes. Every time he stumbled over his words on the tour, they giggled, until the giggling was an underlying current while he tried—and failed—to speak any sense.

He's extra flustered today. First, Tilton's class and the mountain that'll be to climb. But also . . . His eyes drift to his backpack again, where he can faintly see the outline of his phone in the front pocket.

The text came shortly after he fled Josie's house last night. Shortly after his reunion with Ari. He still hasn't opened the message, already anxious over the preview. *hey. sry I was so weird tonite. been thinking about u a lot . . .*

He finishes his shift at the archives, attends one more class, and bikes home before the mounting tension becomes too much. He barely makes it inside, hovering at the bottom of the stairs leading up from the garage as he swipes the message open. Ari is still 'Sexy Runner Guy,' a demand made by an outraged Ari on their third date after Adam revealed that he was, in fact, listed as 'Intersection Stranger.'

hey. sry I was so weird tonite. been thinking about u a lot and it was crazy to see you irl after so long. I'm sry I left things like I did back in April. I shouldn't of bailed. I should've stayed and talked things thru and made sure u we're ok. I get that u don't want to talk to me but wanted u to kno that I'm sry. ~ Ari

Adam stares at the message for so long his phone goes dark twice. He reads it in full, then in parts. He's continually drawn back to the fact that Ari signed the text with his name, as if Adam had deleted his number. Like Adam couldn't recite their previous texts from memory.

He nearly drops his phone when Jon thumps down the stairs on his way to the garage, swinging his car keys. He stops on a dime when he sees Adam. "You good?"

Adam nods, words only slightly behind. "Yes, sorry. You just scared me." He drops his phone in his pocket. "Heading to work?"

Jon's wearing his standard button-up and black pants for his cook position at the IHOP in Daly City. He nods. "This night shit sucks major ass."

"I'm planning to make that buffalo chicken dish for dinner," Adam says, starting upstairs. "Jo's heading over. I'll save some for you so you have food when you get back?"

"See, this is why you're the best!" Jon calls as he leaves. "Tell J I send my love!"

Adam is, in Jon's words, "a Craigslist roommate miracle." They've been living together since sophomore year and have never once had any weird arguments over whose food is whose, why cleaning the house needs to be a joint effort, or delayed rent payments. Jon wants to keep the house nice for his parents, who he's close to, and he's good about giving Adam a heads up before having people over.

He's always "talking to" someone, though his official relationships are few and far between. There was a moment during those first few months of living together that, after Jon had confirmed with Adam that he and Josie weren't a thing, Jon took a liking to Josie. And because Josie enjoys the conquest of many a male, Adam had the horrifying experience of seeing Josie perform the walk of shame from Jon's room to his own one Sunday morning. Thankfully, in a way that made Adam think that Jon is a maker of miracles, Jon and Josie sleeping together was a laughable experience, and one that only resulted in playful ribbing.

Adam's exchange with Jon buoys him enough to formulate a reply to Ari. *Hi. No need to apologize for anything, not now or then. I hope you're doing well.* Practical and clinical. Adam sends the text, and begins preparing dinner, ignoring the disappointment spreading like mold in his chest.

Josie shows up early, which is the first sign something's off.

"You really are changing things up for senior year," he says with a half smile when he opens the door. "C'mon up, dinner's basically . . ."

He falters at her suspicious glare, stomach sinking.

"Did you know Ramona before I moved in with her?" Josie asks.

Adam shakes his head, unable to trust his voice. It's not a lie. Ari mentioned his friends only in passing, and only by first name.

Josie's watching him like she wants to believe him but doesn't. "Ramona was saying some weird stuff earlier. She acted like she knew who you were."

The hurt in her voice is apparent. Adam makes himself speak, hoping against hope there's a way out of this. "I saw her as I was leaving last night. I've never met her before."

Josie nods, the movement disjointed. "You don't have some secret social media account where you're crazy famous, do you?"

At another head shake from Adam, Josie's mouth twists, but it looks more speculative than accusing. "It was *so* weird. You'd have thought she found out her next three lip injections were free when I didn't know what she was going on about."

"Maybe she confused me for someone else?" Adam suggests, fiddling with the sleeve of his sweatshirt. As the lie leaves his mouth, the knot in his chest pulls tighter.

"That has to be it," Josie says. It's clear that even the most vague suggestion is a welcome answer. She steps inside and sends him a sly grin. "One way or the other, you're on Ramona Taylor's radar now. Let me know if Evelyn starts texting you demands."

His responding laugh is weak, but he finds comfort in the confidence taking over Josie's gait once more. He follows her up to the kitchen, a mixture of reassurance and regret for dodging such a critical conversation.

It's for the best, he tells himself. Revealing what happened with Ari would send Josie into hyperdrive. The last thing he needs is his best friend determined to bring Ari back into his life.

Promise me, his mom's voice says in his ear.

I promise, he mentally replies.

When Adam settles into his seat in Tilton's class Thursday morning, Miu gives him a shy smile. Her hair is divided into short pigtails, and she's wearing a long, purple boxy dress.

"Hi, Adam," she says. Her eyes are dark brown, large and guileless. "I still can't believe this is our last semester."

Adam pulls his notebook out of his backpack and sets it on the desk. "You're applying for grad school, right?"

Miu nods. "I'm considering Northwestern next fall, for journalism."

"Wow, Miu, that's really awesome. And Northwestern is a great school. I bet you'll have no problem getting in. They'd be lucky to have you."

Two circles of red appear on her cheeks. She drops her gaze to the floor with a private-looking smile. "Thanks, Adam."

More students take their seats in the classroom, including Elliot, who gives Miu a look Adam thinks is meant to be encouraging. Miu takes a breath. "I was wondering," she says, voice a bit higher now, "Elliot and me and some others are getting together Saturday night to celebrate the start of the semester and everybody back in town. Would you like to come?"

"Oh, um . . ." Elliot's and Miu's stares are intense, Miu's so full of hope he feels guilty saying anything other than, "What time?"

"I'm not sure yet, but I can text you?"

He nods, distracted by Tilton's arrival, the door closing behind her and no Josie in sight. Adam reaches for his phone, but doesn't get any further before Tilton cuts to the chase, telling the class she'll call them up one at a time to speak with her about their story plans. She calls out Adam's name first, and he stands, heart now racing, and walks up to sit in the chair next to Tilton.

He lays out his story ideas, mentioning his primary interest is a piece on a Giants season ticket holder.

The idea is thanks to Jon, who calls himself an "active" watcher of baseball. Meaning if there's a game happening—in person, on TV, streaming—he's constantly running his mouth: observations, statistics, insults, regardless of whether anyone is around to hear him. It was during one of these monologues the previous year that Jon recounted his introduction to a locally famed season ticket holder at a game. "This guy is the definition of dyed in the wool," Jon said to Adam, who'd been reading on the couch but knew to save at least thirty percent of his focus for his roommate. "His mom even went into labor with him at a game back in the sixties. He's only ever missed one game, and that was for the birth of his son who, get this, now plays for the Dodgers."

An intriguing profile subject, Adam decided. He spent the past couple days revisiting Jon's account, then finding and getting in touch with the guy: Barry Keller, a lawyer, who said he'd be more than happy to share his story.

Tilton listens, fingers steepled, leaning back in her chair. When Adam finishes his list of ideas, she goes through the stories one by one, asking follow-up questions, like who additional sources would be, whether Adam might have access to historical photos, and how to expand the story beyond the main tether.

After he answers, she gives him a close-lipped smile. "I think you've got three interesting stories here, some with more obvious strengths, but your passion is apparent. The next deadline will be a formal story budget." Tilton makes a note on a piece of paper. "Solid work."

Adam's face heats as he nods, pleased, and returns to his seat. Miu's called up next, and Adam pulls his phone out to text Josie. *Where are you? It's topic day with Tilton!* He waits for her response while other students trickle up and back, gets a *shit!!!!! I slept in!*, and spends the next thirty-five minutes anxiously tracking her progress to campus.

She shows up wild-eyed just as the bell rings, and marches up to the professor. Adam's close enough to hear her say, somewhat out of breath, "Woke up late. Can I—"

"Deadlines are critical in the world of journalism, Miss Hicks," Tilton says, expression stern. She gathers a notepad from the desk and rises to stand. "You failed to meet today's. You can visit me during office hours on Monday to discuss your missed assignment."

"But—"

"Monday, please."

Josie stands agape as Tilton heads for the classroom door. She's still there when Adam approaches, and he can tell she's gathering steam.

They make it halfway to their grassy knoll before she says anything. "That was total bullshit," she hisses.

"What happened?" he asks.

"Ramona had some sort of get-together last night, and they would *not* stop squealing. I barely slept." She gives an unamused laugh as she rubs at her face. "I still don't have my three ideas for Tilton, so it's probably better that I get the extra time. Doubt she'd have been stoked with me winging it."

Adam swallows a sigh. "You decided not to do the housing one?" They'd spent the past two nights brainstorming ideas. A piece on a workforce housing project was the closest she got to a solid idea.

Josie makes a face. "It doesn't feel strong enough for Tilton. I think you're right about writing a profile, but I need something epic. Like, discovering the person who discovers the cure for cancer."

"Just make sure you have something by Monday, okay? I don't think this class is one to procrastinate in."

"I *know*, Adam." Her voice is sharp.

Adam looks away. "You know I'll help you come up with ideas, right?" he says after a moment.

Her voice is still gruff, but there's a softness to its edges. "Kinda want to do this on my own for once, but thanks."

Without looking, he bumps her side with his elbow. She bumps him back. When they reach their spot, Josie plops on the ground, limbs flung out like she's exhausted. He sits next to her and asks, "How are you feeling about your dinner out tomorrow night?"

Josie looks thoughtful at the question, eyes on the leafy foliage overhead. "Intrigued? We'll see if Ramona's mom fawns over me again. You're still good for the show Saturday night?"

Adam pulls his knees up under his chin. "Yeah. I was wondering, though. In class, Miu was saying she and some others are getting together that night to celebrate the first week of school. I told Miu I might be interested, if you want to come with? Before the show?"

Annoyance lines Josie's forehead as she squints at him. "Yeeeeah, no. I have zero desire to make small talk with Miu."

"She's nice."

"She wants to get in your pants. Why are you leading her on?"

"I'm being friendly," Adam says with a frown. "Please, will you come with me?"

Josie sighs. "Fine. But I can't promise not to punch Elliot when he brings up his stupid bear hike."

It's with relief that Adam heads for his shift at the archives, buoyed by the unexpected ease life has allowed despite Ari's reappearance.

Chapter 9

The following day, Josie's in her room, moseying through a reading assignment, when a text appears from an unknown 415 number. She opens it to find a picture of her bedroom window from the outside. No words accompany the photo. She smiles to herself and, instead of crossing to the window, heads for the patio.

Silas is there, in yet another loose, button-up shirt and dress pants. "You got my carrier pigeon," he says.

"Very creepy," she assures him, relaxing into one of the seats beneath the gazebo shade. "I assume you begged Ramona for my number?"

"Desperately." Silas is slouched into his own seat, ankles crossed, two fingers pressed to his temple. A thin silver chain hangs around his neck, glinting in the late afternoon sun.

"You do have a place of your own, right?" Josie asks, separating a strand of hair to play with.

"Sure. But parking's easier here. And this is too sweet a place to pass up."

The corner of Josie's mouth kicks up at the repeat of her words from the other night. "Can't blame you."

He's watching her with a smile. "Classes have started? How's it going?"

"Fine." She's weaving the strand of hair into a tiny braid. "I'm taking my capstone this semester and have to write a big-deal article for it."

"What does that mean, 'capstone'?"

"It's a class for seniors. Tests our merit as journalists and all that."

Silas arches an eyebrow. "What are you looking for as a topic?"

"Something hard-hitting. Know any slumlords who need to be taken down in the name of journalism?"

"Different circles, believe it or not. How big-deal are we talking?"

"It's basically my chance to wow the judges and get a supreme-level recommendation for wherever I head next."

Silas nods thoughtfully, an earring in his left ear dancing at the motion. "What about a piece on Ramona?"

Josie can't help the sour expression. Is he seriously so devoted a fan that Ramona's name is the first on his tongue? "Hard pass."

He reaches to pull his pack of cigarettes and lighter out of a pocket. With a spark of flame at the end of the cigarette, he says, "Why not? She's well known. You could write a feature on her."

"I said hard-hitting, not a fluff piece about some—" She barely stops herself from saying the word 'bimbo,' "—influencer. I appreciate the pitch, but no thanks."

"Doesn't have to be complete fluff." Silas takes a drag. "And it's the kind of story I would read. Slum lords . . . not so much."

Josie remains untempted. "I'm good."

Silas shrugs. "Your loss. I'll keep my ear to the ground for other ideas. Do you need pictures for your story? I could help, though I haven't really shot *news* photos before . . ."

"I'm supposed to submit photos with my story but I'm not sure if I can use someone else's. Let me get back to you on that because if you're willing, that'd be awesome. I need to get the story published, too, so your name would be in the captions if it works out."

He clasps his hands together and fakes swooning. "I should send carrier pigeons your way more often. An opportunity to have my work *published*!"

The sarcasm isn't lost on her, and she flips him off. He gives her a lazy smile in return and she has to bite back a grin. He's feisty. A little too princely for her taste, but still. Josie likes feisty.

From Silas's pocket comes a muffled ringing. He pulls out his phone, glancing at the screen before answering. "Hey," he says, around the cigarette. "Yeah, I'm out back. No, he's with— Yeah. I mean, you and I both know why. I know. I'll see if I can track him down . . . They're here now?" His eyes shift to Josie's as he listens. "She's with me . . . Yeah, sure . . . Be inside in a few." He hangs up and wags the dark screen at Josie. "Your favorite roommate."

Josie purposely doesn't stick out her tongue. "I'm supposed to go to dinner with her and her parents tonight. Any tips?"

Silas exhales on a laugh. "Get the most expensive thing on the menu, and then get a second order of it for me."

"Not a fan?"

Silas hums, but doesn't reply.

She studies him for a moment, his clear relaxation in this setting, then asks, "So, are you in love with her?"

He meets her gaze. "Ramona?"

Josie gives a confirming flick of her fingers.

The smile he gives her now seems weighted with secrets. "It'd be difficult for me to know Ramona like I do and not love her. But we're not together, if that's what you're wondering. She's seeing a guy named Andrew." Then, before Josie can react to the edge in his voice, he asks, "Do you love Adam?"

"Yes." Her answer is automatic. "Wait, how do you know about— Oh." She recalls Ramona's questioning the other day.

"Tell me about him."

"I mean . . . we're friends, best friends. Since freshman year. Adam is . . . He's one of those people who's genuinely good, you know? He's quiet and sweet and reads way too much." Josie laughs fondly.

"Honestly, if I didn't love him so much, I'd hate his guts."

"Why?"

"Because nice people are annoying." She swings a leg over the arm of her chair. "And he can be timid. Sometimes I have to force him to do things I know will be good for him."

Silas's eyes briefly narrow. "Like what?"

Josie shakes her head. "Stuff. Why do you love Ramona?"

It's his turn to flick his fingers. "History." He stands and stubs his cigarette out in a nearby ashtray. "Wanna head inside? You've got your expensive dinner to get to."

Josie can't help but feel cut off right when the conversation was getting going. "Yeah, okay."

They re-enter through the garage, skirting Ramona's Tesla, and head down the hall. As they approach the entryway, Josie hears Ramona's voice. She's in what sounds like a heated conversation. Josie sees Silas's shoulders stiffen before he takes the single tiled step up from the hallway.

Nara and an older man stand near the front door, conversing with Ramona, who has her hands on her hips. The man has blonde hair, his skin a ruddy red. He's nothing to write home about in the looks department, but that's not to say he's not put together. He's wearing a crisp navy suit and shiny brown shoes. His white collared shirt is open at the top, but he doesn't have the same allure as Silas, who wears his partially unbuttoned shirts like the King of England wears his crown. The blonde man carries himself like royalty, though. Either unaware or uncaring of his displeasing physical appearance, he stands like a man who's commanded Navy fleets: back straight, one hand in his pocket, mouth slightly turned down like he's perpetually disappointed. He stands a foot or so back from Nara, who's once again perfectly styled. This time, however, there's no joy in her expression.

"Mom, you *said* you would lay off," Ramona hisses. "I've done everything you've asked. I'm doing this tonight. Will you *leave* it?"

"When you are living off your father and me, when I am in the position I'm in, we are allowed to have input on the direction you're taking," Nara replies evenly. She catches sight of Silas, his presence apparently doing nothing to improve her mood. The corners of her mouth fall further. "Hello, Silas."

"Nara, Ashland," Silas says with an ease Josie couldn't muster on her best day. He steps back with a nod toward Josie. "Look who I found."

Nara's demeanor immediately shifts for the better. Her eyes widen and her mouth smooths upward into a gracious smile. Even Ashland, who seemed content to have his wife and daughter argue for eternity, looks at Josie with curiosity. "Josie!" Nara moves across the entryway and pulls Josie into a hug. "Lovely to see you again."

Josie catches Ramona's eye over Nara's shoulder and can't help her grin as she pats Nara on the back. "Thanks for the dinner invite," she says as Nara pulls back. "It was nice of you to think of me."

"Why, of course!"

Next to them, Silas shifts. "My cue," he says, heading for the front door. "Enjoy." Ramona gives him a murderous look as he kisses her cheek before slipping out.

Nara drapes an arm around Josie's shoulders. "The car is waiting out front."

Conversation during the ride to the restaurant centers on Josie and is led by Nara, who's sitting across the middle row of seats and turned to face her. Josie can't help but feel pleased. She's thrilled her first introduction to Nara wasn't a fluke, and enjoys the unfamiliar keen attention of a parent as she's peppered with question after question about college: her favorite classes, being around the other students on campus, the independence of moving away from home, and more. Next to her, Ramona is scrolling and tapping on her phone, audio from different video clips blaring.

When the car pulls in front of a restaurant and they climb out, the valet greets them. "Congresswoman. We're grateful your family could join us again."

Nara responds with something about living in D.C., and Josie's eyes widen. "'*Congresswoman*'?" she whispers to Ramona.

Ramona scowls. "Yeah, just ask her."

Inside, they're accompanied to a booth in the back, a private corner. The mood at this place is sophisticated. Exposed brick, trestle wood beams, and concrete walls make up the interior. Bare bulbs hang over individual booths and tables. The kitchen is open, viewed from anywhere in the restaurant; the chef and cooking staff bustle around stainless steel appliances with practiced efficiency.

Josie sits, eyeing the waiters, the patrons, her own companions—a *congresswoman!?*, the menu (where prices aren't listed). This kind of place clearly thrives off rich clientele and probably has a months-long waitlist. Similar to how she feels about living in the Valley house, she recognizes that dining at a restaurant like this is a once-in-a-lifetime experience.

Next to her, Ramona projects a silent force field of fury. Nara and Ashland are having a whispered conversation.

Josie leans over to Ramona, shattering the force field, "How long have they been together?"

Ramona doesn't look up, only says loudly, scrolling all the while: "Mom, how long have you guys been together?"

Nara sits forward and gives Josie a warm smile. She doesn't look like a mom. Not like Josie's, with her casual clothes and comfortable body. But it's not like Josie's mother is the textbook definition of a parent—not even close. "Twenty-three years, if you can believe it," Nara tells her. A fond look over to Ashland, who meets her gaze with a twinkle in his eye. "Best years of my life."

To Josie's right, Ramona is taking a selfie.

"Aren't you in session right now?" Josie asks Nara. "Like, on the other side of the country?"

"We get the month of August off," Nara replies. "And I sneak away fairly often."

A server appears with a bottle of wine, conversation pausing during the taste-testing and pouring. Meal-wise, Josie is easily talked into a crab dish, not caring if it's the most expensive item on the menu. She's surprisingly comfortable in present company, Ramona aside, and is mentally documenting everything—the motion of hands on the stems of glasses, backs straight, flush against the leather of the booth—to give Adam a play-by-play later.

"Are you working on any, uh, bills?" Josie asks. The words feel too casual for what they mean; elected officials like Nara creating laws that govern the entire country. Josie thinks of her needed story idea for Tilton's class. A U.S. congresswoman would certainly be a compelling focus.

Nara looks pleased by the question. "I'm part of a few key conversations. Even though I'm in my first term, my district is reliably blue. There's not a lot of mystery; people know what they're getting with me."

"Does that stop them from trying to change your mind?"

Nara tinkles out a laugh. "Oh, I like you."

A kernel of pride bursts in Josie's chest. "What are the conversations you're having right now?" she asks.

"Well." Nara looks like she's making herself more comfortable in her seat. "Top of the pile is tech, and my district houses more than a few tech giants, so you can imagine how often I'm pulled into meetings on the topic. There's a congressional bill in motion looking to encourage innovation zones across the country. You've heard of them, I'm sure?"

Josie's flattered by Nara's assuming question, but shakes her head.

"They're growing in popularity in a handful of cities with some success. It's like giving a tech company its own town. They can build infrastructure, set policies, even influence local governance—just without the usual public oversight. They end up becoming productive sandboxes for all things tech."

"And they're just allowed to do that?"

Nara nods. "Especially in the current political climate. The race for A.I. dominance continues, and what better way to encourage that kind of brainstorming than by streamlining regulations nationwide? The vote won't happen until November, and you can imagine the speculation flying around over which way things will go. It's a close count."

Swallowing another bite of crab, Josie asks, "Where does your reliably blue voice land?"

Nara swirls her glass of wine and smiles. "That's the question everyone's been asking." At Josie's head tilt, she continues, "I haven't made up my mind yet. There's a fair bit of excitement around the bill, especially from folks in my district. Companies like VYBE—you know it?"

Josie would have to live under a rock not to; the generative artificial intelligence chatbot is so many people's go-to resource.

Nara continues: "Of course, they're already sketching out their wish lists. And I get it: a bill like this could bring investment, jobs, maybe even real infrastructure upgrades. But I represent more than the tech sector. I have to think about what this means for workers, for housing, for public oversight. I'm not interested in rubber-stamping something just because it sounds like innovation."

"Is that the same answer all Democrats in Congress are giving?"

Nara sounds like she's in full-blown politician mode now. "Let's just say a few of us newer members are taking our time with this one. We're asking tougher questions, pushing back on the language, trying to figure out where the guardrails are—or if there *are* any. It's complicated. I'm not opposed, but I'm not convinced either."

"No shi—I mean, uh, kidding," Josie says. "That's a lot to think about."

Nara laughs like Josie's made an intentionally witty remark, but before she can move the conversation further, Ramona groans. "*Ohmigod*, can we *please* talk about something more exciting?"

Nara looks over and Josie doesn't miss her grip tightening on the stem of her glass. "These are the types of conversations adults have, Ramona. You would do well to be more aware of the politics and realities of our home instead of running off to Burning Man."

"I *am* aware of the realities," Ramona replies hotly as the food arrives. "I just don't want to talk about it over dinner."

"Everyone is enjoying themselves except for you. Are you finally seeing how a college education could expand your knowledge base?" Nara is smiling in such a way that anyone not in earshot would think she was gushing. Ashland takes a bite of his potatoes as if this is a conversation oft repeated. Josie watches, wide-eyed.

"Josie here can clearly keep up with elevated dinner conversation. She's studying to be a journalist, and that involves plenty of socializing and research on the internet. Doesn't that sound interesting? You could even pursue *fashion* journ—"

Ramona cracks. "Stop. I am *so* over you controlling literally every part of my life. I'm an adult, and I get to do things my own way. If me living my life how I want is going to affect your, like, platform or whatever, then quit politics."

"Don't you dare act so callous about my career, Ramona. I'm trying to do what's best by encouraging you to pursue a degree that will help bolster your future."

Ramona is all teeth now, mirroring the smiling jaws of her mother. "If you bring up college again, I'll literally scream. I told you: I don't need to spend thousands of dollars to get a piece of paper! You already shoved a roommate down my throat—" A vicious look at

Josie, "—who's absolutely *horrid*, by the way. I'm done with your micromanaging."

Nara looks aghast. "I didn't raise you to be so rude and ungrateful!" To Josie, she says, "I am truly sorry for my daughter's behavior."

"It's really okay," Josie says, fidgeting.

Nara continues like she hasn't heard Josie. "I have tried so hard to support your attempts at social media influence, but the fact is, there is little merit. You've spent this entire dinner staring at your phone when you could be offering your perspective on innovation zones. For crying out loud, don't you utilize VYBE for its social media trend detection tool? A key constituent of mine and major backer of the bill we were just discussing! Engage in something more than like counts for once in your life, Ramona."

"Nara, darling," Ashland finally chimes in.

It's rare that Josie finds herself at a loss for words. She tries to cover her discomfort by reaching for her wine glass and taking a hurried sip. Ramona, to her credit, has shuttered all emotion from her face.

Nara and Ashland slip into a strained but quiet conversation, leaving Ramona to her phone and Josie to place pieces of the puzzle. A parent-child disagreement on the child's future, to which Josie, a college student, is adjacent. It would explain why none of Ramona's friends are living with her. Nara seemed less than fond of Silas, a non-collegiate example in her daughter's life, and if she's often in the limelight as a public figure, wouldn't she want her family represented well? A twenty-something daughter she's still trying to encourage down the college track.

Josie's seed of pride takes root. Proximity to something makes it more of an attainable reality, right? She must be Nara and Ashland's answer to encouraging an education out of their only child. Not the heralded two friends that make up Ramona's entourage, but *Josie*, who doesn't believe relying on a ton of followers is a sustainable way of life. Not that the Taylors would know that, but hey, luck of the draw.

It certainly seems that Adam is yet again right in his assumption: Ramona's hand was forced. What's more, Nara and Ashland—or maybe Nara specifically; Ashland seems relatively chill by comparison on the matter—clearly wanted a college student as a roommate for their daughter. The idea also explains Ramona's hesitations at having her around, nitpicking her existence. If Josie had an entire place to herself and was suddenly forced by her mom to bring in an unwanted roommate who exemplified the life they wanted for her, she, too, would pitch a fit.

It's the first turn of the cog in the machine of Ramona, and Josie's salivating for more.

When they're dropped back off, Nara trills out her fondness for Josie as she hands over a business card, personal cell number scrawled across the back—"Oh, don't call me 'Congresswoman,' just Nara." Even Ashland gives Josie a minute smile. She receives it nobly, maybe a little too primly, but the Taylors just paid a stupid amount of money for her dinner.

Ramona's hair sways like the bends of a river as she walks, back and shoulders straight as Josie follows her inside. It takes balls to stay put-together after such a dressing down, Josie will admit.

When Ramona moves toward her room, Josie calls out, "Hey."

Ramona turns only her head.

"Your parents made you get a roommate, huh? That's why I'm here, right?" She wants to hear the words from Ramona's mouth, but Ramona only stares back. Josie thinks of one of the first lessons taught in her journalism classes: If you want someone to start talking or keep talking, stay quiet; let them fill the silence. She feels the urge to continue anyway and does so.

"I mean, your mom is obviously bummed that you're not going to school, and she's apparently a big fan of mine. That's not normally people's takeaway when meeting me, and what she said at dinner, about you getting a college education . . ." She lets the implication hang.

Ramona looks like she's swallowed a bitter lemon. "Anything with my parents is none of your business."

Josie frowns but tries to keep the edge out of her voice. "It is actually *literally* my business, because I'm the one who's been dragged into the middle of this. If you told me why I was here in the first place maybe I could've—"

"Ohmigod, spare me any goodwill or whatever this is. You are nothing more than a pawn to my mother, and nothing, period, to me. Like, trust me, you're not on my radar in any way."

Recovery from the verbal slap comes slowly to Josie, but it does come. "Well, I'm certainly on a closer intellectual level to your parents than you are," she says, pushing a curl off her face. "Seems like they agree that posting pretty pictures isn't exactly what they hoped for from their only child. Can't wait to fill them in on my experience living here as, you know, the educated example I am."

She can practically see the red burning across Ramona's vision as she swivels toward the staircase. "And quit having Evelyn do your dirty work," she calls out as she begins to climb. "I'm paying to live here, so let me fucking *live*."

Chapter 10

Based on Miu's text, the back-to-school get-together is happening at a dive bar close enough to the Throne Room that Josie and Adam agree to take the bus from her place, then walk.

She's moody on the ride over. No more of the bravado with which she'd called after her dinner the previous evening. ("*Congresswoman Nara Taylor* is Ramona's *mom?*" he'd asked, gobsmacked. "Jo, we talked about her a ton in our media politics class last fall. How did you not recognize her?")

But now when Adam probes, Josie only grumbles something about "mommy issues" and "at least someone's parents care," and he knows without asking what's on Josie's mind.

The bar has an intimate, homey feel: low ceiling, warm lighting, the wall covered with hundreds of stickers: bands, brands, destinations, and more. TVs are mounted to the walls. Miu's group clusters at the far end of the bar, spreading out to an adjacent table. Adam only recognizes one other person aside from Elliot and Miu, a guy who might be a year down in the program. The others are new faces. He can't help but grow nervous as he approaches.

Miu sees him and her entire face lights up. "Adam! You came!" Her voice is high and breathless, pupils large and eyes wide with unfettered joy and alcohol. She's wearing some sort of silky dress, fancier than her usual attire. Her features look more accentuated, too; eyeliner and even lipstick.

"Hi, Miu. Um." He swallows against a hammering pulse, already regretting his eagerness to find distraction in a social situation.

A glance to his left shows Josie's ordering at the bar. She told him when he got to her house that she's coming out to drink, not socialize; pre-gaming for the Throne Room.

There's a hand around his forearm. Adam is pulled by Miu to a seat next to her at the table. Under the influence, Miu is certainly less inhibited, less shy. She's close, still clinging to his arm, as she introduces him to the others. "This is Adam!" she half shouts, even though the music from the speakers is low enough for conversation at a normal level. In exchange for the introduction, Adam receives a few smiles. Elliot is looking over Adam's shoulder, and as Adam turns, he sees Josie walking steadily toward the group, a glass brimming with beer in her hand.

She sits on one of the barstools, above the fray, levels a cool look at Elliot, then surveys the rest of the group. Her gaze lands on Miu, practically in Adam's lap, then, with the arch of an eyebrow, shifts to Adam. *What have we here?* she seems to ask. He gives her a slightly panicked look, but she only widens her eyes in an *I-told-you-so* way and lifts her glass with a cheers! motion.

Miu and her friends begin a hearty debate over something Adam is too distracted to pay attention to, and he's growing increasingly uncomfortable with Miu's fondness for him. Josie's already on her second beer and has devolved into a venomous snake ready to strike. One of the unknown-to-Adam members of the group moves from his seat at the bar next to her to the table, whether in fright or to be closer to the discussion, it's unclear. Regardless, Josie sits alone.

The conversation continues. Miu's hand is high on Adam's thigh, squeezing every time something funny is said, and Adam's face has never felt hotter. He starts to inch away when he's distracted by Josie's angry voice.

"—fuck *off* about the bear hike!"

He looks over to see Josie, a new glass nearly full of beer clutched in her hand, hair wild, glaring at Elliot, who must've wandered over.

"It was just an idea," Elliot says hotly. "Since you were late—"

"The only bears in San Francisco are in the zoo, and I pray to *god* you know that." Josie takes three long swallows of beer before slamming it on the counter and standing. She turns her glare toward Adam and Miu and casts another spear: "Give it up, Miu. He's not interested."

Miu abruptly pulls away from Adam, scraping her chair back. "Oh, I—" Her eyes are even wider now. She swings her gaze from Josie to Adam. Whatever she sees on his face confirms things, and the scarlet staining her cheeks deepens. "I'm so sorry."

"No, Miu, I'm—" Adam starts.

"Let's go, Adam." Josie is standing beside his chair now, arms crossed.

Adam almost doesn't want to. He doesn't want to face the cruelty she'll surely start spouting the moment they leave the bar, maybe even the moment he leaves the table. But there's no delicate way to extract himself from the situation now that Josie's lobbed a grenade into the middle of things. "I'm really sorry, Miu," he says miserably as he stands.

Out in the evening, with a view of San Francisco's high rises, Josie rolls her shoulders back and lets out a long exhale. She staggers once, laughs, then says, "Let's go listen to some music."

Surprisingly, she's in a good mood. She seems satisfied with her jab at Elliot—not the knockout, tear-down fight Adam was expecting, but it was undeniably a point on Josie's side of the scoreboard, as everyone's expressions at the bar suggested. He rubs his face and makes the decision to not engage about what just happened. Not right now, at least. Josie's a mean drunk, and she hasn't even reached her avowed destination: the plastered stage.

It speaks to the weight of exhaustion on his shoulders that he follows Josie to the music venue, a fifteen-minute walk, without complaint. He's been back a week and a half and feels more emotionally dragged down than he did the entire time in Utah—a staggering realization.

At the Throne Room, Josie heads straight for the bar while Adam makes for the outskirts of the gathering crowd. It's still a quarter to nine—he and Josie barely lasted thirty minutes with the others. The shape of the audience is alive, swelling as more people show up, and soon Adam is a few people deep. Josie finds him, beer clutched in her fist, just as the lights dim and the first band stomps onto the stage.

The music pulls in the crowd. It's an indie rock band, an easy vibe for Adam to get lost in. Soon his eyes are glazed over and he's just standing there, letting the music fill him up. Josie is also glassy-eyed, and he thinks that even if he's mopey and she's angry, she's still here next to him and doesn't care about the failures that define him. Even on his worst days, Josie is ready to provide a steadying hand and a pragmatic, if sometimes serrated, viewpoint.

Later, as the first band closes its set, Josie yells that she's going to the bathroom. A cloud of alcohol hovers around her now. He nods and moves out of the crowd so she can better find him on her way back.

But it's another man who approaches, who gives him a slow smile that has Adam's stomach clenching. He looks to be in his late twenties, and his—"Name's Orion," he says, leaning in to make his voice heard over the crowd. He smells like beer mixed with something faintly woody. "Hi."

"Hi," Adam says with knee-jerk politeness. His cheeks begin to warm. No sign of Josie.

"I've seen you here before," Orion is saying. "Swore to introduce myself if I saw you again. So . . ." He shrugs, a self-deprecating-looking smile twitches his neatly trimmed mustache. "Do you live in the city?"

Adam nods, fiddling with the cuff of one sleeve. "I go to SF State."

"Very cool." Orion looks encouraged. "Can I ask your name?"

"Adam."

"Hi, Adam." His smile widens. "Wanna head somewhere quieter so we can talk?"

"Oh—" Alarm bells begin to sound in Adam's head. He thinks of the Halloween party with shame. "I'm not—"

"Hey." There's a sudden weight pressing into his side, and its familiarity instantly soothes Adam. "Everything okay?" Josie asks, dilated pupils on him. He nods.

Orion has stepped back, obviously disappointed but still friendly. "Enjoy your evening," he says before moving off.

Josie continues watching Adam, focused even as she sways. "He was cute. You sure you don't want to—"

He steps away. "No."

Her sigh sounds long-suffering, and he can see the fight bubbling beneath the surface. "Can't you just—"

"Can we get out of here?" he blurts. "Please?"

She stares back for a few seconds, expression flat in a way he hasn't seen before, but eventually nods. "Fine."

It's not nearly as late as they usually leave, but Josie is properly plastered. Adam gives her space as they walk the few minutes from the bus stop to her house, sensing the storm brewing. Thankfully, Ramona seems to be ensconced behind her closed bedroom door when they walk in, the sound of faint music playing. Josie flicks on the light of the entryway with an annoyed grumble, then stomps up the stairs. Adam's on her tail, ensuring she doesn't stumble.

By the time she pushes open her bedroom door, her shirt is halfway off and she's complaining that it smells like smoke. Adam averts his eyes. "I'm gonna head out," he tells her once she elbows her way into her closet. She grunts in response. In a very bad mood, then. "I'll . . . see you tomorrow?" Another grunt. He nods to himself and leaves.

The bottom of the stairs must have a grudge against Adam—the reunion with Ari plays in his mind. Or maybe it has a penchant for confrontation. Because as he takes the last few stairs at a brisk pace, eager to get home to his book and out of his head, the door to his left opens and Ramona appears, framed in the doorway. He gives her what he hopes is an apologetic look and not a terrified one, and continues to head for the front door. Then she speaks.

"So, like, you need to stop coming here." She says it matter of factly, like she's in the middle of a conversation he's only just arrived to. "It's stopping Ari from hanging out with us."

Adam does a double-take, coming to a hard stop at the mention of Ari's name. "S-sorry?"

Ramona crosses her arms. She's in a silky-looking pajama set and her eyes are black. "I don't want you in my house anymore."

"I—" He can't tell if this is some weird joke or one of the power plays Josie's obsessed with catching Ramona in. He looks back at the stairs. "Um . . ."

"He's pretty messed up since he saw you the other night, and after what happened earlier this year between you two, I don't have time to deal with a catatonic Ari. So instead of him shacking up with Isaiah to avoid us and, like, coming to terms or whatever with you being here on the reg, I'm . . ." She flits her hand away, a royal dignitary waving back unwanted admirers. ". . . removing the problem altogether."

Adam blinks, trying to process the request. "I . . . I didn't mean to—"

"It's obvious your little friend doesn't know," Ramona interrupts, with a nod toward the stairs. "I'll keep your secret as long as you stay away, but I don't want to see you here again. No offense." She gives him a smile sharp enough to cut skin.

A sick feeling coils inside Adam's stomach, but his brain is still taking time to catch up. He opens his mouth before realizing he doesn't have anything to say other than a helpless "I'm sorry." His face is hot.

Ramona watches him boredly. He gives her an unsure nod, possibly in acquiescence, but before he can turn to leave, Josie is there, the latest installment of drama. She's in sweats and a baggy t-shirt. Her eyes sweep over Adam. He swallows the humiliation he's feeling, tries to hide the emotion surely broadcast across his face, but it's too late. "I—"

"What the *fuck* did you say to him?" she snarls out to Ramona as she stalks forward. The venom with which she spews the words has been primed for hours, finally let off its leash.

"Nothing," Ramona says sweetly and falsely. The front door opens. Adam's head whips around. It's—not Ari. A different dark-haired man enters—Silas, Adam assumes—whose expression shifts from troubled to curious as he takes in the stand-off: Ramona still relaxing against the doorframe, Josie a tangle of hair and madness, and Adam.

Josie continues. "I don't believe that for a—"

Adam cuts her off, not worth the spectacle this is amounting to. "Jo, it's okay. Every-everything is fine. I'm gonna go. I'm going home. It's fine."

Josie shifts her glare to him. "What's happening? What did she say?"

He shakes his head. "It's nothing. I, um, I remembered I need to do something for a class Monday. That's all."

Josie's eyes narrow. "I'm coming with you," she finally says.

"*No*—" He backs up a step, closer to the front door.

"Yes." She grabs his arm, hand a vice, holding him hostage.

Adam tries to pull away, but she only clutches at him tighter. "I don't want—" The panicked, coiled feeling inside him is rising, ready to choke him. "Please, Josie, please stop."

In his desperation, he looks over to Silas for help, who gives Ramona a hard, frustrated look, before stepping forward. "I think Adam needs some time to himself," he tells Josie.

"I didn't ask for your opinion," Josie snaps.

"But you want his, and he's telling you no."

Josie ignores him, trying to yank Adam toward the stairs, but staggers, movements very obviously still weighted by alcohol.

Ramona laughs, and it's a cruel sound. Josie spins to face her, dropping Adam's arm. "*You*— What did you do?"

"How about you leave this conversation for those who know the whole story, Josephine."

Josie fires off an expletive-laced retort and Adam takes his chance, quietly passing Silas, who gives him a pained look.

His phone rings in his pocket as he drives away, and he knows it's Josie. But he's ruined that too. *I'm removing the problem altogether.* Ramona's words brand themselves across his vision. If he hadn't gone out with Ari, started to fall for Ari, felt comfortable being with Ari, even for a moment, none of this would've happened. Ari would still be hanging out with his friends, not under the assumption that Adam's presence meant his absence.

Adam navigates the roads back to his house. Josie hasn't stopped calling, and he knows it's not fair to leave her hanging, but he can't, he just can't right now.

He tries to steady his breathing, tries to focus only on the road, tries to manage a prayer—pleading for clarity or comfort.

He fails, full of nothing but an ache for everything he can't have.

Chapter 11

Josie has long held a fantasy of punching someone in the face. Maybe it's because of a slight at a bar, or maybe it's in reaction to a thief in the night that she satisfies her wish. But right now, it's Ramona Taylor's face she wants to plant her fist into. Any lingering alcohol in her system has burned off.

Josie has her phone pressed to her ear, calling and calling and calling Adam from the front walkway, and boy, doesn't this feel a lot like the last time he left out of nowhere?

Silas comes outside, closing the front door behind him. For once, he looks uncertain. By Josie's third call, he's sitting on the doorstep, smoking. Because he always smokes. She can see him slipping into his casual, no-worries-here self.

When her fourth-straight call goes unanswered, she yanks the phone from her ear. "Do you know what Ramona said to Adam?"

The hard line of Silas's shoulders has softened. He takes a drag from his cigarette and pats the ground next to him. "Come sit, Juliet."

"Don't call me that. What's going on?"

Another drag. "Not my secret to share."

She stomps toward him until they're toe to toe. "What'd she say to him?"

Silas leans back on one hand, and with the other offers his cigarette. She exhales a violent *no*. The corner of his mouth twitches, and then he's standing up, straightening until he's peering down at her, his height boosted by an additional five inches of doorstep. "I don't think you know your darling Adam as well as you think you do."

"—What?" She's caught off guard, uncertainty closing in as she recalls Adam of recent, dragged down by an unspoken grief. Could Silas know its origin? Could *Ramona*? The confrontation with her roommate in the entryway the other day, something Josie wrote off so quickly, feels ominous now.

Silas offers a small smile. "Come with me." He turns and starts across the pebbled landscaping for the side gate to the patio. Josie follows, growing more confused by the moment.

He settles onto one of the patio chairs, crossing an ankle over a knee.

"Tell me what's going on," Josie demands, refusing to sit.

"Not my place. I'm only stepping in to help a friend."

"Who? Ramona?"

He rocks his head from side to side, then shrugs.

"Fine." She turns away and pulls her phone out to call Adam again. No answer. She calls Jon, who also doesn't answer. She then texts him, demanding he call ASAP. When she faces Silas again, he's watching her, expression unreadable. "Is your car here?" She doesn't even know if he has a car but figures it's a safe assumption; all the rich do.

"Nope." He lets the word pop.

"*Fine*," she snaps again, pulling up Uber. She's going to Adam's house and forcing him to talk to her. The bus or even light rail is too slow for what she needs.

"Trust me on this one," Silas drawls. "He needs some time to himself."

"Oh my god. Dude. Trust you? I barely know you. What I *do* know is that Adam left like a bat out of hell because of something Ramona did. Pardon me if I don't take the word of someone I've known for all of a week and focus on being there for my best friend."

Silas's eyebrows shoot up and he lifts his hands in surrender. Josie is about to place a request for a ride when her phone vibrates with an incoming call. "Is Adam okay?" she asks into it.

Jon's voice is hard. "Bro, what the fuck happened?"

"*Is Adam okay?*"

"Yeah, just walked in looking like someone set fire to his books. What happened?"

"Put him on the phone."

There's the sound of Jon's footsteps moving up stairs, then knocking on a door. "Adam? Hey, J's on the phone and wants to talk. Adam?"

Muffled voices, and then Jon is saying, "Let me call you back."

"Wait, Jon, wait, what—" He hangs up. Josie swears. Her list of people to punch is growing.

She inhales, then exhales before looking at Silas again. He's practically all shadow, except the glimmer of his eyes.

Josie takes three long strides toward the couch he's on and collapses next to him. "Please, Silas. Please tell me what happened. I will beg on my knees if I have to."

He appears conflicted for a moment, but then looks away and blindly holds out his cigarette to her once more. "To help stymie the frustration over things we can't control or have no right to."

Josie gapes at him. "*You* have the right to control this situation by not telling me what's going on, but I don't? How is that fair?"

"Because I know the larger picture here." Silas retracts his offered cigarette and pulls from it instead. His eyebrows briefly draw together. He's still not looking at her. "Just . . . just go with me on this. I'm doing my best."

"Really. Can you say the same about Ramona? That she's doing her best? Because what I just saw in there—"

"I know, I *know*. Ramona could've handled it better."

"Handled *what* better?"

Silas shakes his head and Josie goes back to her phone with a

91

muttered curse. She calls Adam again. Then Jon. No one answers. She lets out a groan as she drops her head back against the couch. "I don't want to just leave him alone."

Silas's head falls back too. He's chewing on his lip, eyes closed. He doesn't say anything.

The silence between them is broken by the sounds of passing cars, a dog barking, and other telltale signs of people's lives late on a Saturday night. Josie chews on a fingernail as she thinks in circles—over Silas and Ramona apparently knowing something about Adam that she doesn't. Something critical. Next to her, Silas shakes another cigarette out of the pack and lights up.

Eventually, Josie stands. Silas arches an eyebrow. "Night, *dude*."

She grimaces. "Yeah."

Up in her bedroom, Josie tries one last time to call Adam. Nothing.

Jon answers, though. He's considerably calmer than when she called earlier. "Sorry about leaving you hanging. Adam was in a bad way. What happened?"

"Something with my roommate," Josie sighs, pinching the bridge of her nose. "I wasn't there, and no one will tell me anything. Is he doing better now?"

"Think so. I made him some tea. He's in his room still, says he wants some space. You comin' over?"

"No . . . I think I'm gonna give him a sec. But will you let me know how he's doing?"

"You got it," Jon says.

"Thanks."

Before Josie settles into bed, she walks to the window. Below, in the darkness, there's the glow of ash. Silas continues to smoke.

The following day is warm, and Josie spends most of it from the small balcony overlooking Valley Street, laptop cradled on her lap and feet pushing against the railing as she balances on the back two legs of a chair. A blank Word document and blinking cursor mock her lack of inspiration and energy.

Ramona's just inside, ping-ponging from videos on her phone, the noise faint, to something on the TV; Josie practically makes it a point now to open the windows despite Evelyn's bossy texts about energy bills. She has half a mind to go in and make her roommate tell her what she knows about Adam, but she's almost—and she'd never ever admit this in a million years to anyone—*intimidated* by Ramona and her loyal followers and unlimited supply of income and congresswoman mom. Being alone with Ramona isn't something Josie wants to do right now.

Her computer screen has gone dark. She taps the space bar to wake it up and resumes her cycle of thoughts: capstone story, Adam, environmental science assignment, Adam, Ramona, Silas, Adam . . .

Below, a black Prius parks out front. Out gets Silas, with his black wavy hair and a gray linen top tucked into blue trousers. He pushes his sunglasses up onto his head as he walks up the path, gaze downcast. After a minute, Ramona's voice greets him inside, and Josie's attention is dragged to the cracked-open windows.

"Any word from Ari?" Ramona asks.

"He swung by the house this morning to pick up more clothes," says Silas.

"Did he say anything?"

"He's gonna stay with Isaiah a few more days." Silas sounds tired.

Ramona's disdain is evident. "You told him how, like, obvious he's being about everything, right?"

"With a little more subtlety, yes. I reminded him what he said last time he hooked up with Isaiah—"

"—that he was an idiot for it, and it hurt more than it helped—"

"—and that he asked us not to let him do that ever again; yes, *thank you*; I know how to relay a message."

"Don't start, Si. I don't need it from you, too."

Oh, fuck you, Josie thinks with venom. Everyone in the world against precious Ramona.

"Sorry, I'm just—" Silas's voice is muffled for a moment and Josie imagines he's running a hand over his face, "—*worried* about everyone. First Ari and his sexcapades, and now Adam is collateral damage. And Josie. I just—"

Josie lowers the chair so all four legs are on the balcony floor, silently begging them to keep going so she can learn what the hell is going on.

"—really wish you hadn't cornered Adam last night," Silas continues. "It's not helping anyone."

"I told you, I'm over giving people permission to control my life. This roommate thing was the last straw. I am so totally done with my mom. She wants me to participate in her politics? I'll fucking participate, and she'll be sorry I did. But if I don't want to go to college, I'm not going to. If I want to influence, I'm going to. If my best friend is having an emotional breakdown because some pretty boy he hung out with for two seconds is back in his life, I'm going to do. Something. About. It."

"You know how much I value you having mine and Ari's backs," Silas says. "And yes, your mom is way too involved, as usual. But there's a better way to go about it all, a way that doesn't involve steamrolling over everyone's feelings."

"I took action," Ramona shoots back. "I'm not waiting around for Ari to *once again* get over some guy he only went on a few dates with—"

"You know how smitten he was with Adam. You can't blame him for taking the time he needs."

It's like a power washer is going off in Josie's head, spraying so hard and fast at the side of her skull that she can't process what's happening in complete sentences—

"No, but I can make sure he doesn't have to face Adam every time he comes over here. Isaiah just fuels Ari's moodiness. You know it's true."

Despite the heat of the day, Josie's gone cold. Adam and Ari . . . *Adam* and *Ari* . . . were a *thing*? Romantically?

"I'm not denying it; I'm just saying there's such thing as bedside manner."

"Did you tell Ari he can come over now? That Adam won't be here?" Ramona asks.

"Didn't get a chance. He, ah, was pissed when I mentioned us worrying about him spending time with Isaiah. Left before I could say anything else."

Ramona groans loudly.

"I'm doing the best I can."

Josie's heartbeat thumps in her ears, realization paired with a sense of dread. It's unbelievable what they're saying—about *Adam*. Her Adam. Friendly-neighborhood-blushing-gay-virgin. That Adam and Ari had some sort of thing. But Adam clearly means something to Ari, based on what his friends are saying, and now that Josie's applying this discovery to Adam's recent moods, she knows that Ari has to mean something to Adam, too.

The urge to punch someone is back. Josie stands, snatching up her laptop and yanking open the door from the balcony to make landfall.

Inside, Ramona sits on the couch. In one hand she holds her phone, scrolling by default. She looks frustrated. It's Silas, though, who Josie locks eyes with, and maybe that's regret flashing across his face as he realizes that she's heard. She's heard and she now knows. He'd told her to give Adam space, to let him have time to sort through things. He'd lied to keep her from drawing Adam back in.

He's standing up, moving forward to meet Josie. "Look—"

"You lied to me." She hurls the words at him, then spins on Ramona. "And *you*. You told Adam not to come over anymore because of someone's hurt feelings? Are you five years old?"

Ramona's face has the hardness of a brick wall. "I was helping a friend."

"By making me look like a shitty one!"

"Josie, let's go for a walk." Silas is beside her, slipping into placating Silas, easy-going Silas from the previous evening. She hates that Silas.

"No way. I believed you and you lied."

"I didn't lie. It just wasn't my business to tell," he says. "And Adam needed time to understand that giving Ari distance was for the best without you—"

She shoves a finger to his chest. "It is *none* of your business whether I talk with him or not! Do you two seriously think you can control everyone around you?"

Ramona looks like she's been slapped. "Don't you *dare* talk to me about being controlling—"

Silas cuts in. "Really, Josie? Like you haven't exerted your own control over Adam all these years? 'Sometimes I have to force him to do things I know will be good for him.'" He raises his voice to stop her retort. "You have no idea how messed up Ari was over him. None of us want to see him go through that for the next year while you're living here and Adam's coming over every day. I know Adam is getting the short straw here, but we were trying to help Ari; we *are* trying to help him."

Ramona attacks from a different angle. "Adam obviously didn't tell you about Ari for a reason. Have you thought about why that is? Maybe he doesn't want you in any of *his* business."

The statement stings, but Josie hides the hurt. Instead, she says with as much contempt as she can muster, "Doesn't look like Ari wants you in his either." She spins on her heel for her bedroom, slinging the door shut with a declarative slam.

Chapter 12

It was date number three that Ari urged Adam to pick the destination for. Adam sent the location of his favorite bookstore, a brightly painted corner shop in the Mission District.

We can go here if you want, he'd texted Ari. *But only if you want. I know you don't really care for reading, so no pressure.*

Ari's reply was swift: *I'm free all sat. name a time.*

There was a live reading going on when they arrived. A local author Adam had followed for a couple years was about to share passages from her latest novel. Ari laughed at the giddiness on Adam's face.

"You have no idea how long I've been waiting for the third book," Adam whispered from the back of the room. He and Ari were hovering behind a small crowd of people sitting in chairs and milling about, waiting for the event to start. "Her second book ended on a cliffhanger *two years ago.*" He pushed up onto the balls of his feet, craning his neck to see the stack of books on the table beside the podium, trying to compare the count of copies to the number of people in the room. Ari placed a steadying hand against the small of Adam's back, and Adam couldn't quite quell the swoop of his stomach as he lowered to the ground.

"I dunno how anyone can wait that long for anything," Ari said after he dropped his hand. "I hate waiting one week for a new episode to come out on HBO. How do you survive?"

"Read the series again and again until you're sick of it or find another novel to suck you in and distract you. But the book hangover is real, especially for this one." Adam nodded to the giant cardboard cutout of the newest book's cover on display.

"Book hangover?"

"Yeah, um, think like . . . like you read a book and you're really into it and invested in the world-building and characters and everything, and then it ends and you're kind of just . . . forced into an unwelcome limbo, stuck thinking about and missing the world even though the story's over? It's incredibly depressing."

"You're not making this whole reading thing sound very fun," Ari teased with a nudge. Adam bit back a delighted smile.

During the reading, Ari had asked Adam so many questions about what was happening that people started glaring, and in horrified embarrassment, Adam grabbed his hand in desperation and begged him to be quiet. Ari simply pursed his lips and squeezed Adam's hand with faint amusement before Adam pulled away.

After the author finished and Adam waited in line to buy a signed copy, they wandered the bookshelves, Adam pointing out some of his favorite books, as well as those he thought Ari might like based on his preferences (healthy eating, self-help, and nothing fantasy). Ari ended up buying the first book of the author who'd read, promising Adam with a friendly eye roll that he'd avoid Googling any spoilers.

It had been such a fantastically perfect day that Adam smiled to himself the entire drive home.

Now, he thinks of how quickly happiness can swirl down the drain. It was barely two weeks later that he'd seen Ari for the last time, had sharply pulled back from the kiss he'd wanted to continue. The summit leading to the inevitable plunge.

He casts his thoughts to the oft-used salve, time spent with his family.

Thinks of good days, laughing with his siblings, taking road trips with everyone crammed in the van, or camping in the backyard. Drives up Provo Canyon in the fall, when the leaves burst into color that put poetry into visuals. Movie nights and family reunions and the anchor of church every Sunday where he was taught about the limitless power of love.

Conditionally, he knows Josie would sneer. She doesn't understand Adam's familial bond. He doesn't mean that in a cruel way. She's said the words herself, during private moments when she's told him in an uncharacteristically small voice how much not having a relationship with the woman who raised her hurts. "I want what you have with your mom, but without the strings attached and the overbearing religion and shit," she said.

Adam's eyes are bloodshot with exhaustion. It hurts, this open wound inside him. He lies on his bed, unable to do anything more than blink. He wants to talk to someone, wants to find a silver lining where there doesn't seem to be any. What he wants is the salve of the good days.

So he calls, heart beating in his throat.

"Sweetheart, I was hoping to hear from you." In the background on his mom's end he hears choral music, the soundtrack to his Sundays growing up.

"Hi, Mom." His voice sounds strangled, a dead giveaway.

"Adam?" She sounds concerned now. "Is everything okay?"

"I'm okay. I just . . ." He drags a hand across his face. His throat hurts. For once, he doesn't want to dance around the words. He channels Josie's bluntness. "Um, do . . . do you think Heavenly Father punishes people for being gay?"

There's a moment's pause, and he imagines her eyebrows pulling down, recalibrating a topic she's always assumed was simple for him. "I think it depends on the situation," she says. There's a slight but clear flatness to her tone now, the kind she reserves for when the breaking of a rule is being flirted with and she needs to make her beliefs clear. She used to rarely use it with Adam. "Did something happen?"

"N-no, I—" He urges his brain to get in front of the panic seizing him. "Um, I've just hurt some people, I think? By being what I am."

The music stops, and he can hear his mom's movement around their house. The familiar creak of the floor in the family room, the soft sigh of the leather recliner as she sits. Her voice is firm, disciplined. "I know it's not easy, your sexuality as a member of our church. It hasn't been easy for me or your father either. But the Lord works in mysterious ways, and you should take courage in that. Maybe he's given you this trial so that you better understand what's on the line eternally? There's no point in involving yourself with someone whose companionship won't matter past this lifetime. Your hurdle is only for this life, Adam. Use that knowledge to find peace."

The misery inside him tunnels deeper. "What if . . ." He swallows. It's the question he's always been too scared to ask. "What if I don't want to be alone in this life?"

"Sweetheart, you have *us!*" she says, sounding like the mother he once knew. "We love you so much, and will always be here for you—and so will your Heavenly Father! We're meant to reach out to Him with our trials and ask for peace." There's emotion in her voice. "This life isn't easy for any of us, but you have an extra weight on your shoulders and I'm so sorry I can't offer anything more sympathetic than that. But you must stay strong. Promise me. For yourself, for me, for whoever is going to help you get through this life. Remember to keep that eternal perspective. As long as you're pure, there are only blessings in store for you."

He grips the phone, clings to it. *You don't know, you don't know, you don't know,* he wants to wail.

"Do you need to come home for a bit? Get away from things?"

"Maybe," he scrapes out. "No. I d-don't— I just need—" He pauses, throat tight around the words. Then, more softly: "I don't know what I need."

"I'll always be here for you. Do you know that?"

He nods, cheeks wet. "Yes."

"You can do this, Adam. You must."

"I know."

He drops the phone onto the bed next to him after hanging up, eyes unseeing on the ceiling. The same words, same message from his mother. They don't feel like enough anymore.

Distantly, adjacently, he knows through the numerous missed calls from Josie that she's worried and that he needs to explain. He'll get there. He just needs—time. To sloppily patch up his aching heart, build up the callus before he can brush off what Josie saw between him and Ramona. He types out what he hopes is a believable excuse.

Sorry about last night. I'm okay, just tired. I'll see you tomorrow?

She doesn't respond, and he's relieved by that.

Chapter 13

J osie is desperate to not be at the Valley house.

She thinks about how she's only living there to satisfy some sort of agreement, an attempt by her roommate's parents to nudge their child down a path they want.

She thinks about her Bernal Heights hole, where things only low-grade sucked.

She thinks about her mom's words to seventeen-year-old Josie, the ones that shifted everything into harsh focus.

She thinks about Ramona and her need to control her corner of the Taylor kingdom.

She thinks about Adam in a relationship with another guy. With *Ari*, one of Ramona's best friends.

More than the anger, or maybe fueling the anger, is embarrassment. Everyone in this house knew about Adam and Ari—and knew that she didn't know. *Adam* knew and said nothing. Her best friend decided against telling her. What does that say about her? Can no one stomach being around her?

She leaves the house Sunday just as the sun is setting, the moonrise bringing a chill with it. She heads down the sidewalk for the bus.

The Throne Room swells with energy when Josie arrives, some singer wailing into the mic. The bar, lining the wall to her right, is backlit, the decanters and bottles of spirits and alcohol glimmering with various colors, from jewel tones to black to clear.

Josie settles onto a stool and asks for a Sam Adams. Behind the shelves lined with bottles, Josie can see her warped reflection in a mirror. She looks how she feels: betrayed.

Beer in hand, she moves closer to the stage, expression guarded. She has zero interest in any mingling tonight, flirtatiously or otherwise.

Josie lets the music surround her, closing her eyes as the guitar's melody thrums through her. This is usually her favorite part, feeling the music, letting it sweep her along—the ballad, the ambient noise flowing through her limbs. Josie and Adam sometimes liked to dissect the feelings different songs emoted, like an auditory Rorschach test. Where she might be reminded of her first summer job at a rec-center, he'd think of his hope for the future. She now wonders if he ever lied to her about that too; perhaps songs reminded him of Ari.

The air has grown hot, harder to breathe. She grits her teeth through the song, then another, before heading for the bathroom. Beneath the unforgiving harsh light, Josie turns on the faucet to splash water against her face.

Adam was her best friend. She only has a smattering of acquaintances, never having bothered with, or considered she'd need someone else. The stability she'd missed out on during childhood had centered into one being as an adult: Adam, who loved her and laughed with her and told her she was the bravest person he knew. Now, she's bereft of everything he allowed her to feel.

Even Jon is off-limits, with his proximity to Adam. And anyway, Jon cares for Adam. It's no small feat that Adam came out to his roommate sophomore year. Even if Jon doesn't know the depth of Adam's issues with the intersection of his sexuality and religion (or does he? Again, what else did Adam lie to her about?), he would surely defend Adam over a lot less.

Josie finds she's suddenly eager to get home and to her bed. Her music sanctuary has grown claws. The current song crescendos as Josie elbows through the crowd for the exit and shoves open the door. The familiarity of city sounds greets her, the low chatter and live music cut off by the closed door. Josie inhales the fresh air, then exhales, dropping her head back to look up at the roof lines of the buildings around her. She wants to scream.

She won't waste time caring for someone who clearly doesn't think she's worth telling the truth to; even her mom managed that much, after all. If Adam wants to wallow in self-pity, she'll let him. If he wants to keep her out of important chapters of his life, she'll just stay out of all of it.

She's up early Monday morning. She can't help but open her eyes at five-thirty, unable to sleep any longer. She lies in bed, poking around on her phone before heading to the kitchen for coffee.

Ramona appears in her workout gear, says absolutely nothing to Josie as she pulls out her blender for another inevitable kale smoothie selfie. Josie can feel the intensity between them growing thicker by the minute. She refuses to leave or to speak because that'd be giving up somehow. Instead, she glares as Ramona adds kale bunch by bunch to her blender, the back of her neck reddened as she does, like she can sense the non-stop torrent of four-letter words Josie is mentally flinging her way.

The blender roars and it's then that the prodigal son returns, Ari's dark curls rising to appear through the slats of the railing, his broad shoulders perfectly framed by the kitchen's arched doorway as he comes to the top of the stairs. The person Adam threw their friendship away over. He's not quite as appealing now.

Josie keeps her face blank as Ari sees her. He's not quick to the draw, eyes flitting to the edges of the kitchen around her, catching on Ramona, then searching for someone not there. He's as easy to read as a roadmap. A sense of territorialism rises suddenly inside Josie; she wants to tell him to stay away from Adam, from *her* Adam, but just as quickly realizes she's cutting off her right to claim him.

Smoothie blended, Ramona looks over mid-pour. She says his name with relief, "*Ari.*"

His jaw is tight. "Silas said you wanted to talk."

Ramona sets her cup on the counter and gives Josie a pointed look. Josie takes a sip of her coffee, eyes trained on Ramona in challenge. She knows where this conversation will end, the one about to happen between Ari and Ramona, and can't help but want to hear it.

"Just—come here," Ramona says, leaving behind her breakfast to cross the kitchen and pull Ari to the stairs. He follows, glancing at Josie as he goes.

"I'm not making this a thing," he tells Ramona as they go downstairs. "I have to go meet with my agent so just say what you have to say."

They're out of sight, and Josie moves to the railing to better hear where they've paused in the entryway.

"How's Isaiah?" her roommate asks.

"Fine." A blunt, emotionless answer. "You don't have to lecture me. Silas already did that."

"Yeah, well it sounds like he didn't get to finish lecturing you before you stomped out."

"Whatever."

Josie doesn't know enough about Ari to recognize vocal tells, has no idea how he'd normally act in Ramona's company. Apparently, though, it's not his standard tone.

"Quit acting like this," Ramona tells him. "And stop wasting brain cells on Isaiah. Silas was supposed to also tell you that you won't run into Adam here anymore. It's taken care of."

Josie holds her breath—terrified, eager, bitter.

"What does that mean, 'it's taken care of'?" Ari says.

"Adam isn't welcome in my house anymore. I talked to him."

"You— Wait. His best friend lives here."

"He can still hang out with her, just not here."

"You told him that? That he wasn't allowed to come here because of me?"

Ramona's voice adopts a warning tone. Josie leans forward. "It's my house. I can do whatever I want. Besides, I wouldn't have bothered if you hadn't ghosted us for the past week. Silas says you've only been home twice!"

"I'm not on a leash like he is. What I do with my time is none of your business. You don't hear me ragging on you about *Andrew*—"

"We're talking about you, not him. And you *are* my business, especially if you're going on sex benders with *Isaiah*, who you've *told* me makes you feel bad about yourself. The fact that you're hooking up with him while trying to get over someone who was barely in your life is, like, lowest of the low. I know you got attached to Adam, or whatever, and I know it, like, sucks that he's friends with my roommate, but you can't just stop coming over."

"Why not? That's literally what you're asking Adam to do."

"Again, Ari, it's *my* house, and you feeling like this is a safe space is more important to me than some random guy who, honestly, babe, seems a little bland—"

"Fuck off, Ramona. You don't know a single thing about him."

"I know he doesn't want to be your boyfriend."

A chilly silence, and Josie imagines Ari and Ramona are glaring daggers at one another. Then, Ari says in a hard-edged voice, "How I deal with shit in my life is my business. And if it means I need some time to myself, you can deal with it."

"I *did* deal with it. The problem is gone and now you can come back without running into him."

"No; now I just have to worry about running into you." There are footsteps across the tile, then the sound of the front door opening and closing with a slam. Josie stays still. She waits for Ramona to react, but there's only a quiet *snick* of her bedroom door closing.

Josie is sickly satisfied by the heavy silence that follows, but there's a nasty amount of hurt there, too. She turns for her room, focus shifting to the day ahead. To Adam, the center of everyone's world, apparently, not just hers.

Ari, a knight in shining armor, running off to save Adam's day. Adam will love that, she thinks with malice. His own romance novel come to life.

Josie was supposed to be the one saving his day. They were supposed to save each other, and the thought of him keeping such a secret from her hits Josie all over again.

Anger rolls off her like a heat wave as she pulls on her bag and heads for campus.

Chapter 14

Adam scuffs his foot against the ground as he waits. Around him, students are loud and happy, the semester still early enough not to completely stress everyone out.

He watches the southeast entrance, needing Josie. He's waded through the weekend's swirl of emotions, and now needs to decompress. Josie's irreverent attitude and practicality will surely remind him that things aren't as bad as he thinks. He's more grateful than guilt-ridden that she knows nothing of him and Ari, because he needs a shoulder to lean on, not someone to analyze.

She's on time, rounding the corner from 19th, and there's a sense of relief at the sight of her, a weight he can finally hand off.

He only becomes aware of her bearing when she stops short in front of him, accusal written across her face. Realization slides over his skin like slime.

"Anything you feel like telling me?" Josie asks. Her voice is as harsh as he's ever heard it.

There's no point in wondering, no other secret Adam has kept from her.

"About me and, and Ari?"

Triumph and betrayal blend across Josie's features.

"Um," he tries, knowing he has to say something, has to try. "I'm sorry for not, not telling you. I . . . it was a new thing, and I was trying t-to work through some stuff with it, and I was scared that you would, um, encourage me to do something I wasn't ready to do?"

Josie cocks her head and says, almost reassuringly, "This happened in the spring, right?"

He bobs his head, hope dawning. "Yeah, it was ages ago. I didn't— It was only, we just went out a few times."

Josie visibly loosens her posture, shifting her weight back on her heels with an air of casualness. "Huh, okay. You kept it from me because I would force you to date him because I'm a shitty friend like that, and then when it ended, you kept quiet about it because . . . ?"

Adam feels himself pale. "You're not a, a bad friend, I just—"

"And when you found out Ari was BFFs with my new roommate, you continued to keep quiet about everything because . . . ?"

"I wasn't ready yet."

"Because I would have pushed you into it still," she continues like he hasn't spoken, her tone still reasonable. "It's okay, Adam, I am now well aware of how you see me."

Adam's vision tilts, then snaps back into place. Students continue to pass by where he and Josie stand on the walkway, flowing like a stream around an obstructing rock. "That's not—"

"You spent our entire friendship saying you wanted nothing to do with other guys. I didn't agree, but I tried not to force it. I tried to respect your beliefs even as I watched you be miserable over them." Her eyes are shining. "And it turns out, you ended up having the romance of the century, one everyone knew about except for me. Ari can't even bring himself to *see* you for how heartbroken he is? Can't stomach coming over while you're around? *Really*?"

"I d-didn't mean to, didn't mean for anything to happen like this—"

"Stop." The word is hissed out between gritted teeth. She takes a step toward him. He takes one back. "I might've believed that if you hadn't lied to my face. I asked! I *asked* if you'd met Ramona before—"

"I hadn't!"

"But you *knew!*" Josie yells. A woman passing by glances over in alarm. "You knew since the day I moved in and you didn't say anything!"

"W-wait—" Adam's mouth is dry, his head spinning. "I'm sorry, I'm *so, so* sorry—"

"Am I that horrible of a friend? Do you really think I'm such a bitch that I would *force* you to pursue a relationship you didn't want? I can't—" Her voice wavers. Distantly, a phone begins to ring. She takes a breath and shakes her head sharply when Adam opens his mouth. "I can't believe you would think so low of me."

His eyes fill with tears. "I don't, Jo. I— You're my best friend."

"No, I'm not," Josie snaps. "If I was, you would have been able to trust me." The ringing continues, and Josie's glare cuts to Adam's pocket. He realizes it's his phone making the noise.

He pulls it out. The screen shows a 'Sexy Runner Guy' calling. His stomach freefalls with dread and joy.

"Who—" Josie starts, but Adam's face must tell her.

Her own expression locks down into white fury and she bites out the cruelest sentence Adam has ever heard her utter: "Just remember that after Ari fucks you, I won't be there to help you put your pants back on."

Adam's hands won't stop shaking. Josie's gone, leaving a gaping path between the others hurrying to classes.

His fault.

She's right. He had his chances to tell her, and he should have. He'd let her walk blindly into a situation where everyone knew the truth except for her, and he let her stay there. She's only ever been there for him. He deserves this, what he's feeling.

Pressing the heels of his palms to his eyes, he takes a few deep breaths and attempts to think around what just happened.

Josie can be vicious. He knows this. She thrives on getting the last word, takes pride in it, hangs a lot of her self worth on it. She certainly got it this time. He's seen many looks flash across her face over the years, but never one with such coldness in her eyes and venom in her voice as she spoke those parting words. She clearly meant them with every fiber of her being, and that is what has broken him down: the deserved why of her departure, and the brutal how of it.

Adam can feel the weight of everything lost crushing down—behind his eyes, in his throat, on his shoulders. A work shift and two classes are on his schedule today, but what use will Adam be? He wants to crawl under his blankets and fade into nothingness. Josie is done with him.

I can't believe you would think so low of me.

He unlocks his bike and walks it to the closest bike lane, the sound of Josie's voice on repeat in his head. Her words, stinging in their blunt finality, leave no room for doubt.

The cracks in his facade have become chasms by the time he arrives home. He leans his bike precariously against the wall of the garage, his fingers fumbling as he unclips his helmet to hang on the handlebars. The motion causes the bike to fall over, crashing to the ground, and it's what finally breaks Adam.

Tears spill over as he kicks at one of the wheels that spins slowly, mockingly. He is so intensely alone, and it's all self-inflicted.

A car door closes, and Adam turns. Parked in the driveway is a white Audi and walking toward him—is Ari.

"Adam?"

Adam's reaction is to freeze, to blink a few times to wash away this hallucination. Ari's in jeans and a zip-up hoodie, a baseball hat on his head and an expression on his face that Adam wants to believe is concern but is more likely disappointment.

He tries to come up with why Ari would be here. There's the missed call not thirty minutes prior. Had Josie talked to Ari? Is he also mad at Adam for not telling Josie about them? Maybe he's making sure Adam doesn't have any plans to return to the Valley house? Did Adam do something else wrong?

"I," he begins with a waver. He rubs his arm across his face, wiping his cheeks.

Ari's gaze is quick but thorough, reading whatever is on Adam's face and somehow knowing it translates into a need. He steps forward and pulls Adam to him, arms bracketing Adam's back, his chest as solid and sturdy as a tree.

Adam stiffens once more, automatically gearing up to pull away from the embrace, but his tears are falling faster now, like they've been cranked up a notch now that someone's here to witness. He doesn't pull away, but he doesn't relax his arms around Ari's waist either. He just . . . stays. Sinks into the familiarity of Ari. His breathing is uneven as he cries. Ari holds him more tightly.

"M'sorry," Adam eventually mumbles. He steps back and Ari drops his hold. Adam doesn't meet his eye as he dries his cheeks again. "Bad day."

"It's my fault," Ari says, and Adam looks up. A muscle twitches in Ari's cheek. "I just found out this morning what Ramona said—" He cuts off the sentence with an angry exhale. "She had no right to ask that of you, and I told her that. You can go hang out with Josie there whenever you want."

He can't, but Adam doesn't say so. "I'm sorry if I . . . Ramona, she said it was because of me that, that you wouldn't go over there."

Ari shakes his head. "After I saw you last week, I couldn't get you out of my head. I didn't want to be around in case you were there, because it hurt to see you and not, like, *have* you." There's no hint of embarrassment on his face; it's like a conduit to exactly what he's feeling: anger, sympathy, yearning. "I didn't think Ramona would blame you for it or make you do something like that." He takes a step forward, ducking his head to press his gaze further. "It's not your fault."

Adam flinches away from the last statement. "Is that why you're here?" Humiliation creeps up the back of his neck.

"I wanted to make sure you were okay. I would've come sooner, but, like—" Ari shakes his head, then readjusts his hat. "I needed to know. And needed to see you."

The tenderness in his voice has Adam's eyes itching again. He's so tired; cleaved in half by the back and forth of it all.

"Thank you," he says. "For . . . for coming. I . . ." But what can he say? *I miss you; I wish I'd been strong enough to try?* No, he chose his path. Pursuing Ari is not in the cards for him if he wants to be loved by his family, let alone live with himself. "I appreciate it."

Ari looks around Adam to his bike. "Here, let me . . ." He crosses over to pick it up and prop against the wall, helmet swinging innocently now.

Adam thanks him again, face hot, then says, "I guess I'll—" at the same time Ari says, "I read that trilogy."

It takes Adam a moment to catch up. "Trilogy . . . ?"

"From the reading we went to." Ari puts his hands in his pockets, then takes them out. "At that bookstore you love?"

Adam's eyes go wide. "You did?"

"Yeah, I couldn't put it down, actually. No idea how you lasted so long between the second and third book coming out."

Wretched as he feels, Adam hiccups out a small laugh. "Told you. It was a brutal book hangover."

There's a grin stretching across Ari's face now. "Did you have any? Book hangovers?" he asks. "Since we— Over the summer?"

"Two. They were . . . pretty bad."

113

Ari nods knowingly, a sudden literary savant, and Adam has to bite back a laugh, stomach flaring with want again. It's the trigger. He straightens, flattening his smile. "I'll, um— Thanks again for . . . for coming. I should probably go." His conversation with Josie has faded to a dull throb, aided by the unknowingly prescriptive Ari.

"Right." Ari reaches a hand into his pocket again, pulling his car keys free. "Well. I'll . . . see you around, Adam." The way he cradles Adam's name on his tongue turns Adam's knees to jelly.

"Um, yeah. Okay." He turns, making for the door. As he reaches to close the garage, he glances back. Ari is reversing down the driveway, hand on the passenger seat headrest as he looks over his shoulder. Adam hits the button before Ari can catch him watching and goes inside.

Like the tide inevitably rising, Adam's misery returns in waves. It's painful how the guilt will recede slightly with a random thought, then return harsher and stronger than ever before. It's an emotionally crippling pain.

Josie's unquestionable ending of their relationship is the shadow in every room—her absence a living, breathing, morphing thing. It grates at him like a play-by-play, a carousel in his head of their greatest hits together: singing along at concerts, watching movies at each other's places, roaming the streets of the city arm in arm and full of a platonic love so fierce both of them wondered aloud if they'd ever find someone they loved more. But here he is, his best friend lost to him.

Friendships, he's realized, die so much faster than they begin, like an ember doused in a lake, ignorant of a history of hard-earned trust.

He's texted and called her enough that the ringing has stopped and he's going straight to voicemail. Josie's been mad at Adam before, punishing him with a deafening silence for a few days—angry over Adam's promise to his mom, timidity over his sexuality. He tries to tell himself this isn't any different, that she'll be back with her loud laugh and rolling eyes in no time; tries to tell himself that withholding information from her won't change things.

Jon knocks on the door; Adam ignores him. He also ignores his books. He sits on the end of his bed trying to convince himself he hasn't permanently damaged his relationship with his warrior-hearted best friend.

The shadows of Josie bleed into twilight. Adam watches the color of the sky out his window and realizes he's been lying on his bed, arms around a pillow, for hours. His phone hasn't buzzed a single time.

Chapter 15

J osie hurries across campus Tuesday morning, full of a panic she's all too familiar with. Amid everything else—she's *not* thinking about him—she completely spaced that she was supposed to meet with Tilton the previous day. The wave of mundaneness so often shadowing her showed up after all. What's more, she still doesn't have three ideas for the capstone project, more like half an idea is rattling around in her head. But she's ready to embrace it; she's ready to burn the world to the ground.

Tilton's door is open, thank god, when Josie shows up. It's thirty minutes before class starts, and she has some explaining to do.

She knocks on the doorframe and Tilton looks up from her desk.

"Do you have a sec?" Josie asks.

Tilton frowns, but nods and gestures to the seat in front of her desk, closing her laptop. The office is sparsely decorated. No framed front page articles of national newspapers or awards on shelves, stuff Josie wouldn't hesitate to display if she earned such accolades, which she knows Tilton has.

"Something ended up happening yesterday and I couldn't make it to your office hours," Josie says. It's not a lie.

"And you're ready to do so now?" Tilton asks.

Josie sits up straight and nods, then verbally adds all her eggs to one basket: "I know the daughter of a U.S. congresswoman who's really

116

diverged, I guess you could say, from the path her parents want for her? She's an influencer—pretty well known, actually, and I thought I could do a profile piece on her."

It's more a delicious form of payback than anything, why Josie's committed to writing about Ramona. She can't take it out this way on Adam because, like, she's exorcizing him from her life, but her roommate? The one who conducted this fallout? Yeah, Josie'll happily return the favor. Forget a profile piece on Nara. Josie's off the rails. This'll be an exposé on the life of San Francisco's spoiled brat, who laughs in the face of education and credibility. *The Influencer Who Ignored Common Sense* might be a nice title. Or, *Selfies at Sixty? All That's Left Career-Wise for This Socialite.*

She can imagine the reaction—the world snorting with laughter over yet another vapid Gen Z example. Who knows, maybe the article will spur Ramona into taking life seriously. Then Nara will *really* love Josie.

She gives a disjointed breakdown of Ramona and what she knows about her. "I'm still coming up with my sources for this one, but definitely her parents. And her assistant."

"Photo ideas? Infographic focus?"

"Yeah, I actually have a photographer squared away." Josie'll need to make nice with Silas if that's gonna happen, but that's for figuring out later. "And for the infographic, I'm thinking . . ." *Shit.* She forgot about that one. "Prrrrobably something about a social media influencer's impact on businesses they advertise for." Josie blinks, the off-the-cuff idea actually a good one. She sits up straighter.

"And your other two story topics?"

Josie grimaces inwardly. "Well, actually, I only have the one. It's just that I feel pretty strongly about it—" lie "—and didn't think any other ideas were worth it."

Tilton's gaze is serious. "I'm sure you'll be able to fine tune the pitch in time for the story budget, due Thursday. I'd like to see a clearer focus on why you're choosing to write about this young woman. Provide the readers with a particularly outstanding aspect of the subject's life, something that they need to know right now. In this moment, I'm not seeing a compelling reason for the story, but trust you'll be able to further frame one."

She sits back in her chair, eyes on the far wall, lips pursed. For a moment, ego only slightly bruised, Josie thinks she's free. But then Tilton continues to speak: "The assignment was to provide three story ideas, including sources for each." Tilton steeples her fingers, elbows braced against the arm rests of her chair. "You not only missed the initial deadline, but the fall-back I offered as well. That's a failing grade for a task I've brought to your attention multiple times now. Brainstorming articles is a cycle for a journalist; you must always be looking for that important factor that people want or need to know about. On the first day of my class, you announced your intention to write a story that would make newsrooms want to hire you. This is not a good start to reaching that goal."

Josie's forehead itches, and as she rubs at the spot, beads of sweat start to form.

"This is a class that will push you. I am here as a resource, but the target is a moving one, and you are already behind. I want to be clear that I am not impressed with your performance."

Josie's "okay" is defeated.

"It's a start, Miss Hicks," Tilton says. "With room for improvement. Please take future assignments more seriously. Is that fair?"

Josie stands. "Yeah. Thank you for your insight."

Tilton nods. "See you in class."

Josie flees.

She keeps her head down in class. How humiliating. She should've done better. Though she wants to hate Tilton for the verbal dressing down, Josie knows she deserved it. An assignment asking for three solid story ideas has turned into a revenge mission, albeit one Josie doesn't feel an ounce of shame over. No use thinking she'll earn any journalistic props from Tilton at this point.

Everyone's talking about their ideas in class and the apparent praise Tilton lavished on each one—all loud, mocking to Josie's ears as she tries to cement a better story. Something about modern-day fame and that it doesn't necessarily mean a host of degrees? Or: an up-and-coming influencer with a politician for a parent, each building a following for their platform.

Nothing feels solid enough, and it's suddenly obvious why: Adam's not there. They'd always brainstormed together in the past. Had she only been riding his coattails? Her entire journalism education has been with Adam by her side. Maybe any success she had was because of her proximity to him? But no, that can't be right, she scolds herself. She had an entire summer at the *Business Times*. Adam wasn't there for that. *And that's why you never wrote anything truly great*, says the nasty voice in her head, ever sounding like her mom. *Enjoy working as a content writer for some shitty marketing company.*

Her reply is clipped, not meant for the voice in her head, but for Adam: *I hate you*, she thinks. *I hate you I hate you I hate you.*

Josie arrives home to a Cybertruck parked in the driveway and a loud male voice from the TV room. When Josie sticks her head in, it's Ramona's manfriend ('boyfriend' feels too amateur for a guy with gray in his beard)—Andrew, Silas said his name was—who has his phone to his ear and is saying words like, "circle back on that" and "run it up the flagpole" unnecessarily loudly. Another thing Josie's forgotten amid all the drama lately: that her roommate is dating an old man.

Ramona's lying on her back, head on Andrew's thigh as she scrolls on her phone. She doesn't notice Josie's arrival but Andrew does. He gives her his smarmy smile as he holds out a finger, like she's some intern meekly approaching a boss rather than a literal tenant of the house passing through. Josie isn't particularly in the mood to have a tête-à-tête with her roommate and side piece, but Tilton's words haven't stopped repeating themselves in her head: *I am not impressed with your performance. I am not impressed with your performance. I am not impressed with your performance.* If she's going to start gaining momentum, it needs to be now.

Josie calls out, "Ramona."

Ramona's dead-eyed gaze shifts to her.

"Hey," Josie says. The word sounds like (and is) a false white flag. "Uh. Can I talk to you?"

Ramona refocuses on her phone. "I don't want to be part of a study group or whatever college crap my mother has you pedaling today."

Josie sips in a breath. *Be nice,* she tells herself. *So, so nice.* "It's not anything like that," she says, moving to sit on one of the armchairs across from the couple. "Well, not exactly. I'd like to write a news story about you. For a class."

Whatever Ramona expects, it clearly isn't that. She openly laughs just as Andrew guffaws into his phone. Josie's too wary to believe the timing is anything other than calculated. She continues, both cautious and defensive. "I would highlight your influencing, do a deep dive on what it takes to be authentic as you grow your following. Maybe pitch it to a fashion magazine and get you more attention."

Ramona sits up, touching her hand to Andrew's bicep. He reacts like she's activated a switch, hanging off his call abruptly and turning toward Ramona. She murmurs something too low for Josie to hear, and they both stand, Andrew zipping up his fleece vest as they make for the hallway. The motion briefly draws Josie's attention to the logo across his chest.

"Apparently I need to make something, like, super clear." Ramona has stopped in front of Josie, standing over her as Andrew disappears. "You've infiltrated the one place I had that was my own and your little tag-along has ruined my relationship with Ari. The literal last thing in the entire world that I want is for you to be more involved in my life." The words are succinct, each one bitten off.

Josie coils back. "I didn't *infiltrate* your house," she says, more shocked than angry. "It's not my fault your mom chose me as the college example."

"*Please*. You're the furthest thing from an example." Ramona places her hands on the armrests of Josie's chair and leans in close. Her breath smells like kale smoothie. "I make more money without a degree than you ever will with one."

A headache thumps Josie's skull. "Yet you're still living under Daddy's roof."

Ramona's black eyes glitter with what looks like retribution in waiting. Her reply, however, seems restrained as she straightens: "Why don't you go play in your room with Adam?" She smirks. "Oh, wait."

She leaves with a toss of her hair.

It's the exact right response to reestablish Josie's fortitude.

The headache spikes as she shuts the door to her room, squeezing like a band around Josie's temples. The last few days have each been a century long. She's suddenly aware of how much empty time she has to fill now without Adam's presence.

The realization nearly smothers the betrayal's sting. All the empty hours over the summer hit her once again, and Josie wants to double over at the reminder of their weight.

She still had Adam, always a text or phone call away. Now she has no one. She's alone in a way she's never been before. The lack of his companionship is akin to a ship adrift in enemy territory—jarring, unfamiliar, dangerous.

She remembers the look on his face when she found him at the Halloween party freshman year. He, the quiet boy in her intro to journalism and history classes, clearly terrified as he turned down a sexual favor already underway.

The naked relief on his face when she appeared.

Anyone would have been drawn to help him, but he'd chosen her. For the first time in her life, she'd been chosen and wanted.

Josie pushes the feelings away, unwilling to mourn someone who cared less than she deserves. Two semesters. That's how long she has to hunker down for. It'll be fine. She'll be fine. She's stronger than a friendship she'd given so much of herself to.

Chapter 16

He's staring at his phone, eyes burning from exhaustion, when a soft voice says his name. "Hi, Adam."

He looks up to find Miu a few feet away worrying her lip, eyes downcast. He's early to the capstone, still waiting for the previous class to be dismissed. His first stop this morning was the archives, where he quickly and quietly found Cal to apologize for missing three days in a row and assure him he won't miss any more. Cal waved the apology away, ensuring Adam was okay and adding that if he ever needed time off, he's welcome to take it: "Your wellbeing is more important than filling a shift."

"Miu, hi," he replies now, trying to stop embarrassment from broadcasting itself across his face. After Ramona's confrontation and Josie's reckoning, the recollection of Miu and her advances at the bar had fallen to the wayside. But her presence brings it all back.

"I wanted to apologize for my actions on Saturday," Miu begins, eyes on the ground. The words are stiff and her hair hangs straight. "I had too much to drink, and I entered your personal space without consent. I'm very embarrassed with how I acted."

"Oh, Miu, d-don't feel bad. I wasn't really thinking and could've been . . . more considerate of your feelings. I'm sorry that Josie said it like she did. She shouldn't have done that." He pauses and tries to quiet his increasingly panicked breaths. "Um . . . I guess I should say that I think you're a great friend, but I'm not— I don't see you as more than that?" His own gaze has drifted, too; he hates this. "I'm really, *really* sorry."

"It's okay." Miu's voice is as small as he feels. She hovers for a moment, as if unsure what to say or do next, then takes a stiff first step, then a second, toward the classroom, now emptied of the other class.

Adam closes his eyes and drops his head back with a long exhale. He's become tangled in a web of secrets he never meant to weave in the first place, planted expectations for others to have of him, only to draw up short. His relationships are fraying left and right; it feels like it's only a matter of time before there'll be no one left.

Josie's approaching when he finally opens his eyes, moving toward the classroom, not shying away from Adam's gaze when he meets hers. Her expression is dangerous-looking, and he recognizes for the first time how scary Josie can be from the other side of a line in the sand.

"Jo?" he manages. "Josie? Can I talk to you?"

She looks back at him over her shoulder, coolly, as she reaches the classroom. Heat climbs up his neck as he waits for her decision. But she only turns and stalks through the doorway without a word.

Adam hasn't used his car in a week, so he's not sure how long the envelope has been there, secured under a windshield wiper. He only notices it after he's begun driving to the grocery store, the white paper flapping. At a red light, he quickly hops out to grab it, assuming a parking ticket. Instead, he finds a fifty-dollar gift card to his favorite bookstore, the one he and Ari went to together so long ago.

So you can find me more book recs is written on a piece of scratch paper in Ari's handwriting.

Adam's stomach does a complicated set of flips and dips as he re-reads the note. A car honks behind him; the light is green. He waves a hand and revs forward, trying to stop the smile that's threatening his entire countenance—a newly unfamiliar action.

He makes himself calm down once he parks the car. Makes himself wander aisles of the grocery store and deliberate over food and wait in line to check out and load the groceries into the back of his car before he gets in and finally pulls out his phone. His thumbs hover over the keyboard a moment before he types out what he decided to say between the bread and cereal aisles.

Hi. I just got your note. Thank you so much. I have a big stack of fantasy books on hold that I can use this gift card to make a dent in.

By the time he arrives home, Ari has responded. *I should of added that gift card only works for non fantasy books sry. it'll be declined if u try*

Adam laughs out loud, the first time he's done so in ages. *Hmm, is it too late to reject your gift?*

WOW, Ari texts back, alongside a frowny face.

Jk. Thank you, really. You didn't have to do that. I should be the one bribing you to forget that you saw me how you did.

Adam sends that one while biting his lip. He doubts he'll ever stop being embarrassed by what Ari saw.

It's all good. glad I was there and hope I helped a little. anyway ur rly cute when u cry.

Adam inhales sharply and shoves his phone in his pocket. None of that, he tells himself, and gets out of his car to take his groceries inside.

Things are still fresh, too fresh, after losing Josie.

Time drags by, slowly and torturously. She continues to make herself known in all the ways she's not around. No numerous missed calls in a row, no texts late at night pleading for help on homework, no flirty exchanges with Jon meant to gross Adam out. Nothing.

When she is present, in their class together, she's a raging wildfire in his periphery. He can't help but glance her way every so often, masochistically magnetized by her presence. She never meets his gaze, but he can tell when she notices him watching. Her jaw gets tight, shoulders stiff, and she glares at whatever she can. He thinks of the glow around her when she picked him up at the airport, a reunion after months apart, and how returning to her side felt like a missing piece of the puzzle finally placed.

The following week, Adam . . . functions. That's as generous a definition he can give himself. If he's not on campus, he's in his room, clutching books in his hands, but only staring at the words, taking in nothing. He fields a couple of texts from his mom of scripture verses that made her think of him. Attending church, seeking out solace there, continues to feel impossible.

At the archives, Cal is quietly diligent about keeping Adam busy, seeming to sense his disarray. Shifts pass by as Adam taps away at the desk computer, runs errands to other departments, gives a few tours, and catalogs new arrivals. In slow moments, Cal brings up his new book club, bouncing ideas off Adam.

"I think I'll make a party out of our first meeting," he muses, eyes bright. "Is that something you'd come to?" Adam nods and says he will.

Jon corners him one evening, knocking twice on Adam's door before pushing it open. Adam, book face down on his chest, hands behind his head and staring up at the ceiling, sits up.

"What happened between you and J?" Jon asks, forehead lined with annoyance. He wiggles his phone at Adam. "I called her and she said you guys are done."

Adam sets his book aside. "Um," he starts out. He doesn't want to go into details. "Yeah, we . . . It was a miscommunication on my part." Or a lack of communication, he knows Josie would correct.

Jon's expression is twisted between confusion and concern. "Did you apologize?"

Adam nods. "It's not really something she can forgive. So." His fingers twist at an errant thread from his bedspread.

"Damn. I'm sorry, man. Is there anything I can do? You wanna hang out this weekend?"

Adam shrugs.

Jon leans against the doorway, arms crossed over his bare chest. "You wanna talk about it?"

"Not really."

"Want me to talk to J?"

He shakes his head.

"I've got some food on the stove. You hungry?"

Adam starts to shake his head again, but his stomach gives a hungry gurgle, protesting on its own behalf. He hasn't been eating very much lately. "Okay. Thank you."

"'Kay." Jon crosses to the side of the bed and holds out his hand to pull Adam up. "Come watch the Giants game with me. Bring your book."

Such is the form of socialization that's thrust upon him in the days that follow. The apartment is small enough that Adam can't sneak past Jon to his bedroom for continued isolation. If his roommate is home, he's inviting Adam to watch baseball on the couch, to stick his feet under Jon's legs while he reads, or to the pizza joint down the street. It's only ever just Jon, but it works. The jagged edges inside Adam's chest are dulled.

The tickets settle them in the lower box level overlooking the third base line. Barry Keller is already there, wearing a Giants-themed Hawaiian shirt, buttons straining at his belly. The seats around them are only half-filled, despite the ten minutes remaining before game time, and the day is warm. What better setting for the interview than a game itself? Barry's law firm had a handful of seats, and Barry was happy to lend two out for an afternoon. Adam welcomes the breeze that plays with his hair.

Jon whooped with joy when Adam invited him along. It was the least Adam could do, he figured, and on the way to the park, Adam paid close attention to Jon's monologue.

A September game means every win matters, he explained. The Giants are in a dead heat for the division title with the Dodgers, who are facing the Diamondbacks in Phoenix while the Giants square off against the Padres. It's game three of the series, the Giants looking to sweep. Jon rattled off names and positions and injuries; he talked about the bullpen and wondered audibly how long the starting pitcher would last in that day's game. Adam nodded every so often, head spinning.

Barry stands when they skirt along the aisle toward him, taking up more space than just physically—his smile is wide and comfortable. "Boys," he booms. "Barry Keller."

Jon's giddiness runs frontman. He grins, hand steady as he reaches out to shake Barry's. "Jon. We met at a game last spring. Thanks for the hook-up, man."

Barry claps his free hand on Jon's shoulder. "Heard you might be a bigger fan than I am. You're in good company in this section. Lots of baseball smarts."

Adam, clutching his notepad and pen, extends his hand a little less confidently. "Hi, I'm Adam. We spoke on the phone?"

He gets his own clap on the shoulder from Barry. "Looking forward to telling you about my love for the greatest sport in the world."

Adam smiles nervously, nods, then sits between Jon and Barry while they swap memories about the season's greatest plays and games thus far, favorite players, gambles for the postseason, and more. It becomes comforting soon enough, the game taking place before them, seats filling in around them, a sunny summer day seeping into the cracks.

Barry's got a portable radio in hand, listening to a Dodgers game happening in Phoenix.

Adam's talking now, wrapped up in Barry's retelling of the game he attended during the 1989 earthquake when the Bay Bridge collapsed.

It's the third inning, still 0-0. Between innings, the Dodgers/Diamondbacks game is broadcast on the scoreboard, during which everyone cheers at the Dodgers falling behind in the seventh—except Barry, who tells Adam, "I thought I'd never feel anything but dislike toward that team. Turns out family blood can be thicker than fan blood after all." He shakes his head with a fond-looking smile. "My son, a Dodger." Adam makes a note.

During the fourth inning, Adam stands, politely excusing himself down the row so he can use the restroom, when he hears his name. He looks up, then around, glancing across the sea of faces for someone looking at him. Then, drawn like a moth to the flame, Adam sees Ari.

He's four rows back and closer to the aisle than Adam is, alongside two middle-aged men who match Ari's skin tone and the way his eyes crinkle when he smiles—which he's doing right now, his grin dazzling. Adam blushes fiercely.

He scoots out the rest of the way, and Ari matches him, meeting him on the stairs and pulling him into a delighted hug that has Adam burning brighter. "What're you doing here?" Ari asks. And then Jon is there, nudging his way into the aisle, asking Adam if he wants any food ("no, thank you") and eyeing Ari curiously.

Ari's smile turns brittle until Adam introduces Jon as his roommate. Ari leads the way up the steps, tossing out comments on the game at Adam, who's still in shock from finding him here. He vaguely remembers Ari mentioning he was a baseball fan, *maybe* something about season tickets. Jon answers for Adam, and by the top of the stairs, Ari and Jon are old pals.

Jon bows out to buy food—this time asking Ari if he wants anything ("a beer and I'll getcha back"), and Adam lingers next to a kiosk selling sushi of all things.

"So," Ari says. "Baseball fan now, huh?"

Adam's face heats again, happy to be here, to spend time with Jon, to be working on a story with such an engaging focus as Barry, and overjoyed, thrilled, ecstatic to see Ari. The ache of Josie's absence dwindles to nearly nothing. "I might be," he says, suddenly helpless against Ari's gravitational pull. And Ari smiles like he knows it. "I'm, um— For one of my classes I have to write an article, and Jon met this guy once who's gone to every Giants game, like, ever, and his son plays for the Dodgers, and—" He's talking a mile a minute but can't seem to stop, "—I'm writing a profile on him, so he invited us to sit next to him and ask questions and watch the game."

"Keller himself!" Ari crows. "Dude's a legend. You know they pulled him onto the field when they won the 2010 World Series? And make sure you ask him about the streaker in '05, too. He gives a great play-by-play."

Adam is jostled by the passing crowd and moves closer to Ari. "You have season tickets?"

"My dad and uncle chip in for a few each year and I come whenever I can," Ari says, raising his voice in time with increased clapping from the crowd. He leans in closer. "Hey, would you want to go grab food after the game?"

"I— Yes," Adam says before he fully processes the question. He's rewarded with a grin, elation emanating off the man, and the crowd seems to respond in kind, a roar going up as someone—a Giants player no doubt—gets a hit, maybe a home run. Adam's not paying attention, high on possibilities, not leaving any room for doubt or regret or self-hatred and maybe baseball really *is* the greatest sport in the world.

It's not a date, Adam repeats to himself after using the restroom and returning to his seat, briefly catching Ari's eye as he sidles along the row. Ari gives him another brilliant smile, the kind that's been glossily printed in magazines, that has Adam's insides doing funny things. *Not a date.*

He tells Jon his plans, all casual-like, ignoring the raised eyebrows—somehow different from the kind his siblings would always give Adam at the mention of a male's name, and returns his attention to Barry and baseball. The game ekes out drama as the innings stretch, and Adam's content to simply sit back and watch as the game extends into later innings, swaying alongside Jon during the seventh inning stretch, and only glancing back toward Ari once—who's talking animatedly with one of the men he's with.

Tensions are high and the stands full by the time the bottom of the ninth inning comes around, and even Adam starts to appreciate the energy as cries from the crowd turn on a hair trigger, each strike met with groans and every successful sprint to a base with cheers. Barry is cackling like the long-suffering fan he is.

Adam's trying to keep track of how many strikes and balls and outs there are, the scoreboard an intimidating grid of numbers, so he's confused when the game ends short of the count, people cheering the impressive hit into the outfield and a player running home and the Giants pouring out of the dugout in a victory that Adam isn't sure has been earned yet.

"A walk-off!" Jon cheers as the team literally jumps for joy around home plate, welcoming the runner home.

"The best way to end 'em," Barry says, shaking Adam's, then Jon's hand. He urges Adam to call anytime to continue their conversation.

Adam and Jon stand and move slowly toward the aisle, caught up in the crowd. Jon recaps plays excitedly, high-fiving with other fans as they go, and Adam smiles along with him for different reasons, though it was an exciting finish to the game. They meet Ari at the top of the stairs, where Jon gives him a victorious high five and says, "Take good care of my roomie," before disappearing into the crowd.

With a tug on the sleeve of Adam's sweatshirt, Ari leads them through the concourse of Oracle Park, offering to buy him a Giants hat at every kiosk selling merchandise they pass by.

"I'm not really a hat person," Adam tells him as they descend the stairs out onto Third Street. It's late afternoon now, and clusters of people are separating to their destinations. "They look weird on me."

Ari protests by sweeping off his own hat and setting it on Adam's head. His mouth quirks to one side as he takes in Adam as they walk, fingers forming a rectangle through which he squints, like he's shooting a film. Adam goes to take it off, flushing and stammering out an "I *told* you—" but Ari stops him, his hand on the crown of Adam's head, then briefly dropping it to cup the back of Adam's neck.

"You look cute," Ari says when he pulls away. "Could easily steal all my jobs."

"Very funny," Adam mumbles, returning Ari's hat, his face on fire. He pats his hair with a shaky hand. "So, um, have you always been a Giants fan?"

"Like my dad would let me be anything else," Ari says. He rolls his eyes with a smile. "Yeah. Played baseball growing up, too, through high school. Lots of baseball in my life."

"You and Jon would get along well," Adam says. "He lives and dies by a Giants win or loss."

"He seems cool. He a good roommate?" They're waiting to cross the street, gleeful Giants fans babbling around them.

"He's great. Really. He's . . ." Adam thinks of how alone he's felt lately, and how Jon's extended his hand. "He's a good friend."

Ari's smiling over at him, corner of his mouth ticked up. Something in his eyes makes Adam want to reach out and touch him, but he doesn't. Ari only nudges him before continuing his questions—any weird roommate quirks Jon has and what Utah is like during the summer. Adam asks Ari about his own intervening months since they last spent time together, an extended job in New York City and a trip to Hawaii with friends.

They end up in front of a Mexican food place, joining the short queue. The woman taking their order gives Ari a lingering smile as they order. Adam can't blame her.

Ari pays. "My idea, my treat," he insists. Adam's cheeks hurt from all the smiling he can't suppress.

They find a two-seater table in the corner. Adam had forgotten how natural conversation is with Ari, how quickly his stuttering dies the longer they talk, how his face heats repeatedly, like the rise and fall of notes in a song, but from the joy of Ari's company. Adam leaps up to grab their food when it's called, grabs a pile of napkins, and settles the food on the table between them. They dig in, grinning at each other with mouths full, Ari bemoaning the fact that he can't get anything deep fried because of an upcoming job. When they're done, Ari leads Adam to his car, parked in a garage off Brannan Street, their pace slowing in an unspoken attempt to drag things out a little longer.

"I'm so stoked I ran into you. Like, seriously." Ari laughs, giddy. "Hey, can I show you a spot? Do you have anything you need to get to? It's a little out of the way by car, but it won't take long."

Adam nods, still basking in the glow of the day and Ari's arm bumping against his as they walk.

Ari drives them to the Russian Hill neighborhood, pulling his car into a two-hour parking spot. The day is edging into evening, cool and clear. Adam gives a waiting Ari a small smile as he joins him on the sidewalk and follows him to the end of the road, where a low wall is centered between two descending staircases, overlooking a small hill of tall trees and leafy foliage. Ari sits, swinging his legs over the wall to face the lookout. Adam sits next to him, eyes lifting to the view before them. The fringes of the city are lit up, on the cusp of twilight, meeting a hard line of water which extends out until, in the distance, the Golden Gate Bridge is on display, its beacon red towers and the steadily moving traffic across. The Marin headlands rise to the right of the bridge, guiding the way toward Sausalito and other North Bay communities.

It's now that the mood shifts. Like clockwork, guilt begins to creep across Adam's skin. The food felt safe, but this—this feels like a date, and he doesn't have time to parse out all the things he feels about that.

"When I started going on longer runs during my marathon training, I'd drive to different neighborhoods, park, and then just run. I found this view one time," Ari is saying, pointing to the stairs below. "I'd just finished climbing those and was totally fried." He laughs at the memory. "It was so fucking hard. But then I turned around and saw all this."

The good day is being swallowed up by the shame of it all. *To act on it is a sin*, whispers his mom's voice. Finally, aware of the lengthening silence, Adam looks over and forces out, "What was your favorite part about running the marathon?"

Ari's already watching him. "Finishing it." He grins, apparently oblivious to Adam's internal turmoil. "It was really, like, rewarding to have my friends waiting at the finish line. All the training . . . It started to get to me at the end. I was glad to be done." He looks back out toward the bridge in the distance. "But it was fun exploring the city on my runs. I found some cool spots—" He nods to the stairs, "—and met some new people."

"People?" Adam weakly teases.

"Person." Ari smiles to himself, and the act twinges something in Adam's chest. "I really missed you. This whole summer."

"I—" Adam tries, looking down as he swallows at the rising panic. Too many emotions, and want most of all. He wants Ari so badly and might fall apart because of it.

A hand on his arm. He flinches and turns away. This was so stupid to do, throwing himself right back into this mix of feelings that he still hasn't climbed out of from the last time. Today was a luxury Adam can never afford again.

"You okay?" Ari's voice is soft.

Just remember that after Ari fucks you, I won't be there to help you put your pants back on.

Adam tries to breathe deep but his lungs won't let him. "I should go," he chokes out, gripping his hands on the edge of the wall. He doesn't stand, though. Afraid his legs will betray him and give out.

Beside him, Ari shifts, lifting one leg over the wall so he's facing Adam, straddling the ledge. His face is earnest and willing and so, so beautiful. "Hey, what's going on?"

If Adam says anything right now, he'll start crying. He shakes his head, takes a deep breath, and pivots to stand.

The parked car waits like a steel trap, and it takes everything Adam has to buckle his seatbelt. He can see Ari's repeated glances, clearly wanting to say something, but Adam stares determinedly forward.

The drive to Adam's house is silent. He meets Ari's eyes for a half second when they pull up. Ari simply stares back, obvious in his confusion and hurt.

Adam can't even bring himself to thank Ari when he climbs out, only managing to softly close the passenger door to show he's not leaving in anger.

Coward, hisses Josie's voice.

Adam feels the truth of it like a battering ram.

Chapter 17

Loneliness still too fresh a demon from summertime, Josie begins to seek out activities good for distraction. Walks through parks, roaming tourist attractions, messaging via dating apps. And the Throne Room.

Similar to last time, Josie finds herself in the crowd listening to music physically, but drifting mentally. She blinks and the first band is done, a new one taking center stage. When this band finishes its third song, Josie sees him, her gaze dragged hard to the right of the stage with the glint of reflection off a camera lens.

He's wearing a silky-looking top and a hat with a brim. The camera slung around his neck is large and expensive looking. Silas Sinclair in action, eyes on the band. As she watches, he lifts the camera up to his face, finger pressing down on the shutter button as he captures stills. Lowering the camera, his eyes flick to the screen, rolling a dial on the instrument to review what he's shot. Then he's moving, to the front of the stage, crouching down, taking photos, then standing up and moving into the audience.

Josie mutters her annoyance, turning back to the band. She manages to stick it out until they're done, but her heart's not in it anymore. She can't have anything for herself.

Outside, she welcomes the evening's mind-clearing coolness. It's nearing nine, the Valley house a good thirty-minute Muni ride away.

"Juliet," comes a voice as she heads for the closest stop, and there he is, sitting on the hood of his car, smoking a cigarette. She should've given it another fifteen minutes if she wanted to bypass him completely.

"Josie," she says automatically, slowing to a stop. His expression is something stuck between humor and wariness. She wonders if Ramona told him about Josie's article request—his original suggestion.

"Want a ride home?" he asks, flicking his cigarette to the ground and sliding off the car. "I'm headed your way."

"No," she says coldly, zipping up her jacket and pulling her hair out of the collar. "And don't litter." A pointed look at the smoldering cigarette.

Silas gives a light laugh, bending to pick it up. "I take it you're still mad at me?"

"I don't care enough about you to be mad."

"Is Adam okay?"

Josie sucks in her cheeks. "Is *Ari* okay?"

A twitch of Silas's mouth tells her he's enjoying her bad mood, which doesn't help her—well, bad mood. "At least he's talking to me."

Josie flinches at the dig but realizes too late that Silas isn't talking about Adam and her, but her and Silas. Silas tilts his head at the tell, but she gives what she hopes is a careless shrug and turns to head to the Muni station.

"Josie, c'mon," he calls after her. "I'm sorry. Let me give you a ride."

She ignores him and fights back the urge to call Adam as she walks away.

The balcony overlooking Valley Street has become Josie's favorite stake-out spot. When she's focused on schoolwork or work-work, the cars driving by, the freeway noise in the distance, barking dogs, people walking by—it's all mind-numbing background noise that Josie can, in theory, think to, be productive to.

In reality, she's once again opening up Ramona's social media profiles, once again searching for a stepping stone to move the capstone story forward. After staring at yet another selfie of her roommate, Josie switches over to Andrew Prosser's profile.

She's been here before, the experience brief and painful. Andrew is a stereotypical tech bro, and it's like he's trying to further prove the point on Instagram. Under a picture of a TED Talk-looking stage, he wrote, *Absorbing thought leadership. May or may not regurgitate it on a future podcast.* Under another one of a stand-up desk covered in papers, *Leveling up—both my game and my posture.* And the crowning jewel: a shot of the same Burning Man-looking landscape Ramona was posting about in August. *Just me, the desert, and a very weak 5G signal*, reads the caption.

Josie wants to barf.

Neither Ramona or Andrew have posted any pictures of each other on their profiles, which Josie immediately chalks up to her roommate wanting to keep Nara from blowing a gasket over Ramona dating a guy with at least a decade on her.

She scrolls further back, past a photo of Andrew wearing a virtual reality headset and giving two thumbs up. A silver letter V shimmers on the band of the headset, which Josie automatically recognizes as the logo for VYBE, the artificial intelligence company Nara brought up at last month's dinner. The last time she saw him, he was wearing a fleece vest bearing the same logo.

Fanboy? Josie wonders, tapping over to the company's profile. The feed is primarily made up of prompt ideas for the A.I. platform. *VYBE Check: Create a two-week meal plan out of ten ingredients that maximizes protein.* Or *VYBE Check: Tell me a bedtime story about dragons and unicorns.*

Occasionally, however, there are videos of people—hip, attractive-looking people—smiling as they talk about the benefits of A.I. The influencers, no surprise here, have arrived at VYBE. Except Ramona, which Josie confirms after a hurried scroll through the rest of the posts. No shots of Andrew either.

She then opens Google and enters *Andrew Prosser + VYBE*.

She's still on the balcony, staring outward, her mind whirring, when Silas's black Prius pulls into the driveway. Josie narrows her eyes.

He gets out, pizza box in hand, and heads for the front door. He glances up once, then double-takes when he catches Josie scowling down at him.

"Oh, come *on*," he calls with a grin, pushing his sunglasses up. He's more casual than usual today, in a black hoodie and black jeans.

"What?" Josie returns warily.

Silas's voice is gleeful. "Now *you're* the one leaning into this Juliet thing." He gestures one-handed to the balcony. "Please drop me a Shakespeare line. It'll make my life."

Josie calls down in a chilly tone, "I'm going for gargoyle vibes." Then, "Ramona's not here."

Silas lifts the pizza box up a few inches. "I know. I'm here for you. With a peace offering—a *pizza* offering, if you will."

"Dad jokes? Really?"

"I'm full of surprises, Juliet— *No*, you can't look at me like that when you're literally talking to me from a balcony."

"This joke needs to die."

"Never. I'm coming up. Don't turn me to stone."

"That's Medusa." Josie briefly considers hightailing it to her room, but she's no coward. She sets her phone on the little table next to her chair and crosses her arms to wait.

Silas comes out a minute later, giving her a smirk before settling into the other chair and opening the pizza box on his lap. "Here. Take a slice. Please."

Josie only narrows her eyes.

Silas clucks and returns the piece to the box. "How many times do I need to apologize?"

"Until I feel like accepting. Or I die. Whichever comes first."

He closes the lid on the pizza and leans forward, elbows lightly pressing on the cardboard. "I'll say this one last time: I'm sorry for how everything shook out with the Adam stuff. I would've handled things differently, but it got away from me. I'm sorry for not telling you everything, okay? I was trying to be a good friend to Ari, and it made me a bad one to you."

Josie gets a shoulder up, feigning nonchalance, but any response gets stuck in her throat, and she has to look away. It shouldn't change anything, Silas's acknowledgement that they were friends, even if just barely. It doesn't change anything, but it does help.

She holds out a hand, still not looking at him. He hands her a slice. "This doesn't mean I forgive you," she says.

He shrugs in her periphery, easy. "I'm done groveling, if that's what you're hoping for more of."

"Fuck off." But she says it through a mouthful of pizza, so the words have less sting.

"How're classes going? Did you figure out a story for that capstone one?" Silas asks between bites of his own slice. The pizza is half olive and mushroom, half pepperoni.

Josie doesn't respond, only glances over at him in silent question.

He gives her a knowing look. "Sorry Ramona said no. For what it's worth, I tried to argue your case."

"I mean," Josie takes another bite and continues with a full mouth, "I know she doesn't exactly care for my winning personality."

"Honestly, I think she's just really stressed about Ari. They're super close—or were, and it's affecting her. And work is stressing her out more than usual. Her assistant just quit, and—" He stops himself with an unamused smile, not meeting her eye. "You don't care. Ignore me."

"Evelyn quit?" Josie asks with genuine surprise.

Silas grimaces. "Ramona didn't say why, but apparently it was a nasty separation."

"Bummer." She pauses, considering what she just learned about Andrew, then asks, "And where does that guy she's seeing fit into all this?"

He makes a small noise. "Should he fit in somewhere?"

The tone has Josie pausing as she reaches for another slice and sitting up instead. She assesses Silas, the fact that he's here and not out with Ramona somewhere, what his best friend having a boyfriend might do to their relationship. It was a problem she never had (or at least thought she never had) with Adam—him dating, splitting his time between her and a romantic partner. Perhaps she's not the only one who's down in friends.

"Seems like you'd prefer if he didn't," she ventures.

Silas chews his pizza in silence as an answer.

"Well." Perhaps a mission will cheer him up. "Any chance you can still convince Ramona to do the story? Maybe it'll put her in a better mood."

"Could we be friends again if I did?"

She waits a moment before responding, then gives a sharp nod. "Fine." She has to look away so she doesn't smile at the relief in his expression.

Silas stops after two slices, Josie after her fourth. Silas sets the box aside and wipes crumbs from his hands, his gray eyes on distant buildings.

"How's Ari?" Josie asks.

"He's not saying a whole lot to me these days." Silas looks miserable about that, but Josie doesn't feel pity given the circumstances. "But he seems better. He was staying at an ex's place for a bit; Isaiah, a perpetual rebound option and it's never ended well with him, but Ari feels things really big and takes things personally and . . . Well, anyway. He came back home, and he's at least saying 'hey' when he sees me, so that's something."

"Still not talking to Ramona, though?"

Silas shoots her a look. "No. It's . . . gonna be a while, I think, before he can forgive her. How is Adam, by the way?"

Josie pauses. "Let's just say you weren't the only one who kept things from me, and his was a bit grander in scale." Her gaze is outward from the balcony, but she sees Silas look at her sharply from the edge of her vision.

"You haven't spoken to him?"

"Friends don't lie." She doesn't want to talk about Adam, now or ever. She can practically hear Silas weighing his next words carefully, takes a weird pride in him being on his toes with her, like he cares enough to not ruin the silk-thin thread of comradery.

Finally, he says slowly, "Do you have anyone else you can talk to?"

"I'm fine."

"You've been here at the house a lot . . . and I didn't see you with anyone at the Throne Room . . ."

"I'm fine, Silas."

The silence is more stilted this time, and shorter. It's only a minute or so before Silas says, "Do you want to go see a movie or something? Get out of the house?"

He's off kilter, she thinks; the dawning realization of Josie flying solo is discomforting to easy-going Silas, liker of all. "I don't need or want your pity."

"Well aware of that, thanks. But maybe I want yours. There's that new Florence Pugh film."

Josie feels the weight of her recent solitude in her bones. Even still, she tells him, "That's a no. I should get back to homework anyway."

Silas taps his fingers on the armrest. "Can I text you?"

"Free country."

"Can I text you and have you text me back?"

"Another pizza offering?"

Silas laughs, his face a map of all the times he's done it before, and it settles something in Josie. It feels like ages since she made anyone laugh. "It's a pretty good line, huh?" Silas says.

"It's pretty bad. But fine. If you text me anything interesting, I'll consider responding."

His smile softens a bit at that. "I'm sorry again."

"For someone who doesn't want to grovel anymore, you sure are doing a good job at it."

"You bring out the worst in me, my sweet Juliet." He stands, picking up the pizza box.

"I'm not going to reply if you call me Juliet," Josie says. She really does hate it, the clichéd romantic expectations of pairs who spend considerable amounts of time together. Whatever this is with Silas, it's not that.

Silas rolls his eyes. "Consider the joke dead. Thanks for sharing my pizza. Had a feeling you were a pepperoni girl. I'll put the rest in the fridge. And I'll work on Ramona for you."

She flashes him a feline smile and a middle finger, is rewarded with a solo finger gun as he heads inside. A minute later, he's walking out to his car. "Text you soon, Josie," he calls without looking back.

Josie scowls, but there's not quite as much venom in it this time.

That evening, Josie pulls up Adam's Instagram, where he rarely posts. His feed is mostly pictures of pretty views around the city, in some of which a stray curl of Josie's or Josie herself make an appearance. There's one of them, a selfie. Josie's smiling hard in the photo, freckles galore and hair a madhouse. They'd been near Pier 39 the previous fall, windswept and happy with all the people-watching they were doing. Adam's hair is blown across his forehead, mouth in a half smile, the one that crawls slowly across his face, as he humored her.

Her eyes start itching so she pulls up Netflix, gets four minutes into a show before she exits the app, turns her phone off, and rolls onto her side as she wonders why it's possible to both hate and miss Adam so much that it's hard to breathe.

Chapter 18

Hi. I wanted to apologize for what happened the other night. It was unfair of me to shut down like I did. I'm also sorry for not thanking you for driving me home. You don't have to respond. Hope you're well.

Adam sends the text nearly a week after the baseball game and subsequent hangout. Nearly a week, but he's still positively humiliated with how he treated Ari. Josie used to always tease him for "pouting," where he'd leave suddenly and not talk to her for a while. It's not malicious. He just needs time to process events and how he's feeling about them. This, though. Ari was nothing but kind and Adam turned into a brick wall.

Ari doesn't respond to Adam's text until the next day: *will u talk to me abt whats goin on?*

Adam sits up, setting the book he's reading aside. A second text from Ari: *I rly just want closure is all*

It's a fair request. Adam knows he owes this conversation to Ari. Ari knows the biggest thing: Adam's very much out with Ari, has kissed Ari, so breaking down his struggles should be a piece of cake. Maybe it'll help Adam move on, too. Move on and lock potential romances up for the rest of his life; Ari becomes the one who got away.

Okay. is what he responds with. Ari tells him he'll come over that night because he's got an early flight out to LA in the morning.

Ari doesn't have the easy, relaxed nature Adam's used to when he shows up. His mouth is a flat line, black eyes distant and wary. He follows Adam to his bedroom wordlessly, then stops a foot or two into the room, taking it all in.

"Do you want to sit?" Adam asks, hovering by his bed.

"I'm good."

Adam deflates. "Okay." He starts to sit, then thinks it might be weird if Ari stays standing while he sits, and bobs back up again. "Um."

Ari's staring at the books crowding Adam's shelves, which crowd his already tiny room, an odd look on his face. Adam's not really sure how to start this. "So, I'm really sorry—"

"Did I do something?" Ari blurts. "Like— I thought things were going really well in the spring, and I kissed you and you seemed really into it for a second but then you seemed really *not* into it, and then you ghosted me. And then the other night, it felt like it had been when things were good, but then you, like, shut off again and I just— What did I do wrong?"

Adam shakes his head, mouth opening. Then closing. Then opening. "Nothing. You—you did nothing wrong." He clears his throat. Takes a deep breath. "Last spring— I left because . . . I stopped it because I was scared."

A beat. "Of me?"

"Yeah. Well, I mean, it was a fear of, of—" It was a fear of wanting Ari, but he won't say that. He pulls back, widens the scope. "I have a hard time with being—with, um, liking guys?" Adam swallows, and there's pain to it, a harbinger of tears to come. He drops his gaze. "How I grew up, with my religious beliefs, has made it really . . . extremely difficult for me to . . . to be with guys. I've always tried to just, to just not?" He stalls out, waits to see if Ari will say anything. He doesn't. "But then I met you and . . . I thought I could just hang out with you or whatever we were doing. But it was all building up, and I kept feeling

146

horribly guilty about, about, um, w-wanting you, and then we kissed and it was all real; so, so real and it scared me. I hated myself for it all: for wanting to be with you and trying to reconcile what I've been taught, about how I'm not supposed to act on this because it's wrong. And I don't mean you're wrong, or anyone else who's—you know, but I . . ." He pushes a hand through his hair.

Still no reprieve from Ari. Adam sighs, swiping at a tear with the back of his hand as he finally sits on his bed. "It wasn't your fault, is what I'm trying to say," he says, voice dropping to a whisper. It's easier to say all this when he's not looking into the ink blots of Ari's soul. "I can't, you know, *be* with you— Not that you even want that. Sorry, I don't want to— I'm not assuming. I can't . . . can't be with other guys without getting really down on myself. But it's not your fault for any of it. It's mine. And, and . . . yeah."

A whimpering end to a pathetic monologue.

Ari's weight shifts, and Adam glances over. Ari is looking at him curiously, but still warily. "You want me, but you don't want me."

It's a statement, not a question, and it's accurate. Adam shrugs and gives a loose nod.

"And that's why you stopped things."

Another miserable shrug.

"You don't like to kiss guys? Or touch or anything else?"

Adam leans forward, elbows on his thighs and head in his hands. "I don't not want to do that. It's how I feel afterward."

"So, what, your religion brainwashed you into self-hatred?"

"No, not at all. It's—" Adam chews on his lip at the accusation, hidden from view. "It's been a beautiful thing, being part of my church. But the doctrine . . . doesn't believe acting on same-sex attraction is good."

A breath that could be a laugh. "'Same-sex attraction,' huh? You're still part of this church?"

147

Adam's reply is more a bob of his head than an outright nod.

"Okay . . . you're, like, trying to not be gay, even though you're gay. Because your church says it's okay with you being gay . . . as long as you're not gay?"

Adam shrugs. Then nods. Then repeats with a whisper, because it still feels like the most accurate description: "I want you, but I don't want you."

He hears Ari exhale, then footsteps toward the bed. Ari sinks onto the mattress next to him, but Adam doesn't look up. "This—you and me—won't ever go anywhere because you'd be absolutely miserable if it did," Ari says.

Adam presses the heels of his hands to his eyes. He doesn't respond. He's so sick of crying.

"Is there . . ." Ari says. "Sorry, I'm trying to process this all— Are you just gonna, like, force yourself to end up alone because of this?"

Adam tries not to flinch at Ari's bullseye aim. "I'm so s-sorry about this. Truly."

"Don't be. I asked for closure, though this isn't . . ." Another sigh, and Ari lets the sentence hang.

Minutes pass. Adam's wiping his cheeks and sitting up straight when Ari turns to face him, pulling one leg up underneath him. He looks calm, eyes dry but honest. "Do you think . . ." His hand moves toward Adam, but he stops short and lets it fall on the bed. "Do you think you could ever . . . be in a romantic relationship with me?"

Adam blinks, then opens his mouth, because apparently everything he just said didn't make sense if Ari's asking him this and—

Ari holds up his hands, palms facing Adam. "Just— *If* you want to try, I'll do it. We can go slow. Like, so slow. You can be in the driver's seat with anything physical. We can work through your stuff."

Adam's eyes are wide.

"The only thing I ask is that you tell me there *is* a destination," Ari continues. "Like, I'm a physical guy and need that in relationships. Ramona says it's my love language or some shit like that. If you want to try things with me, let's do it. But I don't want to not be able to kiss you or anything forever. Does that make sense?"

Adam swallows. "I . . . I don't . . ."

"You said you want this, and so do I. You've missed me and I've missed you. I won't pressure you on anything. I *want* to be with you, Adam. And not just to, like . . . I dunno. From the moment you first biked by me, carefully riding around puddles, trying not to splash me. It was so sweet, and it stuck with me. And then I saw you again, and I kept seeing you, and I started, like, *making sure* I was at that intersection on Wednesdays and Fridays at six-forty-five in the morning. I had the mile count down. I wanted to talk to you and get to know you and then I did and I couldn't stop wanting more." He's gazing at Adam steadily. "You are kind and smart and so fucking gorgeous, Adam—like, seriously. And you are gay and that's okay and all I want to do is kiss you and tell you those things over and over until you believe them."

The words alone make Adam want to pass out. He looks away. "I don't know what to say."

"But you know what you want."

He does. It makes sense to explore taking things slow with Ari, moving forward in steps, testing the waters. If Ari is in fact willing to move their relationship along slowly, maybe that's all Adam needs: Ari, and time.

But . . . "It's not that easy," he says. His forehead is pressed against his palm again. Icy self-hatred circles up his arms and legs, shackling him to dismay.

Ari moves to kneel before him on the floor but doesn't touch him. "You can let it be easy. It sounds like you've lived your whole life stuck in this weird limbo because you like guys. Try a different approach.

149

Try, like, appreciating what makes you, you. Try it with me." A pause. "Even if it's not with me. I know I can't decide this for you. If you don't want to be with anyone, that's your decision. But if you do . . . please, *please* pick me."

Adam flounders, then kicks back up to the surface. "My family—" he chokes out, because at the end of the day, that's what's on the line.

Ari's expression is kind. "Adam, if your family really loves you, they should be happy that you'd be happy."

That's the whole thing, though, Adam thinks: the Hugheses want Adam to be happy for eternity, for the forever *after* this life ends, when his attraction to other men goes away. The happiness up for discussion is a question of now or forever.

Adam finds, suddenly, that he doesn't care.

Eternal perspective on the line, Adam looks at Ari, at the way the other man is staring back, something like desperate hope in the set of his body, his kneeling in supplication—an offering to Adam. Adam looks and finds that he wants something with Ari more than anything else.

Promise me, pleads his mom's voice in his head.

I can't, Adam replies simply.

"If we tried," he says, trying the words and liking the taste, "it's . . . not easy being around me when I get down on myself? I don't want to make you mad or frustrated."

"I appreciate that," Ari says with a small smile. "It means that we have to keep everything on the table, right? We take things slow and we stay honest about how we're feeling."

Adam feels the words drop against his skin like invisible rain. Maybe in order to stop feeling so down about who he is and how he is, he needs to push through the self-hatred. Perhaps a relationship, the kind he's always coveted, is waiting for him; he simply has to face the darkest parts to get there. Ari feels like an elixir. They can take it slow. He'll tell Josie everything. He'll work on his relationship with his family. He'll find a way to make it all work.

The 'but' still hangs heavy on his tongue. "I don't . . . I can't promise to, um, to—" He flicks his eyes to the bed, not wanting to verbalize it. He can't go from zero to a hundred, isn't sure he'll ever be able to. He was firmly taught that premarital sex is a no-go, even without homosexuality on the table.

Ari makes the connection. "Okay. That's—okay. Like I said, we'll take it slow. It's not only physical for me. I want this with you."

Adam looks up at him, their faces not a foot apart. Ari's is wide open, hope obvious across every feature, and it stirs the same feeling in Adam. He could try with Ari. Especially with Ari. Of all people, with Ari.

Adam has thought his way up and down and around his feelings and what might happen if he got a chance, if he was brave enough to pursue something. He's thought and mulled and wanted for months. And even though it's likely that the rawness from the past weeks is lowering his defenses and rationale, maybe this is just right. Maybe not the way his parents would use the word, not the way Cal would use it, not the way their church would use it, but maybe it's right in the way that Josie was telling him all this time: that he's allowed to want and be wanted by another person. He is allowed to love—because that's what this could be, this thing with Ari—others, regardless of gender.

"I want this with you, too," he says, voice low. "I might be—bad— But I really would like to try, um, being . . . being with you." The words end with a whisper, Adam's eyes on his hands. He can't believe he's saying them. A jolt of excitement zips through him.

Ari shifts, exhales. "Will you look at me?"

Adam does.

"You want to? Really?" Ari asks. He's looking at Adam like a man standing before an oasis, unsure if it's real or not.

Adam laughs, a nervous noise that's more than a little hysterical. But he nods and says, "Yeah. Yes. I really— Yeah. I want to." His knees are weak with possibility, so it's good that he's not standing. Is he smiling? He should stop smiling. "With you."

Ari's smiling too. Eyes liquid and white teeth biting his bottom lip. "Okay. Um, shit, of course I'm going out of town now. But that's probably . . . good? I should honestly probably go or I'm gonna end up, like, ravishing you."

Adam stands, legs only mildly weak and face warm with pleasure. "I'll walk you out?" He leads Ari to his car, trying not to grin at the ground but failing gloriously. Ari hesitates by the driver's side door, his signature smile broadcast across his face. Its intensity does something to Adam's insides.

"So, I'll be back Tuesday afternoon, if you want to hang out," Ari says.

"I do. Um, I guess I'll need to put your actual name in my phone now?"

Ari laughs. "Still Sexy Runner Guy?"

Adam flushes with a small shrug.

"Least it's accurate." Ari pulls open his door. "Thanks, by the way. For telling me everything. It . . . helps. It was a pretty shitty summer inside my head."

"For me too. I'm sorry again. Sometimes I get, um— I'm just sorry."

"It's okay. Really. You're here now."

Adam nods. "Travel safe. I'll see you next week."

"'Kay. I miss you already."

Adam's face burns, but it's a welcome embarrassment. "You too."

Ari leaves, and Adam ends up back in his room, falling on his bed and smiling into his hand. It completely goes against who Adam is as a person, how he operates, what he's told himself, what he's withheld—

he knows that. It goes against his nature, yet he can't help but feel like that's the solution; because it's different, it'll work.

Chapter 19

J osie's walking home from the bus stop, a handful of blocks away from home, when a dark SUV pulls up beside her. She moves away from the curb automatically, pulls out one of her earbuds, and glares.

—then relaxes when she sees Nara Taylor lean out of a rear window and smile. "We're heading to the same place," the congresswoman says. "Hop in."

Josie obliges, climbing into the vehicle's dark and tidy leather interior. "Are you picking up Ramona?" she asks, the car moving again.

"Girls' night out before I head back to D.C.," Nara says. She's wearing a black pantsuit with a white silk shirt underneath. At Josie's sideways look, she laughs, a tinkling sound Josie assumes has been practiced in front of thousands. "It's our tradition."

Josie catches the eye of the driver in the rear view mirror and suddenly feels important—conversing with a U.S. congresswoman about family matters in a hired car. She relaxes a bit more into the seat, stretching her legs out in the footwell. "Are you two pretty close?"

It's another lesson in journalism she's applying to real life: asking a question she already knows the answer to out of interest in hearing what the other person will say. It's apparent from outer space what the state of Ramona and Nara's relationship is. Still, maybe they're going through a rough patch and things are usually peachy keen.

Nara gives Josie a sad smile, and for a split second, Josie wonders if her own mother has ever expressed that type of emotion over a lack of relationship with her daughter. "I apologize that we haven't been on our best behavior around you," Nara says, side-stepping the question. "I'm usually a bit more composed than that."

Josie raises both of her hands in an understanding motion. "Hey, I get it. Better than you'd think."

"Ramona and I don't often agree on her future."

The car is paused at a red light. Josie doesn't respond, surprised at Nara's willingness to be candid. Then again, Josie already has many a gold star from the congresswoman for being a collegiate example to her daughter. Maybe it's earned her VIP access.

"It's terribly cliché, but I only want what's best for her," Nara continues. "Though I admit some of my demands are a bit more restrictive than I mean for them to be."

Diplomacy has never been Josie's strong suit—the irony of her conversation partner—so the words probably don't come out as fine-tuned as she'd like, but she wants to prove something, keep up the good graces she earned back at that first introduction. "I think there's a difference between being controlling just because it fits your needs and encouraging someone to do something you know will pay off in the long run."

Nara raises an eyebrow as the car rolls forward. "Is there?"

Josie's mind jumps to Adam and she nods, jaw set. "Yeah."

A sigh. "I hope I align with the latter, then."

The car stops in front of the Valley house and Nara touches her manicured hand to Josie's arm, pausing her exit from the vehicle. "Please don't let a mother/daughter squabble ruin any friendship with my daughter." Josie works hard to not burst into laughter like a hyena. "She is a special young woman, full of great promise."

Josie only nods, not daring herself to even fake a smile of agreement. They exit the car, Nara with infinitely more grace, and Josie realizes this is her chance to make her capstone story more of a reality. She tightens her grip on the strap of her bag as she walks up the front pathway next to Nara.

"I was actually thinking of writing an article about Ramona," she starts. "A profile, to be specific."

Nara looks confused as she glances over. They both pause on the front step. "About Ramona?"

"I think it's interesting to see her on a career path similar to your political one. You both try to gain followers who agree with your beliefs and stuff."

Nara frowns. "Parallels between voter-elected individuals who try to improve their constituents' lives and those who show off their outfits of the day on TikTok?"

Josie would cackle if she could; she and Nara are on exactly the same page. But there's a goal here, so she proceeds with caution, aware she could lose the congresswoman's fondness with a misstep. "I mean, it is a modern-day career, influencing. More than the success and income, it's pretty powerful having such a broad platform. Think about what the most famous influencers have, millions of people invested in their everyday lives. It's no wonder companies pant after that shi—stuff for advertising."

Nara's bracelets rattle as she slides a hand down the front of her blouse; she seems mildly intrigued, but not completely sold. "Well. I can't imagine Ramona saying no to growing her reach. If you can provide me a copy of the story, I might be able to get you in touch with an editor at the *Chronicle*."

Josie nods eagerly just as the front door is yanked open, Ramona's face pinched as she looks out. "What's going on?" she asks, eyes shifting between Josie and her mother.

"Darling, hi. How are you?" Nara says, stepping inside. Josie follows. "I was driving over and saw Josie here walking home."

Ramona gives Josie a look, the slightest narrowing of her eyes, before asking her mom, "Did you want something? I have plans."

That throws Nara. "Our girls' night? I scheduled it with Evelyn and everything." Josie perks up at that, at the recognition that Nara doesn't know Evelyn quit.

"I had something come up," Ramona says. "Can we do this tomorrow?"

"My flight is in the morning," Nara says, frowning. "Really, Ramona, I know you've been having a difficult time lately, but this doesn't—"

Ramona interrupts, but her attention is on Josie. "Ohmi*god*, can I help you? Why are you hovering like a freak?"

Josie doesn't reply other than to smirk. Right on cue, Nara steps in. "Watch your attitude. Josie is interested in writing a story about you for one of her classes, and frankly, you could use some elevated publicity."

Ramona doesn't bother replying. She simply about-faces to her room and slams the door.

Josie hears Nara inhale deeply through her nose before turning to her. "Once again, I find myself apologizing for my daughter's actions." She rubs at her temples as she sighs, "I never meant for you to serve as a casualty from her temper."

"Oh, I don't really . . ." Finishing the sentence with 'care' would be a lie, but there has to be a better reply than 'I'm in the process of socially shaming her, so no biggie.'

"I have thick skin," Josie goes with, pairing the words with a casual shrug. "And anyway, this house is incredible. Ramona would have to do a lot worse to make me want to leave."

The congresswoman chuckles. "I appreciate your patience. I'll be having a long talk with my daughter."

As Nara opens the front door, she adds, "You really are an admirable example in Ramona's life, regardless of whether or not she recognizes it. Thank you."

Josie can't help the rush of emotion she feels at the response, the parental approval she's always yearned for. But she doesn't let it show, only giving a slight wave to Nara before heading upstairs.

You're obsessed, Josie knows Adam would say if he were here, if he witnessed how much energy she spends these days thinking about how she can bring down Ramona Taylor. She wouldn't deny it, either. The most recent conversation with Nara applies a fresh coat of determination to her story quest.

Her first task is learning more about Andrew Prosser—Andrew Prosser the VYBE board member, as it turns out. It's such a convenience in this whole innovation district bill with Nara that Josie can't help laughing every time she thinks about it. The potential for a mustache-twirling, vote-swaying scheme feels too obvious, too easy to actually mean anything, but with a bit of encouragement from Nara, she figures, why not poke around?

A news alert she put on 'VYBE' and 'innovation district' has kept her inbox full of the latest information about the congressional bill. She opens it now to find a particularly intriguing *L.A. Times* article: *Tech Titans Quietly Shape Federal Innovation Zone Bill Behind the Scenes.*

VYBE Technologies, a San Francisco-based A.I. research company, has emerged as one of the most aggressive backers of the legislation, which would create federally supported "innovation zones," which are special districts designed to fast-track tech development through tax incentives, deregulation, and infrastructure investment. Alongside other venture-backed startups, the company has been privately urging California Rep. Nara Taylor, a freshman Democrat whose vote could prove pivotal, to support the bill.

With the vote mere weeks away, stockholders wait with bated breath. A senior Bloomberg *reporter speculates that if the bill passes, VYBE's stock could double in value, as plans for building up data farms across the country become all but a lock.*

Not news, exactly, considering what Nara said way back during that dinner, though the stakes are more clear. A doubling in stock value for VYBE doesn't seem like something to laugh about, even without Josie being financially savvy.

One of the editors at her *Business Times* internship could smell developer corruption from a zip code away. While Josie was stuck writing listicles like *The 10 best for-sale condos with views of the Bay*, she'd hear this guy constantly questioning staff reporters about "following the money" for stories via idioms that didn't make sense much of the time: "Who's pulling the strings?" "Who's wagging the dog's tail?" "Who's billowing from the windfall?"

Now seems as good a time as ever to begin asking herself those questions. Josie starts a new search, sinking deeper into the pillows on her bed. *Average stock amount board member tech company*, she types on her laptop.

A VYBE investor FAQ tells her that a typical board member compensation package ranges from fifty thousand to one hundred and fifty thousand shares.

Cost of one VYBE share, she searches next.

Fifty-two bucks, Google tells her, with the potential to rise with confidence in a passing bill.

Josie does the math. If the stock doubles, and Andrew has one hundred thousand shares? That's millions. Literal millions. Just from the vote tipping the right way.

"Christ," Josie mutters, ignoring the temptation to write out a summary of everything, including screenshots of stock speculation, and tag Ramona in a post captioned, *DUH*.

Next, she looks into Evelyn's departure. The loyal soldier who apparently had little problem telling Josie exactly what she could and couldn't do at the Valley house has now up and left. A "nasty separation," Silas called it. Probably a long shot to think Evelyn will reply, considering how stiff she always seemed, but maybe she'll surprise Josie and want to lambast her previous boss.

She doesn't reply to the few softball texts Josie sends, but the phone call on a Monday morning works.

"Evelyn Michaels." Professional-sounding, but Josie can hear the clip she likes to think is just for her.

The former assistant remains thankfully quiet as Josie rushes to get her pitch in before she's hung up on, then suspiciously quiet once Josie's done.

Finally, after Josie's counted to ten, Evelyn replies, "Ramona *agreed* to this story?"

"Yeah, basically," Josie lies.

There's a surprise-sounding huff down the line. "Does she know you want to interview me?"

"It's not a PR piece. She doesn't get a list of who I'm talking to."

"I'll think about it," Evelyn replies after a weighted pause.

Josie grimaces as she's hung up on, but can't help the feeling of accomplishment at getting that much out of Evelyn. She's still vaguely hopeful Nara will subtly inspire a change of heart in her daughter, or that Silas will help make this one happen.

But she's unlucky on that last one, calling him after a drought of replies to her texts. "Any luck with Ramona?" she asks, brushing past Adam without looking at him on her way out of Tuesday's class.

"Sorry, I meant to text you back," Silas says. On his end there's a garble of voices, the words 'Crop it in a bit, will you? Oh, that's lovely.' Then the sound of a push bar opening a door. The conversation on Silas's end fades. He sighs. "Look, I'm not sure it's a good idea after all to write your story on her."

Heading for the library, Josie smiles like he's joking, but when he doesn't continue, the motion dies. "Wait, you're serious?"

"I spoke with Ramona and I don't think the timing is right for publicity."

Josie's brain supplies fifteen different replies to that. "Isn't she constantly trying to get more attention for her job? How is this not the right time?"

"It's just not."

"But you were the one who—"

"I know. I was wrong." He actually sounds defensive about it. "Ramona's got a lot on her plate, and without Evelyn around she can't juggle things as much as she'd like. A news article is another ball in the air."

"That doesn't make sense. If she wants more followers and more brand deals, a profile piece would only help—"

"Josie." Silas's voice is sharp.

Josie stops on the walkway and echoes his tone: "*Silas.*"

She hears him turn placating. "I'm sorry, okay? I haven't been around Ramona enough lately to understand the scope of things on her end. I can help you find something else. But I'm at a shoot and I've got to get back to work. I'll text you and we'll figure out a different topic, yeah?"

He continues to babble, and Josie tunes him out, tries to understand, until the line goes dead. She pulls back her phone and stares at it.

Josie will be the first to admit that she's not the best student, even in journalism classes where things come a smidge more easily than, say, algebra. But she's heard enough over the years between professors and group projects and Adam muttering phrases from their textbooks to know that if one person pushes back on a seemingly good opportunity, it could be argued as reasonable. If people start acting skittish, one of whom suggested the idea in the first place . . . well, that's when a journalist's hackles are supposed to rise.

Right now, she can sense it. Something off. Ramona's excessive disinterest, Evelyn's surprise, Silas's evasions. Josie may have gone into this story with her figurative guns blazing, but now it's starting to feel as if something is actually going on.

It's as if a layer of static is covering Josie's skin, some sort of awareness she's never experienced before. She adjusts the strap of her bag and continues walking toward the library, feeling, for the first time in her life, like a real journalist on the hunt.

Chapter 20

Adam is—
He feels as if—
Well, like he's made the right choice.

It's not something he's used to, especially in this arena, but since Ari left, the buoyancy hasn't gone away. Adam prepared for the bubble to burst, for reality to sink its teeth into the hope blossoming inside his chest. He quickly busied himself in a book next to Jon on the couch that night and agreed to visit an art museum with him the next day. The rest of the weekend Adam spent smiling privately to himself as he went about his business, Jon side-eyeing him in the car or at the museum, or next to him on the couch. Ari's proposal imbued itself into every detail, the sunshine of him scattering away any doubts Adam might have.

Monday morning, Jon finally stopped narrowing his eyes and asked Adam directly: "You and J make up then?"

Adam was zipping up his backpack, ready to head out the door for his morning class. He fumbled with the zipper. "Sorry?"

"You were cheesing all Saturday at paintings of executions and yesterday while you were buttering toast. Figured you guys patched things up."

"Oh. Um, no. We haven't." A shadow shaped like Josie finally invaded Ari's weekend-long sunshine. She would be thrilled that he's trying

163

things with Ari, would demand they celebrate it over pints of ice cream and dance their happiness out at a concert at the Throne Room. She would match his happiness, maybe even exceed it.

He misses her so much.

There's nothing blissful about her blatant ignorance of him, a cloud of cold dislike around her whenever he's close. It's suddenly hard to remember a time when she didn't terrify him, when she wasn't an unknowable entity who'd built up the walls of her fortress to keep others—*him*—out.

The archives are thankfully busy. Students come in for projects, signing in and out as they access materials. Adam wants the demanding patrons, needs them to keep his mind off Josie. In the few quiet moments, he does his best to force his mind away from the harshness in her gaze by thinking of Ari. They've traded only a few text messages since he left, comments like *my hotel room is dope* and *traffic sux*.

It's one of those moments, Adam blinking happily down at another text from Ari, when Cal appears at the desk, bespeckled eyes large and softly assessing. Adam drops the phone onto his lap, sitting up straight and trying not to immediately apologize.

"Adam, my boy, you seem to be doing better lately," Cal says. He often says things like that—"my boy" and "son," and Adam feels a mix of embarrassment and fondness for it.

"Yes, sorry," he says. "I had some . . . personal stuff going on the other week and was distracted. It won't happen again."

Cal pats the top of the desk. "No need to apologize. Personal things are what life is made of. Speaking of which, can I count on you for the upcoming book club get-together?"

"Oh, yeah. I already finished the book!"

"Aha!" Cal looks immensely pleased by that. "Well, you're welcome to bring a plus-one, regardless of whether they read the book or not. I know it can be intimidating to show up somewhere alone."

Adam bobs his head and Cal leaves. Adam will absolutely be attending solo. Even if Cal doesn't know Adam's parents, isn't a spy for them, Adam knows bringing Ari to such an event would certainly change the way Cal looks at him. Church doctrine is carved deeply into its members. He'll show up, probably stick close to Cal's side, and leave. Easy does it. If Josie was still in his life, he would bring her.

When Adam gets off work, he has a text from Ari: *hey just landed do u wanna hang?*

Adam bites back a smile. *Hi. Yes please. I'm about to bike home from campus. Do you want to meet somewhere?*

come over to my place whenever ur free. He includes his address.

Adam bikes home as fast as he can.

He parks in front of a cozy-looking bungalow. Ari answers seconds after Adam knocks, opening the door wide. He's in a hunter green henley and tan pants, a baseball cap atop his head. He's beaming as he takes Adam in, moves forward to pull him into an embrace, which Adam stiffens for briefly before returning.

"Sorry, is that okay?" Ari asks when he pulls back.

"Yes," Adam says, dizzy.

"I missed you," Ari says, stepping aside to grant Adam entry into the house—all white walls and chevron wood floors, framed photographs everywhere. "I kept seeing all these bookstores in LA that I thought you'd like? We should go back to that one that you love."

Adam's heart soars. "I'd really like that." Then, not wanting to appear as desperate as he feels to be close to Ari, asks, "So, this is your house?"

Ari turns. "Oh, yeah. Pretty sweet, right? Ramona's mom's friend or something was renting it out and we got dibs." He gives Adam a quick tour—two bed, one bath, lofts in both of the bedrooms, kitchen, sitting room, and patio. Adam pauses to look at a picture on the wall of Ari and Ramona, smiling and laughing at the camera.

They end up on the backyard patio, tiled a shiny blue and set with comfy looking couches and a coffee table. Ari sets bowls of chips and salsa down and falls onto one of the couches with a beer. Adam joins him, a tentative space between them.

"How was your trip?" Adam asks.

"Oh, you know. Glitz and glam with a shit-ton of traffic between it all." Ari tells him about the chaos of LAX, then explains about the shoots he was in the city for. "It was for GAP, so keep an eye out for me next time you go to the mall."

"It's kind of weird? That you're a model."

Ari looks over. "Why is it weird?"

"Not in a bad way, sorry. Just that I don't know a lot of people who are. Or anyone, really."

"It just means more pictures of me in places," Ari's saying as he munches on chips. "And lots of standing and sitting while people take photos. I don't really get a whole lot of say in what goes on, just get told if I'm not good enough. My agent tells me where to show up, which I do if I want to get paid." He doesn't seem keen to say a lot more, instead asking Adam about his weekend, the art museum, and a thorough questioning about his latest books.

"How's Josie?" he then asks.

Adam goes still. "Josie?"

"Yeah. She was there when I found out what Ramona said to you."

"Oh. Um. We're not really . . ." He thinks about how he can be diplomatic about it all. "We don't really spend time together anymore?"

Ari looks over, confusion pulling his eyebrows together as he takes a drink. "Why?"

"She didn't know. About you, when we first started— I hadn't told her. Not because I was embarrassed or anything, but I was— I mean, you know, about my family. And then she was living with Ramona, and you were there, and I still didn't say anything, which was, it was

166

wrong. I should've told her. Everyone knew about you and me except for Josie and, and, um, yeah. She found out. Got mad. So."

Ari is frowning. "She ended your friendship over that?"

Adam lifts a shoulder. "I should've told her."

"Does she know about your parents? And the church stuff and what you're dealing with?"

"Yeah."

"And she still blames you?"

"I shouldn't have— She deserved to know."

"Why?"

Adam's brow is furrowed now. "Because she's my best friend."

"But you said she knows all your history? How hard it is on you?"

Adam nods, wary. Ari's quiet, thumbnail tracing the mouth of his bottle. He looks like he wants to say something. "What?" Adam asks.

"I just think she should, like, cut you some slack is all. Especially since she's your best friend. But. I'm sorry you guys are fighting."

"It's not your fault," Adam says automatically.

Ari flashes him a quick grin. "I can still be sorry."

Adam doesn't want to talk about Josie anymore. "How are things with your friends?"

A shadow passes over Ari's face. "Friends don't do the kind of shit that mine did to you. I'm not really interested in spending time with them at the moment."

Adam, reaching for a chip, stops. "Oh."

"It's not anything you need to worry about. I mean, obviously I live with Silas, but he's good at giving space. And Ramona's wrapped up in all her shit. It's not really affecting me."

"Do they know about, um . . ."

"You? Nah. They don't need to. Especially when you're still figuring stuff out."

Adam thinks of Josie, how he kept quiet about Ari for so long that the weight of words unsaid broke their friendship. He doesn't want that for Ari. Not with how much love there clearly is between the group. Adam can tell even in just a picture. He doesn't want Ari to go through such a loss. Even if he's mad at them now, he won't always be.

"I think, if you wanted to tell them, you should," Adam says quietly to his hands. "I don't— You shouldn't stay mad at them. Because I'm okay. And they were just trying to protect you. And, well, I'm here."

Ari's quiet, and Adam doesn't know how to take that. But then Ari asks, "Will you come closer?"

Adam looks over. Ari's arm is draped along the back of the couch, an open invitation against his side. Adam hesitates.

"It'll be, like, an extra-long hug," Ari reasons.

Adam nods and, after a moment, scoots over. He's stiff at first, Ari's bicep against his upper back, the heat of him along his side. He takes a breath and sags into Ari, slowly relaxes his body bit by bit, feels Ari stay still, like he's scared Adam might scamper off at the slightest movement. Finally, when Adam exhales, Ari bends his arm at the elbow, draping it around Adam's shoulder and pulling him closer. "Thank you," he murmurs against the top of Adam's head. Adam isn't sure what he's being thanked for, and doesn't want to ruin the moment of steadiness that Ari is providing by holding him like this. He just nods. Grateful. Happy. Not thinking about if this is acting on his same-sex attraction or not.

"Your house is beautiful," Adam says after a few minutes. "Sorry if I didn't say that before."

"It's all Silas," Ari says, fingers trailing against Adam's arm.

"What's he like as a roommate?"

"Hmm. Messy but not dirty, social but not loud. He's not here a lot, usually over at Ramona's."

"How'd you guys meet?"

"On a shoot for some magazine a couple years ago." Ari pauses, takes a breath, then continues. "I was actually pretty down on myself, like, body image-wise, on set, and he asked to talk to me in private and then gave me this pep talk about how talented I am and how he was really enjoying shooting me and stuff, and that was, like, our first real conversation."

Adam processes that. "Do you still struggle with your body image?"

"I mean, yeah," Ari shrugs, but it's a half-hearted attempt. "It kinda sucks working in an industry that expects perfection—and, like, a specific expectation of perfection, if that makes sense? So, you know. I compare myself a lot and get a little obsessed with not eating too many carbs and maybe have a direct connection from my mood to whether I've worked out that day, but it's stupid. It's nothing you need to worry about."

Adam chews on his lip. "I would like to. Not worry, necessarily—but, um, be there for you? If you're feeling sad about something . . . If, I mean, if you're comfortable talking to me about it, that is."

Ari's arm tightens briefly around Adam; the smell of cider, the sound of his heartbeat and lungs expanding, the heat of him. "Yeah. I would be," Ari says, and Adam can feel the movement of Ari's lips in his hair.

It's a lot, Ari holding him like this. But in a glorious way that instills in Adam a sense of security, physically and emotionally. He wants to make it last forever. Wants to reward Ari however he can.

"Just so you know, um . . . I think you're very . . ." Thank goodness it's dark and Ari can't see the blush washing over Adam's face, his entire body. "Attractive?"

A low chuckle. "Yeah?"

Adam clears his throat. "I mean, you obviously *know* that, since you're a model . . ."

"I like hearing it from you."

Adam's body reacts like he's touched a live wire, sparked by a sudden, mad lust. He wants Ari's hands all over him. There's a stirring between his legs. He likes the feeling but knows he shouldn't, and instead stifles the temptation. Ari must sense it, or at least feel Adam stiffening, because he laughs again, softly, then murmurs, "I think you're very attractive, too."

Adam bites his lip and hopes this is all okay.

Ari walks him out to his car after. After hours of talking. And all the while, Adam is tucked into Ari's side. It's like those times with Josie, Adam realizes; the moments of pure, unfettered joy.

"You're really cool if I tell my friends?" Ari asks, leaning against the hood of Adam's car, hands in his pockets and a vision beneath a streetlight.

Adam separates the keys on his key ring, one by one, eyes on the ground. "Yeah. I mean, I haven't really, um, felt bad about this. Us. That—that sounds bad, but I usually feel guilty? About stuff like this. And I don't. So . . . I guess I'm just hoping that that means I'm okay now. That this works." He pushes his keys into his pocket, mirroring Ari's stance. "Sorry, I know I'm being . . . confusing. I'm being ridiculous. Of course you can tell your friends."

Ari steps closer and Adam looks up as Ari raises a hand to brush his fingers along Adam's jaw. "It's working for me too," he says, and Adam's breathing hitches, his awareness boiling down to Ari's touch. He leans into Ari's hand without meaning to. Ari's gaze drops to Adam's mouth, then his throat when Adam swallows, and Adam—

He steps back, still too cautious. Ari drops his hand immediately, expression appearing forcefully blank, and gives a disappointed-sounding "sorry." Headlights pass over his face. They both turn to see a car approaching. Ari straightens. "That's Silas."

Adam unlocks his car door and opens it. "Okay. Um. Thanks. For tonight."

Silas pulls into the driveway. "I'll text you," Ari says.

Adam starts his car as Ari moves to the sidewalk. He sees Silas approach Ari and peer curiously toward Adam's car. Silas apparently recognizes him through the windshield because he cuts a look to Ari and says something sharp. Adam doesn't know if he should get back out and introduce himself, something more formal than the Valley house's entryway and Ramona's dismissal. But Ari glances over his shoulder to Adam and gives him a nod, a smile, and a flick of his chin, so Adam drives away.

When Adam crawls into bed a short while later, grabbing his current read off the nightstand and going to plug his phone in, there's a text waiting from Ari.

I had alot of fun tonite

Adam feels a sort of expanding happiness inside his chest. *Me too*, he replies.

I rly like u

Adam nestles deep into his pillows at that, cheeks sore with yet another smile. His conscience, perhaps finally having given up the ghost, remains thankfully silent.

Chapter 21

J osie's forgotten what a proper night sky looks like.

That sounds incredibly dramatic. She doesn't mean for it to, but it's also not a lie. In San Francisco, there's not a lot of reason to look up. All the excitement is on the ground here. And in Modesto— Well, Josie's eyes were on the horizon; the future, not the stars.

God, *again*. She rubs her eyes. *Quit it with the dramatics*, she tells herself.

She focuses on a plane passing overhead, high above. The Valley house's backyard really is a nice place to decompress, when you're not being maudlin, that is. Or maybe the backyard fuels one's maudlinness. Maudlinity? Josie takes another swig from her beer. Adam used the word on occasion, especially when Josie would start drinking, and—

She scowls, shifting into a more comfortable position, sprawled across one of the patio couches. She came out here to escape her capstone story, but it seems the only other topics at hand are depressing ones.

Another one of Tilton's deadlines has passed, Josie with nothing to show for the professor's request for two completed interviews and a basic framework of the story. It's not that she's not trying. National media is heating up in its speculation about how the innovation bill will go, and Nara's name appears regularly as one of the key swing voters. Josie knows there's something just under the surface there, with Ramona quietly dating a VYBE board member. But Nara's back on the other side of the country, and Josie herself witnessed mother and daughter leaving things on poor terms. The last thing Ramona seems emotionally capable of doing is conversing with her mom and swinging a pivotal vote in VYBE's direction, which is what Josie assumes any plan would be. The vote is happening in three weeks. Josie has no right to call Nara up and ask if she's decided which way she'll vote. What can Josie do in the meantime? Stalk Andrew until he leads her to proof she's not even sure exists? She doesn't have the time for that. Or patience. Or, to be completely blunt, the skill. Josie is actively out of her depth here.

It makes everything feel useless, the very feeling she's been trying to escape since she was seventeen, let alone her entire life. Giving up entirely seems a lot more attractive at this point. Ramona's made it this far without a degree, why can't Josie? She drinks again. Perhaps if she—

"You made it very clear that brooding in the backyard was *my* thing."

Josie lifts her head to find Silas closing the door to the garage behind him. She hasn't seen him around the past week, and assumes he's been avoiding her because of his lack of delivery with the Ramona story.

"Hey," he says, approaching. "How's it going?"

Josie wags her bottle at him. "Never better. Is Ramona home?"

"Once again, here for you. May I?"

She sweeps her arm wide at the many seating options, but Silas nudges her legs aside and plops next to her, already pulling out a cigarette and lighter.

"What came first," she asks as he lights up, "Silas Sinclair smoking or this backyard?"

He doesn't smile. "Did you know Ari and Adam are seeing each other again?"

Josie sits up. "What?"

"Adam was over at our house the other night. Was leaving as I showed up." Silas looks concerned. "Ari says they're trying things out."

Josie blows out a breath, a current of something zapping through her. She shifts her gaze from Silas to the house, disbelieving at first, and then completely believing. Of course Adam is. First, he'd lied about Ari because he didn't want Josie to pressure him, then he turned around and is now dating him. Adam said a lot during their friendship, but his actions are speaking to his true nature. Did he have this planned the entire time, just wanted her out of the picture? Was she deluding herself in their friendship?

Silas is still talking. "I don't mean any offense to Adam, but I'm worried how seriously he's taking this thing. Ari gets super attached to people and he's already been a mess twice over Adam and—"

"Why are you telling me?" Josie cuts in, voice brittle. There's a distant yowling in her ears, a scratchy ringing sound. She wants it to stop. "I don't care."

Silas watches her, eyebrows pinched. "Josie," he says, "I can see from your face that you care."

She could take a swing at that, tell him he doesn't know what he's talking about, then find a way to needle him, something he cares about to insult him over. She's good at it. She did it to Adam, could do it to Silas. She could dismantle him, if she wanted to. Right now, all she wants to do is cry.

Instead, she gives a shaky laugh. She won't cry, hates crying, especially in front of other people. "I don't know what to tell you," she manages, gripping her beer with both hands. "The Adam I knew wouldn't touch another guy with a ten-foot pole. Would die of shame if he did. But the Adam I knew never met Ari in the first place." It sure feels like the Adam she knew never existed.

"Did you talk to him?" she asks. "Adam?" Silas shakes his head, something verging on pity in his eyes. And that— She doesn't want that. "Don't. Don't look at me like that."

"I'm just . . ." He looks like he's grappling for purchase against a cliff. "I don't want Ari to get hurt. But I'm also sorry that your friendship was ruined in the process."

Josie's quiet for a moment, transfixed by the end of Silas's cigarette as he smokes. She pushes away the compulsion to bemoan Adam's continued betrayal, and instead focuses on what Silas needs. She's realized that he's the kind of person who wants everyone to be okay, and while she won't ever fully trust him, she can at least offer words of solace.

"Listen," she says, adopting the brusque, I-mean-business voice she used to use on Adam when he started spiraling. She sets her beer on a side table. "Adam may be totally different from the version I knew, but he doesn't do anything without overthinking it way more than a reasonable person should. You can bet that if he and Ari are trying things, there's been a lot of blood, sweat, and tears behind the scenes on his part." She reaches out and gives Silas's shoulder a squeeze. "Adam might be a bastard, and a son of a bitch, but he's not going to do something like this if he doesn't mean it." Doesn't mean he'll stay in it, she silently adds.

Silas nods. Even though it's dark, she can see that he's chewing on the inside of his cheek. "Okay." Then, "What about you?"

Josie doesn't expect that. "What about me?"

He breathes out, giving a half-hearted smile as he says, "Anything you can say that'll help me feel better about what happened between you and Adam?"

The corner of Josie's mouth lifts up, but it's not a happy motion. "Kinda feels like our friendship was on an inevitable crash course," she admits. "Moving in with Ramona just sped up the timeline."

"Why do you think it was inevitable?"

Josie's eyes drift to her bedroom window on the second floor. "He lied before I even knew about you people." She looks back at him. "And he kept lying long after."

You people, Silas mouths with a twitch of his lips. "Did he ever say why he never told you about Ari?"

"He's got a lot of baggage with being gay," Josie says with a wave of her hand. "And I spent a big chunk of our friendship pushing him to try things out with other guys. I wanted him to see that it was okay, that it'd be okay and he'd be happy if he found someone. He fought me so hard on it, again and again, saying he cared more about preserving his salvation or whatever than falling in love. So that clearly adds up now. Guess he just wanted me out of the way." Josie rubs her eyes with both hands and doesn't look at Silas as she says, "I honestly thought I was the most important person in his life. I know that makes me sound like an ass, but that's what he was to me—and I thought the feeling was mutual. It was just kind of a shitty way to find out I wasn't."

Silas is quiet, and Josie keeps her head down, afraid her vulnerability will cause him to pity her further.

"I'm really sorry, Josie," he finally says.

She nods, shrugs, leans back against the couch and looks up at the sky. "I'll be okay. I'm not long for this city anyway."

"Well. Until you leave, I hope I can be your friend."

Josie turns her head to look at him. "Why?" When he doesn't immediately answer, she adds, "I know I'm not, like, the *friendliest* person in the world. So, why? You've got Ari and Ramona to worry about."

Silas's mouth quirks, his eyes unfocused. "I like our conversations. And when everything happened with Adam and Ari, you were the only one who came out of things alone. I spent a lot of time alone before I met Ari and Ramona. I didn't like how it made me feel or who I was because of it. I don't want that for you."

Josie hesitates, recognizing that Silas is offering a piece of vulnerability to match her own. "Like, growing up you were alone?"

Silas takes a drag. "Plenty of people who ditched me in one way or another growing up. Lots of time for resentment."

Josie stays quiet, kinship stirring in her chest.

But then Silas smiles, and there's life to it. "Then I met Ari and he looked at me like I was the greatest thing that ever happened to him. He's like that—all in with people pretty quickly. To have someone like that after losing so much meant a lot."

"And Ramona?"

Silas grins with his teeth now. "Made me feel like a real person after I got lost in all the photography." He scratches his cheek, then says, "I think I'm like Ari in that I got all in with her really fast. It feels a little bit like losing a limb whenever she starts dating someone."

"You miss her." Even if Josie tried to make the words sound accusatory, they wouldn't be believable. She can relate; Adam's absence is as loud as crashing cymbals.

Silas meets Josie's gaze. "I know she hasn't been kind to you, and I'm sorry again about the story thing. I shouldn't have offered her up like that. It's all a bit . . ." He trails off, hesitating.

Josie nudges him. The topic only brings about a sense of numbness. "You can talk about Ramona. Promise I won't wig out."

He laughs like he's tired. After a moment, a deliberate pause, it seems, he says, "It's just frustrating, seeing friends make poor decisions, and not being the first person they turn to."

Josie tries to keep her interest in check as she asks, "Is Andrew the poor decision or the one she's turning to?"

Silas squints but doesn't answer.

"Does Nara know about them? Could you talk to her?"

Silas scoffs this time. "I'm not going nuclear."

"Doesn't she just want her daughter to have a stable job and the education to back it up? I mean, is Ramona planning to be an influencer at forty?"

"I have no doubt that if Ramona wants something, she'll make it happen, no matter what others think," Silas says firmly. His annoyance is clear. "She and Ari made up, by the way." Josie feels his next words like they're cutting into her very skin, the underlying accusation clear as day. "I guess Adam said it was important for Ari to maintain his friendship with us and encouraged him to reach out."

She says nothing, just goes cold and looks away. She squeezes her eyes shut, tries to push down whatever's building inside her. Her roommate, who brims with good fortune. Honest friends invested in her wellbeing; responsible parents who give a damn; a romantic partner who's smarmy but makes her happy; and a lifestyle that, vapid as it is, she loves and it loves her back. Josie has none of that. That Adam said those words like he knew they would get back to her somehow.

Silas's hand lands on her wrist. "I shouldn't have said that."

"Don't." The word wavers; she moves away from his touch. Even as her ribcage creaks, threatens to snap in half over the hurt, she wants Adam back at her side. Silas has his own first string of confidants; Josie lost hers.

They're quiet for a long while before Silas asks, "Do you want to be alone?"

Josie doesn't reply. Still he stays, meeting her silence with his own.

He gets through another cigarette before standing. "I'm sorry," he says. "Really."

When the door clicks shut with his departure, Josie fiercely wipes at her cheeks, flings the wetness away from her. There's anger, of course. There's been almost nothing but anger since this whole thing blew up. But more than that, for the first time, there's grief, too. At the loss of Adam.

Josie pulls her phone out and navigates to Adam's contact info, still listed as her emergency contact, number one on speed dial. She blocked him ages ago. Still, she hovers her thumb over the call button. She wants to ask him why, why he never trusted her with the information about Ari. Not wanting to be peer pressured is one thing, but Josie wouldn't have, would have sacrificed a long list of other people, places, and things before purposely throwing him under the bus in such a way.

The emptiness next to her, the space left by Silas but permanently held for Adam, seems to pulse, and Josie finds herself holding her breath. It's faint, but it's present: a yearning for the most important person in her life despite his turning toward another.

Their friendship was so much more than something to maintain. It gave them both life, a will to keep going because each of them knew the other person would always have their back no matter the situation, the hour, the repercussions.

For the first time, Josie wishes she wasn't herself, wasn't the type of person who pushed Adam away when everything came to light. Instead, Josie wishes she had stood there when Adam faced her and told him, *I'm sorry you didn't think you could trust me with something this important. Let's figure it out together.*

Would he still have ended up with Ari if she tried? Where would that have left Josie, the active BFF instead of the scorned ex-one? Has Adam told his family, to which he'd originally pointed as his reason for withholding himself from a relationship? Has his life worked out now that Josie's out of the picture? There are so many more questions than answers and it's a terrifying space to exist in.

Josie doesn't call Adam, but for the first time, she considers what it would mean to get him back, to return their friendship to something not to maintain, but to celebrate.

Chapter 22

Adam is busier than he ever has been in his college career ("Can you really call it a career?" Josie once teased. "Or are you a professional student?" "I mean, I am getting paid," he'd pointed out in reference to his partial scholarship). His classes are all demanding, Tilton's in particular. What was supposed to be a slow but thorough burn has become a hurried flare. Because he's selected Barry Keller as his story focus, Adam and Tilton agreed the best timeline for publishing the story will be right as the MLB postseason is starting, in early October (a good two months before the capstone project would be due). Adam grilled Jon on projections and timelines for the Giants—Jon using lots of words like *clinched* and *wildcard* and *divisional series* that Adam wrote down to understand later. Basically, his roommate said, with both the Giants and Dodgers locked in for the postseason, they'll be facing off the second week of October. "That's your sweet spot," he told Adam.

Sweet spot. Meaning Adam has days left to finish interviews, then hours and minutes to craft the story before he needs to have Tilton edit it and send the piece off to happy takers. He's had a second, more formal interview with Barry. Next up is Barry's son, Dale, the Dodgers player. Then there's Barry's business partner, his ex-wife, and a nanny who helped raise Barry and took him to many baseball games. In other words, work to be done.

180

"I have a connection with *The Athletic*," Tilton tells Adam during the last week of September, "which I think would be an ideal publisher. I'll CC you on an email to her and let you pitch."

The story is published the day before the Giants face off against the Dodgers in a divisional series. Adam can't help but smile as he endures classmates and professors congratulating and, in Jon's case, picking him up and spinning him around in victory. Barry sends his gratitude. Dale the Dodger shoots Adam a text. Ari, who's been out of town since Adam last saw him, picks Adam up from work, comes *inside* and is chatting with Cal before Adam can get a grip on the situation. Adam prays his face doesn't give anything away to Cal, tries to hide the infatuation he knows is transparent whenever he's in close proximity to Ari. He hurries Ari out, ears burning, and doesn't give Ari a hug until they're safely in his car.

They watch game three of the series at Adam's, Jon and Ari on the couch, Adam on the floor, shoulder pressed against Ari's leg. When Ari brushes his hand across Adam's neck, Adam pretends it's accidental, arming himself against imaginary conversations with his mom. When the announcers mention the relationship between Dale the Dodger and his father, referencing the article, Jon whoops and Ari squeezes Adam's shoulder, leaning forward to murmur how proud he is—"seriously, babe. You kicked ass"—lips brushing Adam's ear, sending a delighted shiver down Adam's spine. He spends the rest of the game dazedly wanting Ari's mouth against his. But he's appropriately gagged the urge by the time Ari leaves, trying to ignore the hopeful-turned-disappointed look Ari is unsuccessful at hiding completely.

Ari said he'd go as slow as Adam needs, but it's obviously more difficult in practice. Not just for Ari, who's had many boyfriends, many sexual partners, and has likely never had to hold back on physical intimacies before—but for Adam too, who no longer has a massive capstone project to distract him from his want. And oh, how he wants.

Jon hasn't acknowledged what he's witnessing between Adam and Ari, nothing more than silent smirks that have Adam stammering out answers to questions that have nothing to do with Ari, but somehow Adam knows what's turning up the edge of Jon's mouth.

When Adam calls his mom and tells her in a small voice that a project he worked hard on was picked up by a national media company, she's overjoyed, calling for the rest of his family to gather 'round the phone and putting Adam on speaker to explain once more. There's a chorus of admiration and Adam smiles into his phone, emotional over their support.

"How have you been?" his mother asks when she has him back to herself. Her voice sounds pleasant, neutral. "I'm only getting your voicemail lately. Everything okay?"

"I'm sorry. Things are very, um, demanding right now?" he says, repeating the words he's practiced, toeing the line so nothing he says will be an outright lie. He *has* been avoiding her calls, wrapped up in a cocoon of schoolwork and time with Ari. But the pressure is building, his nights' sleep growing more and more fitful. He doesn't know how much longer he can go without telling the truth. It feels like he's choking on the words he needs to say.

"I can imagine," his mom says. "Will you be able to join us this year for Thanksgiving? It's at Grandma's."

Adam usually stays in the city for the holiday, keeping Josie company, but that's not on the table this year. "Yeah, I'm looking forward to it—" He stops himself too late, the lie already out. Looking forward to it? Not fully. Adam's dad's side of the family is loud, combative over anything from politics to child-rearing to modern medicine. And while Adam's parents are tolerant of his inactive sexuality, the other Hugheses, unaware, tend to opt for more old school barbs.

"I have a new pie recipe for us to try out," his mom continues. "Sarah's become quite the little chef. Oh, and I have a couple books I read recently that I think you'd enjoy! Goodness," she laughs. "Can you tell I'm excited to see you?"

The joy from celebrating his publication has dissipated. Talking to his mom is calling attention to everything he hasn't had the courage to tell her. His heart pounds as he gets out, "We have a lot to catch up on."

It's not a lie.

The conversation is still weighing on his shoulders when Adam goes out to dinner with Ari, a belated celebration, Ari'd demanded, of Adam's article. Adam drives them at his own insistence, and as soon as Ari opens the passenger side door, settles in next to Adam, and leans over for a quick hug, Adam can tell that something's off.

"How's it goin'?" Ari asks. The words are clipped, his movements tight.

"Are you okay?" Adam replies, not shifting out of park quite yet.

Ari blows out a breath. "Shitty day. Shitty week. Whatever. It's fine." His tone doesn't invite further questioning, and Adam focuses on quietly driving them to the restaurant. Ari pulls out his phone a few times, frowning at whatever messages keep appearing on the screen. Adam is too new at this thing with Ari to know how to approach it. With Josie, he'd stay quiet until she'd crack and let it all out. That was her preference, but he doesn't know with Ari.

They pull up to the restaurant, Adam finding a spot near the entrance. He turns the car off and gets out an "um" when Ari says, a hand loosely gripping Adam's wrist, "I'm sorry. I found out today I didn't get a job I really wanted and my agent was a dick to me about it."

"Oh. Oh, Ari, I'm so sorry." Adam rotates his hand, pulling it back so he's holding Ari's. "Why was your agent mad?"

Ari squeezes Adam's hand, his shoulders relaxing a bit. "I was kinda off my game for a while. Like, after I saw you at Ramona's place and was hooking up with Isaiah and not eating like I should've. It's catching up with me now. I deserved him chewing me out, but it was on top of hearing I didn't get the job, and . . . and I just, like, you know, want to be able to touch you without feeling skeezy about it and it's been a little frustrating."

Adam looks away, out the window toward the restaurant. "I'm sorry," he says. "I know I'm going—slow."

"You're doing exactly what you said you would," Ari says on an exhale. "That's the thing. You're not being, like, unreasonable. I mean, maybe, but you're doing what you said you would. I just— I'm just not used to it and it's turning into me thinking—or feeling shitty about myself and thinking that you're not attracted to me enough to want to be physical with me."

Adam whips his head back toward Ari. "That's not— I, I like you so much and—"

"I know, Adam," Ari says with a small smile, thumb rubbing the back of Adam's hand. "I'm just in my head about it. But we promised everything on the table, so that's what I'm doing."

"Y-yeah." Adam feels caught out, and rightly so. What did he think would happen, taking his time with Ari—that he'd actually stay immune to his growing feelings? His growing urges? Ari is someone who likes to touch others, in friendship and romance and acquaintanceship. Even with Jon, casual shoulder claps and hugs. Ari told Adam how important physical touch was to him and Adam took the information and continued at his own speed; at the most, up until this moment, allowing Ari hugs and close proximity but nothing more. Now, his hand flexes automatically, and Ari loosens his hold, starts to pull back. Adam shakes his head, clinging to Ari's grip. "I'm sorry about your agent. And, and I'll try—harder," he chokes out, even as the phone call with his mom wraps its reminder around his vocal cords.

"I'm not asking you t—"

"No, I know." This is his choice, the fork in the road: to hide or hang on. "I— I want to. You deserve it. I like you so much, and I'm sorry."

With the hand not holding Adam's, Ari reaches over and grips the back of Adam's neck. "Hey. Look at me." Adam does. "It's okay. It is. We're going at a slower speed and that's okay. I think, when you said the other week that you weren't really feeling guilty about things, I thought it meant you'd want to try stuff. But I'm not, like— I do *not* want to pressure you. I like you, too. It's just, you know, shit on shit and it was piling up. I'm sorry. I already feel better about it, just saying it out loud, y'know? I'm okay. You and me—we're okay."

Adam nods mutely, pressing his forehead against Ari's. He makes a silent promise to push himself. If he's going to be in this relationship, he needs to be okay with it being a relationship. *For Ari*, he thinks. *I can do this for Ari.*

After dinner, a tentative dance of apologies from each of them, they watch a movie at Adam's, on his laptop, on his bed. Adam's foot nudging against Ari's, hand in his, a white flag.

After the movie, lying on their sides, facing each other, Ari reaches out with a "can I?" He touches his fingers lightly to Adam's face. "Just this." He traces across Adam's cheeks, his chin, his eyebrows, his nose, his lips; Ari's eyes dark and face wide open, Adam watching Ari as Ari touches him. "You are so beautiful," Ari whispers. Adam closes his eyes, can't handle the sincerity. Ari traces his eyelids. And Adam wants.

Because of his inkling that Cal is Mormon, there's a lot more than simple social apprehension as Adam drives across the Bay Bridge to Cal's place the following week. He's been dreading the book club for many reasons. The Hughes household presents its religious beliefs to every single visitor: photos of prophets and apostles, framed prints of proclamations stating only marriage between a man and a woman is acceptable to God, figurines of Jesus Christ. When Adam was home over the summer, he was reminded daily of his shortcomings. He can't help but expect more of the same from Cal.

The house lies among the grid-like, tree-laden streets of Alameda. It's small, blue, and lit from within with warm, yellow lights. Adam parks, locks his car, and takes a deep breath before walking up the front path.

Cal answers within moments of Adam's knock. "Adam, my boy, you're here, and you're the first! Come in, come in."

Adam steps into cottage-style warmth—in decor and aura; whites and creams and faded golds. Patterned fabric couches, a million frames on the walls and propped atop any flat surface. There's a piano in the front room, bookshelves that Adam automatically itches to explore. Through the sitting area is the kitchen, a two-seater wooden table, cushioned chairs, a spread of homemade goods Cal is most definitely responsible for.

"Your home is very nice," Adam says truthfully as he takes it all in.

Cal gives him the quiet, sparkly-eyed smile he often shares at the archives. "It's been a comfort to me since Linda passed. She filled this place with many, many good things." He looks around fondly, then returns his attention to Adam. "I was hoping you would bring a plus-one? Like the young man I met the other week? Ari? He seems delightful."

Adam has to physically pinch himself through his pocket to stop from passing out or scampering right back out the door. "Oh. Um. Sorry, I— It's n-not, not— I didn't mean for— He's—"

The doorbell rings. Cal slips into host mode with an ushering of Adam toward the kitchen before turning to answer it. Adam's steps are ungainly at first, like a wobbly colt, as he tries to recover. His mind whirs, questioning whether Cal can tell, has been able to tell this entire time, especially when Ari showed up at work, if he's sensed that

Adam has acted in sin. Adam shakes his head, trying to clear it of the assumption.

Proof of Cal's religious beliefs isn't difficult to come by. No picture of Jesus front and center, no scriptures on the coffee table, but Adam grew up in Utah, the mothership of Mormonism, and he knows the signs to seek.

One of them is what he already knows: Many of the photos on display show Cal and his late wife, Linda, from their wedding day: a dated white gown for her and tux for him in front of an ornate, white castle-looking building—the temple where they were married, where Adam's own parents were married. Other photos show familiar landscapes in Utah that Adam has been to himself, Cal and Linda surrounded by many, many family members, all white, all paired up— men with women, plus a billion kids.

Adam enters the kitchen, heart continuing to race as he glances over his shoulder to see Cal welcoming a group of people in the doorway, some of the older, permanent staffers in the library. On the kitchen island are platters of quiche and canapes, brownies and macarons, cheeses and meats and little cups of jello. So much food, much more than the small amount of people Cal said were coming will be able to eat. Adam has an overwhelming rush of affection for his boss, for the time he's poured into making all this food and bringing people into his quiet little home where he spends his day-to-day life missing his wife and living without her.

The fridge catches Adam's attention, and he circles the island to get a better look. Further proof, found. Held by a magnet to the fridge's front, a young boy is pictured on an announcement in a suit and tie, *Emerson is 8!* scripted at the top in gold cursive. The age when kids are baptized into the church, and something many members announce like a Christmas card. *We're so proud Emerson has decided to be baptized as a member of the Church of Jesus Christ of Latter-day Saints . . .* Adam lifts his eyes to a different type of announcement. A piece of paper advertising a get-together for singles over fifty, a regional event for church members. Words and phrases like "testimony-building" and "service" and "hear from Elder So-and-So" cement Adam's assumption.

Seeing proof of his religion in black and white on Cal's fridge is a reminder of how simple everything used to be—before Adam understood that living his life as a member meant doing so incompletely.

He turns to see more people have arrived. It's a gathering now, edging on party in numbers if not noise level.

Adam stays quiet through the discussion, nodding along with commentary about the book's literary style. On the other side of Cal, an older woman catches Adam's eye and winks.

Forty-five minutes have passed when Adam checks his phone after using the restroom. Jon's texted him a picture of a bowl of mac and cheese (*saved you some*). Adam replies with a smile. Both Jon and Ari have been in perpetual bad moods the past few days over the Giants' postseason run ending in a whimper.

He's sliding his phone back in his pocket when Cal approaches. The others are migrating to the kitchen for more food.

"Found the restroom okay then?" Cal asks. He's bobbing slightly on the balls of his feet, eyes bright, cheeks flushed, no doubt overjoyed at the many people filling his home. Adam wonders if the Emerson from the fridge is a grandson.

"Yes, thank you," Adam says.

"I'm thrilled you were able to make it," Cal says. "I've always enjoyed melding my worlds. I haven't had a get-together like this in a long time."

Adam has the slightly hysterical thought to ask Cal point-blank if he knows that Adam is gay and has a boyfriend, but Cal keeps talking. "If you don't mind, Kim asked for a more official introduction."

He gestures over Adam's shoulder, and Adam turns to see the woman who winked approaching from the kitchen. She looks to be in her sixties like Cal, with the same kindness lining her features.

"Kim is visiting from Utah," Cal says. "She's one of my oldest friends."

"I resent that description," Kim says. "You've got a year on me." But she's smiling, and says to Adam, "Adam! You were quiet during the introduction round. Cal says you read more than is healthy."

"Oh, I—" Adam looks to Cal, who's started to splutter.

Kim flaps her hand. "That's alright. It's a sickness I share and one of the reasons I wanted to meet you. Tell me, does science fiction make you feel as dumb as it does me?"

"Goodness, Kim," Cal manages. To Adam, he says, "I apologize for her aggression."

"You call it aggression, Maggie calls it conversation," Kim says easily. "This is why you and I never stood a chance in high school. You're too soft, Callahan, old boy." She winks at Adam again, whispering, "He had these coke bottle glasses that made his eyes look the size of dimes!"

Adam's face is suspended in a part-amused, part-awkward smile, unsure of how he should play into the dynamic. Then he hears Cal's next words: "I never stood a chance because you and Maggie were only ever meant for each other."

"I suppose, after nearly fifty years together, it's time I finally accept my life with her," Kim agrees with a solemn nod, then says, "But also, the Coke bottle glasses."

She and Cal continue their light bickering while Adam's mind reels. He's not sure if he correctly interpreted what he just heard, the implication that Kim is with another woman. If he's going based solely on Cal's reaction, he must have heard wrong. Adam's never seen his parents interact with a queer couple before, but he can imagine how well it wouldn't go over, all pursed lips and wide eyes directed at Adam, silently telling him to stay true because there's no way this couple will be together forever. But Cal doesn't seem to care, wearing open adoration for Kim.

Adam comes back to himself in time to hear Kim ask him if he's from the Bay Area.

"Orem," Adam manages as an answer, voice scratchy. His face feels too hot to think he can get away with not acting embarrassed. "In Utah. I grew up there."

"The bubble," Kim says knowingly. She opens her mouth to continue, but Adam, flooded with a fear of the conversation continuing in, frankly, any direction, interjects.

"Sorry, I, um— It's been nice to meet you," he says to Kim, "but I actually n-need to go?" To Cal, whose eye he has trouble meeting, he adds, "This was— Your home, it's beautiful. I'm so sorry, I— My roommate—"

If Cal's offended, he masks it well, only settles a hand on Adam's shoulder. "That's fine, that's fine. An old man's house isn't the best place for Friday night frivolities. Drive safe, son. I'll see you next week."

"Give Cal some book recommendations so he can pass them along," Kim says.

Adam nods, backing away. His mind is garbled. "Thank you, and, and sorry again."

He escapes into the night air with an exhale.

Chapter 23

Added all up, the moments over this semester that critically changed its trajectory—overhearing about Adam and Ari and realizing Adam had lied to her; confronting Silas about it, then confronting Adam; deciding to write about Ramona—amounted to maybe thirty minutes in total? Not a whole lot of time considering how much Josie's spent suffering over it all.

October is halfway over before she realizes it's been a month and a half since she's spent time with Adam. A month and a half since he arrived back from Utah and helped her move and they'd watched movies and ate ice cream and danced to music and texted nonsense and lived and breathed each other's day-to-day life. Josie thought the ache would dull with time.

She guesses it has in some ways. She's stopped swinging by the ice cream aisle at the store to automatically grab a pint of Adam's favorite. And she's stopped, like, *expecting* him on her heels everywhere she goes.

Maybe that's what hurts the most: He was always waiting, and he needed to start going. And he couldn't be around her to do that.

That's what Josie tells herself whenever she sees him now. She's getting in her own way of wanting him back, focusing too much on the sappy expression he wears when he pulls out his phone in class, apparently receiving infinite gooey texts from Ari. She's embarrassed—that he was so miserable while she was in his life and now that she's gone, everything for him is coming up roses. He's so obviously fine without her, and it kills Josie to know that she's the one at fault.

The ache continues, but so does life. And she has Silas now to distract her from her perpetual flying solo. She's a little uncomfortable that he saw her in such a vulnerable headspace in the backyard, but he has the good graces to not bring it up. She asks him only once how Adam's doing, willing to hurt over the topic later: "Have you talked to him?"

They're on the patio again. Silas must hear the emotion in her voice, must clue in to exactly who she's speaking about. Thankfully, he doesn't turn to look at her, just continues to smoke. "A little bit, the other week." He pauses, as if hearing the silent follow-up question. "I think he's doing good. I don't know him that well, but he seems happy. Ari's absolutely moon-eyed over him." There's silence for a moment. "I'm grateful he still gave Ari a chance after what we did."

Josie gives a small nod. "Adam is good people."

She eventually invites Silas to the Throne Room.

He's coming from Oakland, out there for some shoot. She's braced herself for his arrival, not exactly sure why, though it's probably something to do with the fact that there's only ever been one other person by her side for this stuff.

Silas is in a cream-colored turtleneck sweater and loose tan leather jacket when he shows up. He told her that of all the settings he gets to shoot his photos, live concerts are at the top of his list. "Right after being an Instagram husband for Ramona, right?" Josie asked. Silas only chuckled, denying nothing.

Music is already happening when they walk inside, the floor a cluster of bodies, the bar a cluster of clinking glasses. Josie and Silas get drinks, people-watching while they do.

Silas is different in how he witnesses the music. Where Josie is a bulldoze-her-way-into-the-middle-of-the-crowd type of person, Silas likes to hang back, maybe too settled into his method of seeking the best angle for a shot. He takes a few photos with his phone; Josie only lunges in front of the shot once, a blur of hair and teeth. Then Josie drags him into the crush of bodies, where he stands, smiling apologetically as every other person before the stage dances except for him, acting more Adam-like than Adam.

Josie dances, hair wild as she bounces to the performance.

"I want to take a picture of you!" Silas yells over the music. "A proper one!"

She bares her teeth in return, feels like she's floating six inches off the ground and thankful that gravity is finally giving her a break from the weight of reality.

Well after midnight, Silas drives Josie home, both of them buzzing about the music and the crowd and the energy between it all. Josie's got Silas's phone, surfing for different songs on Spotify, playing them through the car speakers and telling him why she loves them and when she first heard them. She zones out to a full song, a smile on her face as late-night, glittering San Francisco passes her by; she's missed this kind of companionship.

"You cool with swinging by a drive-thru first?" Silas asks from her left. "I'm starving."

"I'm always down for the drive-thru," she agrees.

They eat in Silas's car, still in the Taco Bell parking lot, discussing how they'd spend a full fifty-dollar gift card for the fast food establishment in one go.

"And at least two Baja Blasts," Josie is saying. "To wash it all down. Maybe three. You've gotta think ahead."

Silas laughs. "You've thought way too much about this. It's starting to make sense why you don't have more friends."

She flips him off. "I operate best as a lone wolf, dude. Makes me mysterious and shit."

"Yeah, people are really missing out on your breakdown of Doritos Locos tacos."

Josie gives him a light shove. "Didn't you say you spent a lot of time alone before Ramona and Ari?"

Silas's mouth twists. "I had to get away from my dickhead of a dad somehow. Think moody teen with emo bangs who spent lots of time at parks."

"Oh, I had you pegged since the moment I met you," Josie says in jest. "What did he do, your dad?"

"Like, for work? Or to become such a dick?" Silas asks, toying with the keys hanging from the ignition. "Work, he has a pest control company. Dickishness, controlling demeanor plus alcohol. Nothing groundbreaking. He shoved me and my sister around a bit, but he was mostly verbal in his abuse."

"Was anyone else around?"

Silas glances at Josie with a weighted smile. "Mom died when I was thirteen." He shrugs and looks away again. "Anyway, I don't have to see my dad anymore. He's in Vegas. Jess—that's my sister—lives back east, but we see each other every so often." Clearing his throat, he continues, "What about your folks? Did they purposefully breed you to be a fast food connoisseur?"

"One parent. And, totally. Her dream is that I become a Taco Bell influencer."

When Silas raises his eyebrows, an invitation to continue, Josie shifts in her seat. Vulnerability has never been her strong suit, and this topic is the peak. She doesn't meet his eye as she says, "It was hard, with my mom. Growing up, she was always working, and if she wasn't working, she was complaining about everything I did. We fought a lot, but it got really bad my senior year of high school. She lost her job."

She grimaces, looking out the window. "It finally snapped something in her, and she went off about how I was the child she never wanted. The pregnancy was an accident. One that her parents didn't let her get rid of as a lesson, and she regretted it every single day. And— I mean, I always kind of figured, you know? But to have someone say that directly to your face . . . Well. Wouldn't recommend."

"Shit," Silas says.

"Yeah." Josie clears her throat. "So I left. For college. To prove something—to her, to myself. I don't— I don't talk to her. Haven't since I left. I'll text her once a year, on my birthday, to remind her I'm alive, but that's mostly to piss her off."

Silas makes a sound of understanding.

Josie gives him a sideways glance, hesitating. Then: "Adam always tried to get me to talk to her, saying that the relationship was worth it. He said she probably never meant to say what she did." She lifts a leg to set her heel on the dashboard. "He was always so Pollyanna about it, which made me feel shitty for not wanting anything to do with her."

"I never believed in forcing a relationship to work," Silas says. "And I know it gets complicated when parents are involved, but if something drags you down this much—and it sounds like your mom's said some pretty cruel things, you're allowed to step away. That's what I did with my dad, and it legitimately saved my life."

They're both quiet, aside from the ice clinking as Silas swirls his cup.

Josie says, "I never knew what it was like to be loved, actually loved, by someone. Not romantic or anything—just, like, having someone who cares about you, who's there for you no matter what, who wants the best for you, even when you disagree."

"And then you met Adam?" Silas asks softly.

Josie bites her lip, hard, until she's sure she can speak without her voice wavering. "Then I met Adam."

Josie's wrapping up a work assignment at her desk—data entry for a nonprofit in New Mexico—when her phone buzzes. There's a new email in her inbox. *Innovation Zone Bill Narrowly Fails in House Vote, Delivering Blow to Tech Industry Backers* reads the news article from the *New York Times.*

A shudder passes through Josie, and she sits up straighter. In her self-preserving effort to ignore her capstone story, she'd forgotten that the vote was today.

Washington, D.C. – In a surprising defeat for Silicon Valley lobbyists, the U.S. House of Representatives narrowly voted down the Innovation Zone Act, a contentious bill that would have paved the way for semi-autonomous technology districts across the country.

The bill, backed by companies like VYBE Technologies and other venture-capital-funded firms, fell short by just seven votes. Among those voting no was Rep. Nara Taylor (D-CA), a freshman Congresswoman whose swing-district seat and prior silence on the bill made her a closely watched vote.

"I believe in innovation," Ms. Taylor said in a floor statement, "but not at the expense of democratic oversight, labor protections, or corporate accountability. This bill was a blank check."

Ms. Taylor's vote, viewed as a key defection, appeared to swing several undecided members of the Progressive Caucus. Her opposition also marks a significant rift within the Democratic Party, where some younger members have been increasingly vocal about unchecked tech influence.

VYBE Technologies, which had positioned itself as a cornerstone tenant of the first planned innovation zone in Nevada, saw its stock drop 11% in after-hours trading following the vote. Industry analysts say the company may now struggle to secure federal incentives for its planned expansion of A.I.-focused data campuses.

Josie doesn't finish reading, instead repeating her searches from the other day. Sure enough, VYBE stock is down. Whether a reality or only in Josie's head, Andrew's woo-ing Ramona to woo her mom plan didn't work after all.

He's gonna be piiiiiiissed, Josie thinks.

Knowing just how much he's been impacted by this vote stock-wise suddenly becomes an urgent need. She hovers her fingers over the keyboard, thinking things through. On the *Business Times'* real estate beat, staff reporters would occasionally have to look into stock reports associated with developers. And for that, they would use—

Josie pulls up the Securities and Exchange Commission website. She's never visited it before, never had a story important enough for her to need to, so it takes some clicking around and a lot of Googling in a separate tab before she finds a promising route.

Since VYBE is a public company, its insider transactions are published on the SEC site. With Andrew being a board member, he has to file a document anytime he buys or sells stock. What's more— and Josie thanks the government gods for this—a private company insider like Andrew must file within two business days of making a move. Not enough time has passed to see the vote decision impacts, but there was likely lead-up movement with how much everyone was talking about the bill. Josie searches his name with no small amount of anticipation.

She's bracing herself for a large number, and she gets one. But—

Josie stops breathing for a moment, distrusting what's on the page in front of her. She refreshes the page; the results stay the same.

The awareness from the other week begins to buzz across Josie's skin again. Surely, *surely,* this can't be what it's suddenly seeming like it might be.

She takes a moment to sort her thoughts, recalculating what she assumed, then opens up her phone contacts.

The call is answered after three rings. "Evelyn Michaels."

Josie doesn't say anything at first, intensely aware of the importance of handling everything delicately.

"Josephine?"

"I'm here." She stands and moves to the window. "Sorry."

"Did something happen?" It's the first time Josie's ever heard Evelyn speak with caution, like she knows.

"Yeah." Josie takes a breath, then starts small. "Hey, I was wondering: does Ramona dating a VYBE board member have to do with her mom's position as a congresswoman?"

She hears Evelyn inhale, sharp, but doesn't get an immediate reply.

"How about we grab some coffee?" Josie says. She tries to keep her words gentle, like Evelyn's a spooked horse. "Just to talk. I won't say anything to anyone unless you want me to. But. I think we should have a conversation about this."

The silence on the other end of the call is deafening, but Josie forces herself to not push things. She counts to ten, then to twenty before there's a response.

"When can you meet?"

Chapter 24

"Hey," Ari says when he gets in Adam's car. "What're you doing for Thanksgiving? You get it off for school, right?"

Time together continues to be limited; Ari's working more and Adam's studying more, prepping for the slow ramp-up of finals in a month. They're resorting to small moments: Ari picking Adam up from campus, or Adam going grocery shopping for Ari since he's already out, devotedly sticking to the list Ari sends him so the food stays in line with his diet. Or the perfect evening at Ari's: Ari playing video games, Adam beside him on the couch, glowing with happiness when Ari paused his game, settled his chin on Adam's shoulder, and started pronouncing some of the sci-fi names and words from Adam's book. "Kwisatz haderach?" Ari said incredulously, butchering the pronunciation. "Seriously?" Adam began laughing, harder so when Ari started tickling his side. Adam imagined a million more nights just like it.

"I'm going to my grandma's in Yuba City," Adam says, pulling onto Monterey Boulevard. They're heading to his favorite bookstore, the one they visited months ago.

Ari tucks his hand beneath Adam's thigh. Adam's been better about keeping up physical contact lately, and casual touches like this have become almost normal. He can't stop thinking of Kim and Cal. Her openness, Cal's acceptance.

"Ramona's doing a big friends-giving thing up at her parents' place in Tahoe," Ari says. "Figured you had plans, but still wanted to put the offer out there."

Adam's attention is pulled back to the present. "Oh. I'm sorry. That would've been fun."

"All good. Hey, will you help me find some healthy cookbooks? I want to get more handy in the kitchen."

Adam looks over. "Are you just using me for my bookstore prowess?"

Ari gasps, eyes wide. "Is it that obvious? Damn. My former bookworm quit and I was on the lookout when I met you." He pulls his hand from under Adam's leg and cups the back of Adam's neck. "You weren't supposed to seduce me like you have."

Adam turns his head to smile out the window.

The bookstore has two stories, and Adam knows its sections religiously. He enters with Ari, the bell jingling above the door, and gives a wave to the clerk behind the desk.

"Adam, hello!" she calls out.

"Hi, London," he replies, then catches Ari grinning at him.

"Adorable" is all Ari says, fingers briefly tangling with Adam's.

"C'mon," Adam mutters, face heating. He leads Ari to the fiction section, pointing out books he's liked, loved, and didn't care for. Other ones he'd like to read some day.

"How many books do you read a year?" Ari asks, eyes skating over book spines.

Adam shrugs. "Depends."

Ari nudges him. "How many so far this year?"

"It's a lot," Adam admits. "Too much. It's embarrassing. You know I don't go out a lot and my boss lets me read at work and—" He stops as Ari gives him a look, something fond. "It's . . . about ninety?" It's ninety-six, but that suddenly seems like too much.

Ari's jaw drops slightly, and Adam is momentarily transfixed by the color of his lips against his white teeth, his pink tongue. A lick of desire up his spine. He shivers, flushing, and turns away. Ari's response doesn't help: "I like you so much," he says with a startled laugh, phrasing it like an admission. "Like—" He cuts himself off. "Will you show me where the cookbooks are?"

The cooking section is upstairs, near the back. Ari toils, pulling books off the shelves, leafing through, keeping one or two and putting others back. Adam watches him, how his shoulders shift as he leans and stretches, the brown of his hands as he lifts his hat to scratch the top of his head, the bob of his throat when he swallows.

Another shiver up his spine, but Adam doesn't turn away this time, only glances to see if other customers are nearby. They aren't. He takes a step forward. He doesn't even need to remind himself of his promise to try harder for Ari.

"I've had some success with the Keto diet," Ari is saying, thumbing open a book, "but I'm kinda interested in this intermittent fasting, you know? I heard Hugh Jackman had a lot of success with it."

"Ari?" Adam's next to him now, hands on the books under Ari's arm. He gently tugs them out, same with the book Ari's holding, and sets them on a shelf nearby.

Ari frowns slightly. "Do you not like those? I don't have to get them. I just wanted to try something new."

Adam shakes his head. His heart is pounding so hard and fast he's surprised his body isn't shaking with it. "Can I, um—" He bites his lip, then reaches out to grab Ari's arm, both a question and for support. This close, he can see the individual hairs of Ari's stubble, smell the clean scent of his clothing. Adam rises on the balls of his feet, his other hand lightly pressing against Ari's abdomen for balance and leans in to kiss him.

He can feel Ari's surprise, a stiffening under his hands, mouth slack against Adam's. Adam pulls back, clearly having misread something, starts forming a "sorry" when Ari shifts into the right gear. His arms slide around Adam, pulling him in, destroying any distance between them as he catches Adam's mouth once more, now fully engaged. There's a sound from the back of Ari's throat, desire made audible. He's all over Adam, enveloping him arms and teeth and tongue.

Adam can feel himself opening up, eyes fluttering close, body stirring after a long wait. His hands flatten against Ari's chest, each muscle cut to aesthetic beauty. The melting starts, just as it did in the parking lot long ago; Adam's body lining up with Ari's, like Ari is the sun and Adam is a planet delightedly trapped in his gravitational pull.

There's the press of a bookshelf at Adam's back. It's overwhelming in the best way, Adam lost to Ari's practiced techniques of kissing and caring. He's trying to keep up, match Ari stride for stride until he can't and he just—lets go, gives a shuddering breath as Ari takes control. His mouth drags across Adam's jaw to his neck, where he can surely feel the jackrabbit pace of Adam's pulse. Adam makes a soft sound he doesn't mean to.

It's so much . . . *good*. So much want put into motion. This is what other people do together, people who are attracted to one another can kiss all the time and not feel bad about it. Adam's only difference is that he's male and Ari's male and maybe that's not right to some people, but he doesn't feel evil in this moment. All he feels is Ari's lips on his and Ari's hands on the skin of his waist and the goodness of Ari and it can't be bad. It shouldn't be bad.

He's gripping a shelf, an attempt to stay grounded, when the first whisper of his mom's voice slithers into his ear. *To act on it is a sin.* He pushes it out and away, focusing on Ari.

Promise me, Adam.

As long as you're pure, there are only blessings in store for you.

Adam doesn't realize he's shaking until Ari pulls back, baseball cap knocked askew, face flushed, and hands at Adam's elbows. "Whoa," he says, expression clearing as he takes in the wild look that must be evident across Adam's face. "Whoa, whoa, whoa, you okay?"

Adam nods, then shakes his head wordlessly, cringing away from Ari's touch. "Sorry," he manages, blood pounding and thoughts racing. "Sorry, I . . . um . . ."

"Don't worry at all. Was that you feeling bad about things?"

The door at the front of the shop rings, and Adam can hear a group of people talking loudly entering. He begins edging to the end of the aisle. "Is it okay . . . Are you okay if we leave?"

"'Course." The books Ari had been considering are left on the shelf, Ari not sparing a second glance.

Adam hurriedly gives the clerk a wave on their way out. He unlocks his car and they both get in. Ari moves slowly, obviously still cautious of spooking Adam. "I'm okay," Adam says, and he hears the edge to his voice. "Sorry, I didn't mean— I'm, just, I'm okay."

He's not, actually. The dawning realization that he will truly never be able to be involved with someone he's interested in and attracted to has taken hold. He thought if he'd just been able to push through, fight the hesitations, he could find the self-acceptance he sought, find a way to BandAid his relationship with the church. If Adam were straight, if he were out with a girl his age, a make out session would be natural, expected. Even his conservative parents wouldn't bat an eye at Adam doing what he just did with Ari if he was a she— Well, maybe a little. Ari is . . . really good at kissing, and Adam's body was starting to respond appropriately. But Adam is gay and his entire life he's been told that what he's doing right exactly now is bad, will cut him off from salvation and an eternal relationship with his family. All Adam really thinks, though, is that it's unfair. Intimacy with Ari becomes a Pavlovian response of self-hatred.

Ari doesn't speak until Adam's pulling up to his house. And then he doesn't unclip his safety belt. "Will you talk to me?" he asks softly.

Adam drops his head back against his headrest and looks determinedly forward. His frustration pushes the words out succinctly, not a hesitation or stutter to be heard. "Nothing to say. I just had one of my stupid panics because I can't function like a normal human being."

He waits for Ari to tell him that it's okay, or for him to pull a Josie and tell Adam that he needs to suck it up and quit falling victim to these episodes. Instead, Ari asks, "What is it like? Like, what's going through your head when it starts?"

Adam frowns, disbelieving of Ari's intent, but a glance to his right shows Ari watching him earnestly. He hesitates, defenses wavering. "Um, it's . . . it's usually my mom's voice."

"We were making out in a bookstore, and it was your mom in your head?"

Adam looks at him quickly; Ari wears his teasing smile.

Adam gives a weak laugh. "Yeah . . . I know, I know it sounds weird but it's like everything she's ever said to me about staying strong attacks my brain anytime I think about another guy. Or do something with another guy."

Uncertainty passes over Ari's face. He asks, "I don't know why I'm waiting until just now to ask this—I think I just assumed—but how many other guys have there been?"

"Um. It's mostly been pining from a distance until you?"

"Was I your first kiss?"

"No. I . . . There was a girl in high school." One of his lower, more desperate moments to fight his sexuality.

"Your first kiss with a *guy*?"

Adam shakes his head.

"Well, what did you do with that guy when you heard your mom start up?"

"It was just a . . . one-time thing? And my thoughts kinda killed the mood."

"But kissing is the furthest you've gone."

Adam takes a deep breath, tracing a fingernail along a leather seam of the steering wheel. Everything on the table, he reminds himself. Then he shakes his head. "A few years ago there was a Halloween party I went to, and, and there was this guy there and we started dancing, and then we kissed?"

Ari's wearing an odd, tight expression.

"And then we went to an, um, empty area of the house and, well . . ."

"Well, what?" Ari pushes fast enough it's almost a snap.

Adam's face is burning. "He did some stuff." The words are barely more than a whisper.

"'*Stuff*'? What, a hand job? He got on his knees and blew you?"

Adam recoils at the accuracy. Ari's eyes go wide. "Really."

Adam slumps miserably.

"But you won't even—" Ari cuts himself off with a shake of his head. The mood in the car has shifted. "Never mind. You start hearing your mom's voice when you do anything from kiss your boyfriend to get a blow job from a stranger. Then what?"

A one-shouldered shrug. "I d-don't really wanna talk about this anymore."

"I'm sorry." Ari's voice still has a clip to it. "It kinda hurts my feelings that you've gotten head from a random guy you knew for fifteen fucking minutes but I had to wait, like, a month and a half to even kiss you. But whatever. It's fine. I get that it was probably really difficult in the aftermath."

There's a roiling in Adam's stomach. His mom's voice is a low, non-stop murmur in the back of his head, and now Ari's heading a frontal attack. "Can you, um— I n-need to go home."

"Adam . . ." Ari says his name on a sigh, like he's disappointed. The dial in Adam's head is slowly turning up, more words from his mom: *Repent. Repent. Repent.*

"I need to be alone, please."

"Can we talk about it?"

"No, thank you." A tear slides down his cheek.

"But—"

Repent. Repent. Repent.

"*No.*"

"Fine, fuck this," Ari snaps, unclipping his safety belt and shoving open the car door to get out. He slams the door closed and then Adam is driving away—a punctuation mark on the situation.

Chapter 25

Josie's waiting for Evelyn at one of the campus coffee shops, bag puddled on the table. She can't help fidgeting, still wired from what she discovered about Andrew. The burgeoning idea as to what this all could be makes her want to tell everything she suspects to the next person she sees. Frankly, it's Adam she needs, but what else is new?

Her phone buzzes. She expects a text that Evelyn's running late, but tenses when she sees an email from the property management company that handles her rental agreement at the Valley house, the subject line: *Notification of Rental Lease Discontinuation.*

Her body goes cold as she swipes the email open. The message is brutal in its brevity: *Ms. Hicks, This email is to inform you that your rental lease will expire sixty days from today in compliance with California state law, no-fault termination. Please contact our office with any questions.*

Josie's brain activity flatlines.

A joke. It has to be. There's absolutely no way this can be real.

She rereads the email, the two sentences dismantling her life. Rereads it again. Did her setting up an interview with Evelyn trigger this? She opens up her phone's contacts before any coherent thought appears, needing to call someone. Silas? Nara? The president of the United States? Someone she can absolutely rip into, someone she can—

"Hello." Evelyn's there, primly taking the chair next to her.

"Hey." The greeting is both bark and bite. Fingers pressed to her eyes, she tries to wrap her head around reality. Is the email even real? Two months to find a new place to live? Her chest feels hollow. The cost of housing—she's been too lucky, her rooms have been too cheap. There's no way she'll score such odds again. Would Nara agree to be a reference? Maybe a U.S. congresswoman's clout could help speed things along? Oh *god*, will she have to move back in with Feather? Go from her own room and tons of personal square footage to dirty gray walls and sharing a room with someone who's probably a fervent member of a cult by this point?

There's a hand on her arm; Josie sits up fast. She didn't realize she'd been leaning forward, head on her arms. "Are you okay?" Evelyn asks.

Josie falls back in her chair with a laugh. "Oh, you know. Just your former boss screwing me over." She runs a hand through her hair and takes a shaky breath. This is not where her attention needs to be right now.

She pulls a notebook out of her bag, willing herself to focus on Evelyn, who's taking a sip from her drink, unflappable as ever. "I told you we'd just talk. Nothing has to be on the record if you don't want it to be." Josie clicks her pen. *Focus, focus, focus.* Eyes on her list of questions, it still takes a moment for her mind to interpret what's written. Finally, she says, "How did you end up working for Ramona?"

Evelyn sets her drink on the table. "About two years ago, one of my professors was asking for resumés of people who'd be interested in a personal assistant job connected with Nara Taylor's family. She was friends with Nara, who was still in state legislature at the time, and offered to put the word out. I'd like a career in politics." A loose gesture with her hand. "Clearly, I got the job."

Josie frowns. "Nara hired you, not Ramona?"

"Ramona was my boss, but Nara paid my bills. I was brought on as a support system, to add organization and goal orientation to Ramona's life. I put together a specific business plan for Ramona's influencing, I created an LLC to formalize her brand deal pay-offs, things like that. This was right around when Nara began running for Congress, and when her concern over her family's public image took root."

It's not surprising information, but still. Brutal. "I assume Ramona didn't love it?"

Evelyn lets out a soft laugh. "No. She put up with it, though. For a while. Then I guess Nara decided to entice Ramona in a different way."

A dip of her chin toward Josie, who says, "Along came me."

"Along came you." There's something like a twitch of Evelyn's right eye. "Living under the thumb of your parents can be difficult, especially when you rely on them financially. Ramona has an impressive income, but not nearly enough to match the luxury she's accustomed to. This has resulted in years of Nara holding prized possessions over her only child's head as a way to keep her thumb on the scale. I'm not here to offer judgment on the Taylors' personal relationships or to condone anything. I'm simply sharing my interpretation of what fueled Ramona to do what she's done, at least partly."

The housing fiasco is no longer forefront in Josie's mind. She sits forward, pen gripped tightly.

"When Ramona was informed she would be gaining a roommate at the house she's lived in by herself since she was twenty, she perceived it as the final straw in a challenging relationship with her mother. She was angry, and asked me to pursue branding deals that would get her away from her parents' rulebook—high-paying ones, the content didn't matter. This is where my focus was when Ramona went to Burning Man for a few days in August."

Her words, formal before, now sound borderline rehearsed. Josie wants to tell her to relax, but knows better than to break the rhythm, especially when she's being so forthcoming.

"Ramona was approached last year to help market VYBE's generative A.I. She turned it down because it didn't align with her passions, but knew plenty about the business. So, when she ended up at the VYBE camp on the playa, there was likely some mutual recognition."

"She met Andrew there," Josie says. It's a long-held assumption she's had.

Evelyn nods and spins her coffee around on the table. "I'm not sure she knew much about the innovation district bill before Burning Man, but she came back a lot more knowledgeable, if biased."

Josie finds herself momentarily speechless. *She knows!* she wants to say. *Ramona knows she's being used!* Instead, she asks, "What did she say to you?"

"That she met someone."

"What did she say about the *bill,*" Josie clarifies, annoyed.

"That a man named Andrew wanted to know if she had a finger on the pulse of her mother's political mindset, and," Evelyn replies, "if she could ensure a yay vote."

"Bold of him."

Evelyn tips her head side to side, obviously not sold on Josie's statement. "I'm sure VYBE had a fleet of opportunists looking out for intel about the bill."

The sound of grinding coffee beans momentarily stalls their conversation before Josie asks, "Okay. So, a few months ago, VYBE, in the form of Andrew, asks Ramona to be a spy for them, basically, and Ramona says yes. Then Andrew plugs himself in as the boyfriend to keep tabs on her." Josie's back to questioning how much of a grip her roommate actually has on this whole situation. "Did he threaten her?"

Evelyn's frown is back. "Nothing like that, I'm fairly confident. My conversations with Ramona after Andrew entered the picture were primarily her probing to see if I'd go along with things. While I don't have the full facts, Ramona maintained that it was a mutually beneficial relationship."

"Sex? Money?"

"Visibility boosts, advanced content tools, brand deals? Nothing concrete that I heard. There was certainly mutual romantic interest, but that seemed like an added bonus." Evelyn shrugs. "I didn't stay long enough to find out. I'm not interested in being part of political bribery."

"What'd she say to you leaving?"

"That she didn't need me."

Josie moves her pen down the list of questions in her notebook. Thank goodness they're there, too, because she can't think straight with everything coming at her. "The bill failed. Does that mean Ramona failed?"

"I can only speculate; you've spent more time with Ramona than I have since September." She hesitates before continuing, Josie for once able to suppress her need to interrupt. "I wouldn't have been surprised, I guess, if Nara did switch her vote in connection to her daughter's prompting."

It's the first time Josie is fully caught off guard in the conversation. "Really?"

Evelyn's mouth twitches like she's trying not to smile. "You don't think Nara wouldn't be thrilled if Ramona approached her with a convincing argument on why she should vote in favor of a certain bill? She's never cared for her daughter's lifestyle approach, but using government lingo? Entering what Nara sees as an intellectual debate? It's not exactly a reach that Nara would see it as her daughter taking a serious step forward in cementing a career."

"I mean, I guess . . ." Josie has too much respect for Nara to think the congresswoman would fold before such a flimsy attempt.

"But with the bill failing, it's a moot point."

Josie can see Evelyn slowly returning to the stiff-but-courteous-enough assistant, a hand down her sleek low ponytail, then a glance at her Apple watch.

"You think Nara ever found out?" Josie asks.

"Ramona was never going to let her mom know the extent of things. If it does come to light—" A nod toward Josie's notebook, "—it'll be handled in private."

"And you haven't said anything to anyone else?" Josie asks, eyebrow raised.

"You're the first."

"Why?" A question Josie didn't realize she needed to know the answer to until she's asked it. "Why are you trusting me with all this?"

"I was planning to let everything play out from a distance," Evelyn finally says. "But when you called and put things how you did, it . . . changed things."

Josie doesn't buy that completely. It's likely the bill's failure added what Evelyn saw as a layer of security to her involvement. She watches as Evelyn fiddles with the lid of her coffee, then asks, "Enough that I can use you as a source?"

At Evelyn's alarmed look, she raises her hands. "I'm not going to do anything you don't want me to, but I'm breaking this story, and it'll look a hell of a lot better to have you coming forward on your own instead of letting Ramona and VYBE control the narrative. I really think this is a stance you need to take. Publicly."

Evelyn doesn't immediately respond. "I worry about retribution. I don't want anything coloring my future political paths."

Josie sets her notebook on the table. She needs to be delicate. "This is the kind of shining knight shit people love, especially in the face of the wealthy. You quit when you found out what was really going on instead of going along with it, and then you were willing to speak with the media about it? I think that's pretty powerful."

Silence from Evelyn. Josie waits, hoping she's pegged things right.

Finally, Evelyn's stiffness loosens. "Only what I've said about VYBE and Ramona. Not the history with her mom. And only the facts of what I experienced. I don't want to speculate."

Like a ghost from the past, Evelyn's watch chirps. She glances down at the notification. When she meets Josie's eye again, she nods. "I need to go. Good luck."

Only when the door of the shop shuts behind Evelyn does Josie collapse back in her chair, overwhelmed by being on the cusp of something that feels real—close enough to be tangible if she continues to play her cards right.

A U.S. congresswoman wishy-washy about a significant bill that ultimately fails. Her daughter in cahoots with a pro-bill company. With Evelyn's perspective in place, it seems more likely that even one seemingly interested question from Ramona to her mom could have resulted in Nara sharing how she was going to vote with the daughter she's so long wanted bigger things from. Ramona apparently tells Andrew, who—and this is what Josie discovered on the SEC site—sold off thirty thousand shares of VYBE stock right before bill decision day. What's more, he did it alone; no other board members sold off pre-vote.

VYBE might have been plunged into panic mode, but Andrew knew enough to go rogue and come out majorly unscathed.

This is insider trading. Capital-I illegal. SEC-illegal. Go-to-prison illegal.

There's significant proof here, but is it enough? Josie drums her fingers on the table, staring out the windows of the coffee shop for far too long, wondering how Ramona could have benefited from the deal, and how Josie can prove it.

By the time she arrives home, Josie's simmering. The property management email is back at the forefront of her mind, but now Josie wields her story like a weapon of opposition. *You think you can get rid of me so easily? Just wait.*

She's leering by the time she climbs the stairs, intent on scouring the fridge for something to snack on before she heads to her room for a Netflix binge. She's earned it.

Silas's voice sounds from the TV room and Josie hesitates, bursting with the need to share.

Two dark heads lounge on the couch; Silas uses Ramona's lap as a pillow, one of her hands running through his hair. Ramona's just said something that causes Silas to burst out laughing, clear and loud and honest in its delivery. Ramona joins in, the two intertwined in their moment of unrestrained closeness.

Josie doesn't have time to analyze the root of jealousy in the pit of her stomach at the sight of them. Silas pulled back into the Ramona tractor beam now that her business with VYBE is done; Josie the placeholder no longer needed.

At that moment, Ramona glances to her left and catches Josie's eye. Silas—does *he* know Josie's being kicked out? That his beloved Ramona has dipped a toe in dangerous political territory?—is talking with his hands, saying something about a photoshoot gone wrong in a hilarious way.

Josie stares her roommate down, Ramona's expression giving nothing away, not even triumph at Josie's sixty-day countdown.

You're done for, Josie thinks.

Ramona looks away, back down to Silas, her hand now still across his forehead. She glances back once more at Josie, then away just as fast. Like she can sense something just underneath the surface.

Josie smiles, lets it bloom across her face in conquest, then turns for her room.

Chapter 26

He wakes with tears in his eyes, whether from panic or anguish, Adam doesn't know. He wipes them away. His phone tells him it's after two in the morning. There are still unread texts from Ari in his messages.

C'mon, dude, says Josie's voice in his head.

Adam sighs, rubbing his eyes. He can't figure anything out. Not since the kiss, the *kiss,* then subsequent fight with Ari. Is this thing, this trial period with Ari, over? The aftermath of the kiss—he can't stop reliving it—had been ugly on both sides, jealousy and shame vying to swallow him whole.

He hasn't responded to Ari to talk things out because what happened, maybe it's for the best. Maybe being with Ari isn't meant to work out and cutting the cord now will be considerably less painful than it would be further down the road. They kissed, and it was glorious, perfect, Ari's mouth on his, Ari's hands holding him tight, the way Ari's body felt against Adam's . . . Adam shivers, trying to suppress the lust. *That's* what he's scared of, of how much more he wants of Ari and how much further he can let it go. His mind is screaming at him: *No acting on your same-sex attraction* and *no premarital sex* and *sin* and *repent* and—it is very loud in his head.

C'mon, dude. He thinks of Kim, Cal's friend. Kim, who's with another woman. How Cal so obviously loved her. Adam wishes he could have that, that proximity to and understanding from members of the church.

Adam looks at his phone again. Fewer than four hours before his alarm will go off and his day formally begins.

He closes his eyes, but sleep escapes him, worries chasing one another in his head until they're not worries but memories of his time with Ari. Is he already considering them part of the past? Events from another life? He thinks about the way Ari focuses so intently on each person he's speaking to, or how he always tries to subtly find his reflection in windows or glass doors—a self-conscious act, Adam learned—making sure he looks how he thinks he's supposed to. Or the night after the movie, when Ari touched Adam's face, marking invisible brands that would never allow Adam to forget. Adam relives the touch now, the intimacy between them subsumed into the brushing of fingertips against Adam's temple, re-lives it until the jingle of his alarm pierces through the memory.

If Adam expects or hopes for any sort of sympathy from Jon, the one person who's been consistent this semester, he's sorely out of luck.

Jon finds out about the fight with Ari, and he's pissed. At Adam.

He stomps up the stairs when Adam's in the kitchen making a grilled cheese sandwich for dinner. "Hi, do you wa—"

"Man, you need to cut the shit," Jon says.

Adam freezes, spatula in hand. Jon has never spoken to him like this. "Sorry?"

"Ari called me, trying to get a hold of you." Jon comes to stand in the kitchen, blocking Adam's exit, arms crossed.

"Oh. Um, I don't w—"

"I don't care. We're talking about it. I'm sick of you pushing everyone away."

Adam's face heats. "I'm not—*pushing* anyone away."

"Josie? Ari? Two of the most important people in your life you've kicked to the curb."

"I— Josie doesn't want anything to do with me. I've tried."

"If I know J then you definitely know her. You obviously haven't tried very hard to get her to talk or she'd be back by now. She gets angry but she burns out quickly."

Adam grips the spatula. "This isn't my fault. You don't— Everything that happened, you don't know."

"Fine, but you're clearly miserable without her, or you were until Ari, but now you've shut him out too? Adam, what is going *on?*"

The grilled cheese sandwich billows smoke on the stovetop; Adam flips the charred form onto the plate he had waiting and turns off the burner. "I'm just trying to figure things out and I promise I'm n-not trying to push anyone away."

"From what Ari said, he's been trying to apologize for days, and you haven't given him a chance. Sounds like pushing away to me."

Adam wills himself to stay calm. "That's not—" he starts, then stops.

"Talk to me, man. I'm here." He's here but others aren't, is what he doesn't finish with.

"Jon, please—"

"No, we're doing this. I gave you space last time, with Josie. I'm not doing it again. I'm not leaving until you tell me what's going on. I don't care if you give me the lite version; I want something."

Adam closes his eyes, heart pounding in his throat, his ears, his fingertips. Jon is safe, he tells himself. Jon knows Adam is gay and has only ever been a friend, has been there for Adam, knows and loves Josie, knows and loves Ari. He's safe. He's—

"Hey." Jon's suddenly in Adam's space, hand to his shoulder. Adam flinches and opens his eyes to Jon wearing a soft smile, as gentle as the touch on his shoulder. "Hey," he says again. "It's okay, whatever it is."

It's all so far from okay, how much Adam misses Ari but can't bring himself to reach out because he's terrified of what he's feeling, what's been growing in his chest, what the endgame will be if he admits it, the losses that'll start to accumulate. Maybe it's admitting something else to Jon, something just as scary; a diversion to the tectonic plates shifting and cementing inside of him whenever he thinks of Ari.

"It's . . ." He swallows, squeezing his hands together in front of him. "I'm not . . . *supposed* to, to do this, to date another guy." He inhales deeply, lets it out after a few seconds. Then, eyes on the ground, he says, "It's— My parents— It's not how I was raised? With the church. I don't not want to— But it's just, um, become too much. With Ari—" He takes another breath, shakier, and doesn't, can't, continue.

Jon squeezes his shoulder. "Come sit?"

Adam nods, then follows Jon to the couch in front of the TV. "All right," Jon says. "Tell me what happened, whatever you're comfortable with."

Adam tells him. Navigating his sexuality in the Mormon church, his family, his ongoing guilt, Josie, and Ari. He hugs a throw pillow to his chest while he talks.

Jon stays quiet throughout, his gaze a weight on Adam. When Adam finishes, glancing over at Jon, his roommate's mouth is twisted. "You need to give yourself a break."

"That's not—"

"Hold up. Let me get this in, okay? Thank you. For telling me all that. It means a lot, even if I did kinda push you into it. Now . . ." Jon shifts his position, sitting up straighter. "It sounds like you have some seriously unresolved issues with your family and the church, yeah?"

"I think 'issues' sounds a little bit harsh . . ."

"Go with me here. It also sounds like maybe you made some choices that you haven't really come to terms with, like not going to church anymore and getting with Ari. Are those conversations you're willing to have with your folks? Because Adam, bud. I've *seen* how you look at Ari. Like he's some all-books-ever access card or something. Your family really wouldn't want you to be happy like that?"

Adam's head is bowed. "That's not how they see it." He doesn't know how to explain it in a way that won't make Jon immediately condescend like Josie always would. "It's just hard," he whispers. "I . . . I like him so much, but I can't . . . I can't turn off what's happening in my head. And I d-don't want to not be able to talk to my family." That's the crux here: a choice Adam might make now that has no credence after this life.

From the kitchen counter, Adam's phone vibrates with an incoming call. They both know who it's likely from. "I think," Jon says, once the call goes to voicemail, "you're pretty fixed on this situation being black or white. Family and church or no family and Ari, right? Personally, I think you should talk to your family and tell them what you're feeling. I bet they'll surprise you. But if you really don't want to, maybe your answer is in the gray area and you just have to be okay with being there." He reaches out to grab Adam's arm and pull him in for a hug. "That means talking to Ari, regardless, 'kay? He sounded miserable when he called. He doesn't deserve the silent treatment."

Adam nods against Jon's shoulder.

"And one more piece of advice? I mean, you're obviously coming from a place with a whole lot of unacceptance over anything not heteronormative, but if you keep up that mentality and go around thinking that who you are is bad because you're dating a genuinely good guy, it's gonna spill into relationships with other people. Like, I know you'd never hurt a fly intentionally, but if I didn't, and you said what you said to me, about not being brought up to be gay or whatever, I'd assume you were a massive homophobe and not want to be your friend, and definitely not your roommate."

Adam pulls back, looking at Jon, eyes wide with horror. "I truly didn't mean anything by it—"

"*I* know that, and I'm sure Ari gets it, but you saying you hate yourself for being into guys can't help but rub off on others sometimes, like you're implying that you hate them deep down too. You're in the wrong city for that attitude. And the wrong century."

Adam shields his eyes with a hand, more mortified than ever before. "You're—absolutely right. I'm so sorry."

Jon ruffles Adam's hair. "No biggie. Now, you were saying something about a grilled cheese sandwich?"

Adam returns to the kitchen, grabbing his phone off the counter as he passes. It was indeed a missed call from Ari. Adam pulls up their text thread with shaking fingers. Ari's messages since the day after their fight follow the same tone:

sry abt last nite I got jealous

hey will u call me?

I fcked up w wut I said im sry pls answer ur phone

Adam please

look I cant do this if ur gonna ignore me when I'm trying to talk to u and fix this

if ur braking up w me will u at least tell me?

just forget it

The last message was sent a few minutes ago, right after the call. Adam swallows, eyes burning. He didn't mean for it to happen like this, but he has no excuse. He hasn't said anything to Ari in almost a week. Ari's reaction, this feeling—Adam deserves it. The least he can do is face Ari and hear his own faults.

Still, Adam takes a breath, holds it as he types, *Can we talk tomorrow? I can meet you somewhere, or I can come over. Whatever's easiest.*

Ari's responding, typing up a reply before Adam's phone even goes dark. *u can come over to my place I get back from la at 2 but have plans at 6*

It's a far cry from cheerful Ari. Adam, worry gripping his insides, somehow manages to focus on prepping dinner for Jon, hoping all the while the next twenty-four hours will pass as slowly and quickly as possible.

Adam is staring out into nothing, finger marking his spot in a book he hasn't read a word of, when he realizes Cal is hovering at the desk, watching him. He snaps to attention, dropping his book.

Cal's eyes twinkle with kind amusement. "Head in the clouds, my boy?"

"Just distracted, sorry. It won't happen again."

"Not a worry. Now, I wanted to ask . . ." Cal sets his palms flat against the desk, and Adam knows what's about to happen, like his brain can sense the words Cal will speak before they're processed into existence. "My daughter and her family recently moved," Cal says. "Not a far launch, only a couple of hours south from where they were in Ogden. They're in Orem now, and she was telling me about some of the new people they've met. Mentioned a Hughes family full of redheads. Linda, my wife, was a redhead, and my children and I always like to comment on kindred spirits of hers. I mentioned you, of course, the first day you started . . ."

A cold dread pools in the darkest place inside Adam.

". . . and I wondered, with you coming from Orem, if it's your family? I understand Hughes is a common enough last name, but as I said, that hair. Do you happen to have family in the Orem Fourth Ward?"

There it is, at long last. Adam swallows, nods. "Yes, that's— I grew up in that ward."

Cal looks positively gleeful at the connection. He starts to ask, "And how are—" but Adam turns frantic, blurting out the exact words he doesn't want getting back to his parents, to his mom: "I'm not— Sorry, I didn't mean to— I haven't really been going to church lately?"

He forces himself not to look down to escape Cal's reaction, the inevitable disgust and disappointment, and wonders if his boss will know now, sense that Adam is a sinner in the worst way. Not that—he internally berates himself, reminded of Jon's stern suggestion.

Cal raises his eyebrows, something assessing turning his gaze over.

"Sorry," Adam says, trying to amend his obvious misstep. "It's not that—um—" He doesn't know what he's trying to say, doesn't know if he's even trying to say anything specifically. "It's important to me, but I'm not— Please, don't tell my—"

Cal's hands, lifting from the desk, turn placating, patting the air. "Adam, my boy, it's okay, not a worry to be had."

Adam jerks his head into a nod, eyes humiliatingly hot with tears. Now he's looking down at his hands, gripping the armrests of his chair.

"I'm not the Christianity police," Cal says. The delivery is gentle even if Adam can't quite believe the message. His nightmare of a spy placed by his parents, and Adam spilling his secret under no form of duress but kindness. "Your practice of religion is certainly not my business. Forgive me for implying anything of the sort."

"No, that's— You didn't, I just . . ." Adam exhales, looks up. "Could you not, um, if you don't mind, could you maybe not tell your daughter about me? About how I'm . . ."

Cal mimes sealing his lips. "Not a word. I'll play up the old-man-being-forgetful card. 'Must've misheard the last name.' An easy excuse to pass."

Adam rubs his hands across the tops of his thighs. "Thank you. Sorry, it's . . . Um, just—just, thank you. For not."

Cal watches Adam, on the cusp of saying something else.

Sure enough, when he pats the desk, it's with a weighted farewell. "I know the church can be . . . demanding in its expectations, and members are sometimes a little too quick to build walls of judgment and forget the love of Christ. Whatever your relationship is with it now, if you left in anger or in hurt, know that you have a place to talk about it with me. I have my own frustrations with its actions toward and treatment of those who might not fit ideally within expected lines. It can be a difficult separation from that world. I know better than you think." He removes his hands, pausing briefly before adding, "And if it has to do with— Well." Cal shakes his head, smiling slightly. "One lifetime is a long enough time to live with a decision that doesn't make you happy, let alone forever."

He departs, Adam's eyes itching all over again in his wake.

"Ramona and Silas will be here in twenty, FYI," Ari says as soon as he opens the door. His movements are stiff, features forcefully relaxed.

Adam manages to nod. "Did, um, did you want . . ." he says, looking past Ari into the house.

"We can do this right here," Ari says, crossing his arms. He's in a three-quarter sleeved pale green Henley and so obviously does not want anything to do with Adam that it's like he can barely look at him, gaze chilled.

"Okay," Adam says, voice wobbling. His nerves quickly get away from him. "Um. I w-wanted t-to— I'm s-so sorry. For what I did—"

"Deep breaths, Adam. Breathe."

Adam nods, palms pressed to his eyes. Manages one stuttering breath.

Ari sighs, a hand on Adam's back to nudge him inside. "Just—c'mon."

They settle onto the couch, all the distance in the world between them, and Adam takes a moment to salvage any amount of calmness he can muster. But Ari speaks before Adam can continue. "Look, I'm sorry again for how I reacted. I got jealous and took it out on you even though I had no right to judge you for something that happened before I even knew you. I really hate that I'm a jealous person, and it's something I'm working on. But, like, ghosting me for a week was pretty fucking uncool. I called you like fifty times and texted you even more, feeling like absolute shit, and you couldn't even bother to respond."

Adam's throat is tight as he says, "You're right. I— It was unfair of me to not reply. I'm so sorry. Truly. I get—" He looks down at his hands, hot and clammy in his lap. "I have a difficult time processing things quickly and I end up, um, isolating myself? when I'm trying to figure stuff out." He swallows and thinks of Jon's words last night, of the hope Cal gave him today—of the possibilities. "And I'm sorry about how I've been about this, us. But I want to be better. I want to, to be with you and figure this out. I know it can work. It *was* working until we kissed, but that's because my guard was down and—"

"Adam." Ari's voice is soft, and Adam looks up to find his eyes are wet. "I don't think I can do this anymore."

The sole flicker of candlelight in Adam's chest is snuffed out.

"I know you're still figuring shit out," Ari continues, "but it's really starting to weigh me down. Like, I'm starting to feel bad about my sexuality and wanting you, and I'm not into that. I don't want to feel any worse about myself than I already do."

Adam manages to say "right," and the word is broken clean in half. He looks away, across the room, taking in nothing.

"I'm so into you, but I think this is the best move for both of us, you know? You still need to figure out things with your beliefs, and I . . ." Ari stalls out. "I need someone who's more secure about being with me, I think."

Adam's nod is automatic. His insides feel cold. "Of course."

Of course, his mind echoes. Of course this is what happens. Hasn't he spent his entire life understanding that acting on his attraction is a sin? What did he expect would happen, a happily ever after?

He doesn't move, too numb to do anything more than breathe. Ari doesn't either, like he can sense the slowly unraveling connection between them and wants to make it last as long as Adam does.

Then the doorbell rings, and Adam panics. He reaches out and grabs Ari's hand.

"I want you to know," he says, "you deserve someone who doesn't— who isn't afraid of being with you." He swipes the back of his free hand across his cheek. "I'm just, sorry. I'm sorry for everything that's happened. I'm sorry it's not easy for me l-like it is for you, being, being gay. And I'm sorry that I'm not brave. And I'm sorry that I was going too slow. And, and I'm sorry that you had to m-meet me and feel this way." He takes a breath. "I mean, I'm not sorry that, that I met you? You've been everything and I am so, so grateful that I got a chance to t-try things." His tears are falling fast and loose now, hot against his skin. "And I'll p-probably feel this way about you forever. I like you so much and I'm just, just— Even with everything that happened, I'm glad I got to try it with you."

When Ari pulls him in, Adam goes willingly. Neither of them speak, just hold each other until there's a second ring of the doorbell. Ari pulls away and covers his face with a soft curse.

Adam stands and makes for the door. A mirror in the entryway shows his face as splotchy and tear-stained, no surprise but he quickly tries to fix it, hands to cheeks in a useless movement.

Ari appears over his shoulder, and Adam turns for a final goodbye. They don't touch. "This is breaking my heart," Ari says, open as ever.

Adam only manages a small smile in return before opening the door, skirting Ramona and Silas, who wear twin expressions of hatred, and leaving.

Chapter 27

I f Josie thought she was obsessed with her roommate before, it's nothing compared to the feeling she has now that her rise into professional journalism is coordinated with Ramona's downfall.

She can't stop looking at Ramona's posts: a close-up of her lying on a bed; a video of Ramona, Silas, and Ari eating sushi together, chopsticks as utensils and weapons as Ari spears one of Ramona's rolls; an over-the-shoulder picture, Ramona's hair wavy and her lips glossy. Her life still perfect, no sign of grief over the loss of whatever connection she and Andrew Prosser had; her friends as loyal as ever, her follower count rising. A bigger bang on the horizon.

Josie's actively ignoring her housing situation for the moment, too determined to make progress with her capstone project to think about the elephant in every room of the Valley house. And if she navigates this right, she can hold Ramona's threat at bay.

The purposeful ignoring becomes easier when she sits before Tilton's desk and tells the professor everything she's learned.

Tilton is quiet at first, once Josie finishes talking, and Josie can't help assuming she's messed up somehow. Finally, the professor exhales and leans forward, forearms resting atop her desk, hands clasped. "You haven't yet approached Representative Taylor or her daughter on the matter?"

Josie wants to point out that Ramona had her chance to cooperate, but doesn't. "I'm waiting until I have more solid proof that Ramona took the deal—something that can show she was the one to pass on the information to Andrew."

Tilton's nodding before Josie even finishes. "If you're going to claim Ramona benefited from her mom's voter intel, you need three things: movement, motive, and access. The SEC files show a strong movement likelihood; the access is an assumption you could possibly corner Ramona into admitting; and the motive—which, as you said, is your top priority. What is or was Ramona set to receive in exchange?"

Josie closes her mouth, trying to not be awed by Tilton talking to her like an equal.

"You'll need to approach Andrew as well," the professor continues. "Though I suggest reviewing his SEC filing more thoroughly to see if there are clues as to how he's been able to avoid scrutiny so far. There are watchdog groups that cut their teeth on this type of information. Why haven't any flags been raised publicly yet?"

Josie scribbles in her notebook, hand aching for how fast she's writing.

"Don't leap to guilt. Build the trail. Let the facts hem in the story until it can't squirm away."

When Josie finally looks up, Tilton is watching her closely. Then she smiles, freezing Josie like a deer in headlights.

"If you're correct about this, Miss Hicks, it'll easily be the most impressive story to come out of this class," Tilton says. "If you pull this off, I'll give you that letter of recommendation. I'll hand deliver it myself to the newspaper of your choice."

Josie's looking for a bag of Cheetos she swears she didn't empty completely. It's not in her room, and so far, it's not on any of the reachable shelves of her cupboards in the kitchen. She's dragging a chair over from the banquette table, ready to search the top shelves with a fine-tooth comb when she notices the gang quietly gathered at the dining room table, audience to her slamming of cupboards and drawers.

Ramona ignores her, but Silas gives Josie a withering glare from his seat facing the kitchen. Ari's back is to Josie, but he glances over his shoulder, a quick motion, but not fast enough for Josie to miss his red eyes. Red, she realizes after a moment, because he's crying.

Josie goes cold, mind jumping to the worst. Adam hurt, dead in a ditch, kidnapped by his family and submitted to electric shock therapy. Silas continues to accuse Josie with his eyes. "Is—" she starts, and he stands with a sharp shake of his head.

"I need to talk to you." There's a little too much demand in the words for her liking, but Josie's so overwhelmed with worry that she nods, retreating deeper into the kitchen. Silas only jerks his chin to the hallway, and she ends up following him to her room.

"Adam?" Josie says as soon as he shuts the door behind her. Did she wait too long to finally reach out to him, too wrapped up in her burgeoning story?

"Ari ended things with him."

Josie bites on her lip, a mix of emotions rearing up in response to that—hurt for Adam, but relief most of all. That's for analyzing later, though, especially with Silas looking at her like she forced Ari into action. "Okaaay," she says.

"So, Ari's still cut up about it, and I thought . . . I thought what you said, about him, Adam— I thought it would last." His voice is an eddy of emotion, frustration lining the words' edges. "I believed you, that Adam was taking this seriously."

"I'm not his programmer, dude. I told you what I knew from my experience. Why did Ari break up with him?" But Josie has her assumptions, suspect number one starting with L and ending with O-I-S.

"He says it's private." Silas scrubs at his forehead. "But he's absolutely miserable and I can't— I *don't know how to help him.*"

Josie moves farther into her room, kicking aside a pile of worn clothes. Eventually she says, back to Silas as she stares out the window, "Why do you have to help him?"

"Because he asked me to."

Josie breathes out with a control she doesn't feel. Adam never asked her for help.

She doesn't speak for a long time, instead watches the pieces of San Francisco through her window. The cars and houses and people and buildings and cloudy sky above it all. This city that's been her home for the past few years. She thinks about how she'll leave in a few short months, and how the events that unfolded as a student shaped her. How Adam shaped her. She'll leave him too, and he'll go on with his struggle to find purchase on a thin ledge of happiness because he thinks that's all he deserves.

Silas is gone by the time she turns around, back to those he loves.

She grabs her phone off the bed. She won't call Adam, scared to break him further, but she will call Jon.

"Hey," he answers.

"How is he?"

Jon blows out a breath. "Not great."

Josie's fingers tangle in her hair, twisting at random strands. She just wants to hold Adam. Pull him to her and squeeze all her love into him and tell him it'll be okay. *Let's figure it out together.*

"J?"

She swallows. "I'm here."

"Will you talk to him?"

"I don't know if I'm the right person."

"This is bigger than your fight," Jon says, voice sharp. "He needs you."

Josie's eyes drift to the framed photo on her desk, facedown for eons because she couldn't stand the reminder of herself and Adam in such a happy state. "I'll try."

Approaching someone you used to be inseparable from is underrated in terms of awkwardness, anxiety, and humility. Josie can't say she's a fan.

She's late to class Thursday, but clocks that Adam's there. He's like an anchor, pulling the entire weight of the room toward him, all slouching lines. Josie worries, but can't help the small bit of vindication inside her, too. Like even when she's recognized her role in what went down between her and Adam, she's hyper aware that maybe things didn't work out with Ari because she wasn't there to nudge Adam forward. It's not nice, the feeling, but Josie's never been nice.

When class ends, she stalls, waiting for the others to leave. Adam remains seated, chin in his hand and staring zombie-like at the whiteboard like he hasn't noticed class is over.

She moves slowly, wading through water. "Adam," she says when she reaches him. The room is empty.

He blinks twice, sitting back to look up at her. His skin is sallow beneath the classroom lighting, face puffy and eyes rimmed in red. He doesn't say anything.

"I heard what happened," Josie says softly. "Are you okay?"

His gaze, only halfway focused on her, drops. He mutely stands and moves for the door.

She stops him with a hand to his arm. "Adam." He yanks away from her touch, and there's a painful throb in her chest because of it. "Was it because of your family?"

He stops on a dime at her words. She can see how tense he's become. He still hasn't said anything, but she knows she's right on the mark. Ari might've pulled the lever, but Josie knows Adam well enough to

230

see the deeper trajectory.

"Why couldn't you just let yourself be happy with him?" she asks.

He whirls around at that. "Let myself?" His voice is strained. "I tried that and it ruined everything. I was lying to my family and I was hurting Ari and I— I'd already lost you over it."

Josie moves forward automatically at that, but he shakes his head, turns ninety degrees, and eyes the door of the classroom like he wants to bolt.

"I'm sorry, okay?" she says, practically pleading now. The sorrow she's been stifling for months now is stripped down, raw inside her chest. She needs him to understand so he'll let her back in. She needs to push back the vindication she feels and figure out how to make Adam better. "I'm sorry about how I reacted. It wasn't fair. But you clearly had something great going on with Ari. Why is it always your family and religion getting in the way of your happiness?"

"Don't." He looks over at her sharply. He's clearly trying to be standoffish, but there's a quiver to his chin. "You don't get to do that. Not again."

Josie's temper spikes. She finds a way to drag it back down. "What do you mean, 'not again'?"

"If you hadn't pushed me to date, I wouldn't have . . ." He's fighting hard against crying. "I wouldn't have done anything with Ari and he wouldn't have become so unhappy and I wouldn't b-be feeling this way."

Josie sucks her cheeks in. "That's not exactly fair. I was only trying to help. You very obviously hated your life, and your religious ideals were following you around like a grim reaper. You made a promise with your mom and she was using it to control you—"

"*You're* the one who wants to control me!" Adam sounds hysterical now. Josie's head jerks back; she's never seen him react like this. "By making me do something I might not have done! And always saying I

231

should go on dates! And when you found out about Ari, you pushed me away because you couldn't stand that I didn't tell you something! Because that's what you do, Josie: You force people to bend to your will, and when they don't, you hate them for it." He's fully facing her again, his chest rising and falling quickly, hands clenched into fists. "I should've t-told you about Ari. I know that. But you pushed me away with such cruelty. I needed you then. I don't—" He swallows. "I don't need you now."

Josie swells like a frog in anger. "I only ever wanted you to be happy," she spits back. "I only ever wanted you to realize that you deserved more love than you were getting from your family. Just because I didn't sugar-coat my beliefs in scripture doesn't make them any less valid. And it looks like you finally got a chance at happiness with Ari before you decided to blow the thing up." Adam makes a pained sound and a tear spills over. "I didn't *push* you to do any of that so don't you *dare* make it my fault that your life is a dumpster fire. I just want what's best for you."

"I don't— I don't believe you," Adam replies. "You were worse than my, m-my family," he says after a moment, voice breaking on the last word, "because you p-pretended to care until it inconvenienced you. At least, at least they've been honest with me from the beginning."

Josie's mouth falls open. *"Really?* I'm worse than your family who raised you for slaughter by their own hands?"

"They raised me to be *righteous!*" Adam half-yells. He seems taken aback by his anger because his next words aren't as loud, but they're dripping with desperation: "They're thinking of my salvation."

Josie laughs loudly but it's not funny. "And I assume *'they'* knew you were dating Ari?" Adam flinches, turning his head away. "Did *'they'* know you were acting on your 'same-gender attraction'? Were you so concerned about the opinions of your family and religion when you were *literally* sinning against them by having a boyfriend?"

232

She waits for him to answer, and when he does, after an extended silence, he only whispers it, eyes squeezed shut.

"What was that?" Josie asks, taking a step forward.

He opens his eyes to look at her, gaze steeled. "I said at least *my* family thinks I'm worth being saved."

Josie feels herself shut down. She doesn't look away, doesn't react in any way, won't give him the satisfaction, except to brush past him, heading for the door.

Only when she's left the building does she realize her face is wet with tears.

Chapter 28

Road trips growing up were one of Adam's favorite pastimes. His parents would pile him and his siblings into their van and they'd set off. Weekends during school, weeks during breaks, exploring by car much of the western United States, national parks in Southern Utah, ski resorts in Colorado, lonely motels in the middle of Nevada that were decorated with clowns or aliens, or had a pair of bunk beds set up for the kids, who would bicker over who got the tops. Sundays on the road, of course, meant his parents looking up the meeting time of the closest church and a mad scramble to iron dress shirts on the motels' cheap ironing boards.

The trips were a staple part of the Hughes family, and Adam still thinks fondly of them. He can't help but feel a sense of anticipation at what the road will bring every time he gets in his car for a long stretch.

Like now, driving across the Bay Bridge, car pointed northeast for Yuba City, where family awaits him. Adam needs a break from the city, where everything is snarled. Distance from the depressing cave his bedroom has become. He's lost weight, lost a little of his will to live, if he's being perfectly honest, though he knows Josie would harp on him for being dramatic—*pouting*, she'd say.

He doesn't really care if he's being dramatic. He's grieving. Not just about Ari, who he thinks about constantly, the memory of him bombarding all of Adam's senses. He's also grieving over Josie and their decisive argument. *At least my family thinks I'm worth being saved,* he'd told Josie, a twist of the knife to her secret wound. The words feel like ash on his tongue.

He pushes his foot harder against the gas pedal. Forward and onward, Adam pleading with his brain to adopt the same anticipation from road trips of old.

It works, sort of. A little over two hours later, Adam's pulling up in front of his grandma's house, a white, single-story home with blue trim, a manicured front lawn, and an American flag happily waving in the light breeze. He's early by a day, wasn't supposed to show up until Wednesday, but his grandma welcomed his presence when he called and asked if it was okay. "I'll get you all to myself for a few hours," she said.

She greets him in the style of all grandmothers in the movies: open arms, smiling face, and a batch of cookies just pulled from the oven. He sits at the kitchen table and tells her about classes and work. She doesn't know he's gay, would be just as concerned about his salvation as his parents, but at least she doesn't lambast him for living in California, which he's sure everyone else will do at least once over the next few days. Might even be a Thanksgiving meal conversation; they all hate California.

She asks him if he's dating anyone, and he says he's too busy. She tells him the most important purpose in this life is to create a family, and he says okay. Then she asks him to help her get all the bedrooms set up for everyone to arrive.

The Hugheses show up in fits and starts over the next twenty-four hours. Adam's dad is one of four boys, all of whom are married with at least three kids apiece, and all of whom are coming for Thanksgiving.

His parents arrive late afternoon on Wednesday, caravanning with two other Hughes families who live in Utah. They're all a pile of bad moods; it's a long drive from central Utah, and apparently the weather entering California delayed things further. Adam's been wondering how his mom and dad will react upon seeing him, if they can sense anything amiss. His dad only claps him on the shoulder, but his mom greets him with a hug. He hangs on to her, needing the comfort of the mother he grew up with. His mom squeezes him back, likely her finely tuned maternal instinct keeping him close. When he finally pulls back, she looks at him closely, eyes darting across his face. Her hand cups his chin and she nods without saying anything, then continues deeper into the house.

Adam doesn't hate anyone, but the person closest to the mark is his Uncle Kirk, his dad's oldest brother. Even Adam's mom minimizes her preaching of Christlike love when Kirk's name is part of the conversation. Uncle Kirk is on the heels of Adam's family through the door, corralling his kids ahead of him as he loudly complains about snow, California, traffic, California, and all three at once.

"—cars spinning out everywhere; I should've run them right over," he's saying to no one specifically but everyone all at once. He sees Adam, standing by the door. "Adam! You're still a scrawny kid, aren't you? Always said your parents kept you kids too sheltered, need to turn you boys into real men!"

Adam doesn't sleep. Or if he does, it's short-lived and he can't remember. He's sharing a bed with Ben, his sixteen-year-old brother, who sleeps like a starfish. Adam is shunted to the very edge of the bed. On the floor of the room lie male cousins and his brother Matty in sleeping bags and beneath blankets, mounds of slow and steady breathing. Adam has never felt more alone.

He says a silent prayer. He thinks of Ari. He uses the restroom but can't look at his reflection. Back in bed, he thinks of what he said to Josie, of the look of betrayal on her face.

Adam doesn't sleep, just lies in bed, living with the consequences.

236

Thanksgiving Day dawns gray and rainy. It's not an issue, because the Hughes family tradition of a gratefulness-themed devotional means they stay inside all morning, dressed in Sunday best, the women flitting in and out of the family room to work on the food, Adam's sister Emma sharing messages of God and Jesus Christ and eternal family.

They get through the morning, and Adam is feeling pretty okay, the listing out of blessings they all enjoy helping him to sip from his half-full glass. He hasn't thought about Ari in at least three hours or Josie in two.

For dinner, multiple tables are crammed in a zigzag pattern in the dining room so everyone can fit. Adam ends up closer to one of the ends, Matty to his right and Uncle Kirk a table-length away. Adam snaps a photo of his plate, heaped with turkey and stuffing and sweet potatoes with the marshmallows melted on top and a roll and— He's half-tempted to type his full meal out line by line to Jon, who may be on a cruise ship, but there's no way he's enjoying food as quality as this. He opts for just the picture, which Jon replies to immediately with a frowny face.

The food is prayed over, and everyone dives in, Matty talking animatedly to their cousin Daniel across the table, Adam smiling privately at their conversation, a mix of organized sports and sixth grade and video games.

A comment down the table drags his attention away from the happy corner of innocence, the hair on the back of Adam's neck rising. It's Uncle Kirk, because of course it is.

"—understand that marriage should only be between a man and a woman, don't get me wrong," he's saying. "Fully support it; that's the way God intended it. But I think we should let the queers do their thing with each other."

Adam, mid swallow a bite of green jello, freezes, catching his mom's eye. Her face looks carefully blank. Adam can't help but feel a confusing glimmer of hope at what Uncle Kirk is saying, of all people and all insults aside. Adam's dad, next to his mom and across from Kirk, looks as perplexed as Adam feels. He doesn't glance at Adam, though. Only says, hand halfway to his mouth with a buttered roll, "How can you say that?"

Kirk laughs. "Trust me, Luke. Makes my stomach turn just thinking about it."

Adam's trying to shut his ears to the conversation, trying not to hear anything that'll sink him further in the mire. He stares hard at his plate of food, trying to recall the music playing at the last concert he went to with Josie, where it was so loud any thoughts were drowned out, and what would he give for that now. But Uncle Kirk is still talking and he's the only thing Adam can hear.

"Hear me out: The reason the queers are the way they are is because God doesn't want 'em reproducing. Darwinism at its finest! Ha! Far as I'm concerned, send 'em off to the pasture of Sodom and Gamorah. That gene or whatever it is, the one turning them, it shouldn't spoil future pools by marriages of convenience, right? Keep them away from our children and our schools and, ideally, the state of Utah entirely. No offense, Mom, but California's a great place for them all. Put them all here—San Francisco's already a cesspool as it is." He raises his voice to call down the table: "Don't know how you stand it, Adam! Anyway," he pauses, mops up some gravy with a forkful of turkey, takes a bite, then swallows, "quarantine the queers and they'll die off, easy-peasy."

Adam's staring at his sweet potatoes without seeing them, face and neck assuredly scarlet.

"What's a queer?" pipes up Matty.

"Now, Matthew," Adam's mom says just as Uncle Kirk shoots out, "Word for the gays—the ones who like their same kind. And don't get me started on these transgenders."

Adam's hands shake as he sets his spoon to the right of his plate.

Matty looks at Adam curiously, and Adam knows it's coming, but can't figure out how to stop it. *This* isn't a premonition, this is an if-then situation: If homosexuality is brought up, then Adam will be shoved center stage. "You're a queer then, right, Adam? Because you like boys?"

The table doesn't go quiet instantly. Instead, it's drawn out, from the seats around him, spreading to the edges like a slow earthquake rippling out from Adam at the epicenter. The tinkling of glasses stops, conversations die, and heads swivel.

Kirk laughs, loud and brash; Adam fails to not flinch. "Hughes stock doesn't breed that trash, Matty. Your brother might be living in that sin-bath that is San Francisco, but he isn't one of 'em. You're trying to bring 'em back to the light, aren't you, Adam? Doing the Lord's work in that city of liberal snowflakes and fa—"

"Kirk," Adam's mom says stiffly, "You know as well as I do the church's stance on same-sex attraction. We are to love—"

"But my dad said he was," Matty interrupts, then adds over a scolding *Don't interrupt, Matthew,* "That Adam likes boys. We always pray for him, don't we?" He looks toward their parents in question. "To ask Heavenly Father to make sure he doesn't kiss another boy?"

Adam's heartbeat is so loud in his ears he can only faintly hear the conversation continue.

"Adam is staying true to the doctrine," his mom is saying. "He's not acting on his attraction and—" She raises her voice as Uncle Kirk starts to splutter, "—you are not to insult his challenge in any way, Kirk. I mean that. We love Adam just as much as we would if he had a normal attraction."

Uncle Kirk mutters something about Adam sharing a room with his sons, and Adam's mom snaps, "Judgment is for God, not you. Adam might deal with temptation more profoundly than the rest of us—"

"Mom—" Adam tries.

"—but he has promised to stay true, and at the end of this lifetime, he will appear spotless before the judgment seat. It is not your place—"

"Mom, please." Louder now. She looks over at him, cut off mid-speech. "I n-need to talk to you."

In the silence that follows, his mom trades a tense look with his dad. Adam tries not to see the realization in everyone's eyes. They have to know, can probably smell it off him—all his lies and the fact that he's so boldly sitting here and pretending otherwise.

She stands and he follows her, a wave of whispers at his back. She leads him to the bedroom she and his dad are sleeping in. Adam closes the door with shaking hands; he's never been so terrified in his life.

When he faces her, she's already crying. "What happened?" she asks, voice choppy.

He stares back at her, empty of an answer. He knows their similarities only increase when they're both crying, her face splotchy like his, eyes reflective with tears. "Mom." The word is a plea and a bargain. *Don't make me say it*, he thinks.

She gives him no such option. "Adam." Her voice alone has dropped the room's temperature by degrees. "What did you do?"

Adam closes his eyes and sees Ari's face. "I met someone," he whispers.

There's no sound of a reaction, and when he opens his eyes, his mother simply looks back at him. Adam, caught up, keeps talking, the words spilling out of him. "I, um, just wanted to try and see? See if I could— I, just, I liked him so much and thought that it might be okay if I tried taking it slow with him. But I was making him miserable and he ended things with me. And it feels like I'm broken, and my insides are f-falling apart and I just m-miss him and I wish I wasn't born like this. I wish, I wish I hadn't b-been born at all because it *hurts* and—"

He stops as something like hope overtakes his mom's face. "It's over? Your relationship with this other man?"

"Y-yes, I—"

"And your bishop? Have you gone through the repentance process?"

"That's n-not—" he starts. *That's not the point*, is what he doesn't finish saying. But it is, isn't it? The whole reason he struggled over being with Ari was because he was lying to his family. He should've come clean a long time ago. "I haven't," he tries again, "been to church in months."

"Months?" She perches on the edge of the bed, grappling blindly for the bedpost.

"I—" He swallows thickly. "I wasn't happy going. I hadn't been for a long time."

"Then you need to try harder." His mom says it like it's the most obvious and easy thing. "There are many members of our church who struggle and overcome. They continue to attend church and keep their covenants with God. If you're so miserable, Adam, that's on you. It truly hurts to know that after everything we taught you, after what you promised me, you still chose this. We all have hardships and trials, and we're invited to give them to the Lord to make our burdens lighter—"

"I *d-did* that, Mom. I prayed and I went to church, and I tried to be a good person. And all the while I felt wrong for wanting someone and knowing I have to be alone to stay worthy. I want so badly for things to go back to how they were before, before I came out to you because not a d-day goes by where I don't have to convince myself that you wouldn't, wouldn't trade me in for a better—" Adam tries to compose himself; fails, "—a b-better version."

"The only thing we want for you is to stay true to the gospel so we can be an eternal family." She's crying again. "I thought we'd been clear that if you were to act on your attraction, there wouldn't be a place with us in the afterlife. I don't understand— What happened to the boy I raised? Do you not want to be with us forever?"

"I *do!*" Adam sobs. "It's all I ever w-wanted! But I'm so unhappy trying to keep my promise to you."

"No. Absolutely not," his mom says, holding a hand out like she's warding him off. "Blaming me is not the answer. If you were doing what you were supposed to, you would have the strength to endure. It wouldn't be easy, but it would work. I know you think I'm being unsympathetic, but I want what's best for you in the long run. I want our family to be together eternally, and that will not happen if you continue down this path. Heaven does not have a place for you."

Adam sinks to the floor. "Mom, p-please."

Her voice shakes as she says, "If you are here to begin the repentance process and put an end to your sin, then we can talk. If you're not interested in being with your family in the afterlife, I am not interested in having a relationship with you in this life. You need to choose, Adam."

Suddenly, it feels like everything is on the line. A series of snapshots are cycling in his mind's eye, moments from the past few years: classes and concerts and cartons of ice cream with Josie; baseball games on the couch next to Jon; Ari jogging in the early morning fog, flashing a smile Adam's way that tipped him into love. All of that, erased with the start of a new direction, guided by his family. Guided by, but not as companions. His parents and siblings would serve as touchstones for a complete life he'd never be allowed to measure up to; no family to call his own, no one to look at him or touch him like Ari had.

Josie's voice is in his head, angrily telling him she only ever wanted him to be happy. *Just because I didn't sugar-coat my beliefs in scripture doesn't make them any less valid.* Had he rejected her reasoning because of its serrated delivery? She'd pushed him—yes, too far sometimes, but wasn't it only ever to help him see that stripped of religion, he's still a good person and he should be able to show his love for others in the way that works best for him?

If love is the point—of man, of God, of self, then that's the religion

Adam wants to continue to seek.

He looks up at his mom, wiping his face—soaked in tears, his nose running. "Can't I have both?" The gray area Jon had been talking about, romance and a relationship with his family, is it as simple as asking?

She stands, arms wrapped around her waist, and shakes her head. "I'm not going to give you permission to both act on your attraction and expect eternal blessings. The doctrine is clear—" Her voice breaks and she turns her back to him. He can see the tremble in her shoulders.

But a moment later, when she turns back around, a calmness has descended, clearing her countenance. She reaches out to grab his hand and pull him up. "Sweetheart," she says, "I will never deny my belief in the doctrine that marriage is the union between a man and woman. I won't. I have a testimony of that belief, and I put it above my role to support you as a parent. I love you, Adam. You allowed me to become a mother, which is the greatest blessing of all, but I don't want you to confuse my love for you with me condoning your behavior. Our Savior Jesus Christ didn't withhold his love from anyone, but he also never exempted anyone from keeping his commandments. The action you took in involving yourself with another man is in direct violation of everything you were raised to be, and maybe that's on your father and I, not being clear enough, so I want to be now: If you are going to act on your same-gender attraction, you are not welcome in our home."

She pulls him close, into a hug. Her voice wavers only slightly as she says, "You need to make a choice, Adam. And this time, if you make a promise, I expect you to keep it."

Chapter 29

Ramona is late getting out the door for her Thanksgiving extravaganza. It doesn't help that she had a small army clogging the entryway of the Valley house, babbling about useless topics like so-and-so hooking up with so-and-so and "Did you see what she posted? So cringe, right?" and taking selfies between it all.

Josie only caught a piece of it, passing through on her way back from the grocery store with bags hanging from her arms. Silas, sitting on the bench and looking minorly aloof next to Ari, nodded his hello. Ari stared at the floor. No sign of Andrew. They all left by noon, and Josie began the day alone.

Adam romanticized the holidays more than the average person, but made a point to stay in town for the week of fall recess, keeping Josie company instead of returning to his Hughes fold. She didn't say it as much as she should have, but Josie was always grateful for his presence and the way it filled in the suffocating absence of others. They'd get a ton of pre-made meals from the store, except for the family green jello recipe Adam always made from scratch, and happily gorged while watching Hallmark Christmas movies. Josie, inevitably, would fall asleep before each climatic breakup, and Adam—

Josie stops herself with a curse. She's spent too much time mourning over the reality of his parting words last week.

She takes another bite from the tray of crappy microwave pasta and returns her focus to the laptop screen.

She's been working through an ever-shrinking list of where a breadcrumb trail could start with this whole collusion thing.

Already there's a handful of figurative misfires. Ramona's public-facing persona continues to stay streamlined, all about beauty and nothing about tech. Nothing that screams scandal.

And VYBE, as a private company, isn't required to report payments to influencers or other third parties.

She's already used up her luck with public records on the Andrew front; there's no magical receipt of one VYBE board member wiring over a big thank-you check to a certain San Francisco influencer.

Josie reaches for another bite of pasta. Her back aches from how much time she's spent hunched over her computer. *Think*, she tells herself. The deadline for Tilton's class is next week, and the further away time gets from the congressional bill's failure, the more likely any proof of the deal has already been swept aside.

"C'mon, Ramona," she says to no one. "You had to get something for this."

She starts again, taking VYBE out of the equation completely. The company continues to suffer: a further drop in stock, and the CEO resigning. Amid the chaos, Josie hasn't seen any media specifically pointing out Andrew's offloading of shares, let alone the reason behind it. For now, she's maintaining her hold of the scoop.

She refines her scope. If everything between Andrew and Ramona was happening behind closed doors, then any exchange of goods would be, too. Not a wire transfer or a suitcase full of cash. Something cleaner. A brand partnership, a consulting retainer—something that looks legitimate from a legal distance, but quietly reeks if you follow the timing.

Something twitches in Josie's brain, and she reaches for her notebook. Barely legible, halfway down page one of her notes from the conversation with Evelyn, is 'LLC.' Evelyn mentioned creating an LLC for Ramona back when she was first hired.

Josie turns first to Google for instruction, and then ends up on the California Secretary of State's business registration portal. She runs a business entity search for Ramona's name. Nothing. Tries again, using initials, full legal name, even Nara's. Still nothing.

It's not like Evelyn to lie. If Ramona has an LLC, it should be in here . . . unless it's not being used, maybe. And that thought—

Josie clicks the box to include search results from inactive or suspended LLCs, types again, and hits enter.

There it is. Taylor Media Holdings, LLC. Ramona listed as the principal owner. Evelyn Michaels as the organizer. The LLC was registered two years ago, then went quiet—no filings, no action.

Until: five days ago. Just after Nara Taylor cast her deciding vote against the innovation zone legislation.

Josie's eyes flick over the filing, heart thudding against her ribs. A defunct LLC, suddenly back from the dead, means it was revived—formally. Someone paid the fees. Someone wanted this entity alive again.

Searching the LLC's listed address, a Palo Alto one, tells Josie the location is tied to a corporate law firm, one that a separate search reveals—and Josie tenses so hard she bites her tongue—is known for anonymous financial structuring and "quiet transactions" for high-net-worth clients.

Josie backtracks on the Secretary of State website, searching the law firm's address and hoping this is a trail with a pot of gold at its end. A few dozen or so LLCs are connected to the same place. Sorting by date puts a Westward Strategies, LLC, at the top, registered right before the vote. The registered agent name isn't familiar, but Josie didn't expect Andrew's name in actual print. That would be too easy.

The LLC's purpose, however, is similar to Taylor Media Holdings: *Strategic consulting and corporate advisory services.*

Josie pushes away from the desk and paces the TV room, wrapping the end of her braid around her fingers and pulling.

LLCs. They're often used to keep ownership and money paths out of headlines. Could Ramona have done the same to hide a massive payout? Another yank on her braid. How she wishes she would've worked harder at the *Business Times* to earn more in-depth stories. She could have walked this very line before and would better know how confident to feel.

While there's no active proof Westward Strategies made a payment to Taylor Media Holdings, the timeline's too neat to ignore. One gets filed just before the vote; Andrew offloads a chunk of shares; the other LLC, dead for a year, is resurrected right after. And the fact that they both used the same law firm—

The doorbell rings, and Josie jumps nearly a foot in the air. *VYBE assassins*, she immediately and nonsensically thinks as she hurries to slam her laptop shut, then barks out in laughter at the thought.

Still, her heart is hammering so loud she nearly misses the tentative knock that follows.

Adam is on the doorstep, and every single thought of Ramona and Andrew and LLCs evaporates in an instant.

He's wearing a creased white button-up shirt, blue slacks, and brown dress shoes. He looks like he's spent the last year crying.

Every ounce of hurt she's been working to bury since his biting departure rises like bile. Josie wants to slam the door in his face.

She almost does so, has a bullet-pointed presentation in her head listing exactly how she'll tear him apart piece by piece, followed by a door slam. Another part of her recognizes, however, that it's five o'clock on Thanksgiving Day and the perfect Hughes family should be enjoying singing Jesus's praises over funeral potatoes, or maybe burning an effigy of queer people everywhere. Yet here Adam is.

She allows him a greeting: "What."

His face crumples further. "I'm s-sorry," he says, the words a scrambled mess. "Jon's gone and I d-didn't want to be alone."

Josie crosses her arms. "What, did your family stop caring enough to try to save you?" Bullet point number one, check.

Adam covers his eyes with a shaking hand. "I'm so sorry about what I said. Really, Josie. I'm truly, *truly* sorry for not t-telling you about Ari, and for what I implied about your mom. It was horrible of me. Your friendship means so m-much and, and I let my brain justify things I shouldn't have."

"Like saying I wanted to control you and only pretended to care when things suited me. Got it." An adaptation of bullet point four, check. "Why are you here?"

"My—" He drops his hand and squeezes his eyes shut. "My family."

Josie doesn't let herself be fooled. Adam perpetually carries the weight of the Hugheses' good graces on his shoulders. "Yes, the ones whose opinions you worship at the altar of and allow them to suck any happiness out of you like vampires. Did one of their masks slip?"

"My m-mom told me to leave."

If Josie hadn't watched the words leave his mouth, she might not have believed them. Still doesn't, fully. "What does that mean?"

Adam's shoulders are slumped in defeat. "She made me choose."

"'Choose,'" Josie repeats dumbly. "Choose what?" But realization is dawning.

"*Jo*," Adam pleads.

She's not comprehending, not completely, as she steps back and jerks her head for him to come inside. He does so, and she leans against the closed door, arms crossed once more. "Them or Ari?" she asks. She can't help that she's hurt by her lack of inclusion. "He's not here, so I don't know why you are."

248

Adam stands in the middle of the entryway, looking like a ship lost at sea. "Them or, or everything else," he says. "Ari, the city, Jon . . . you." His hand goes to his tie, loosening it further. He's not meeting her eye. "I couldn't do it. I couldn't lose any of you."

"You didn't have a problem pushing me away last week."

"I was wrong," he says. "This whole time. I've been so caught up in how my family wanted me to be that I missed what I had." He lifts his gaze to hers. "I should've fought for you. Back when you first found out about Ari. But I was . . . scared?—about what everything meant, and then things happened with Ari and I, I was worried about my family's reaction and I forgot. I forgot how much I needed you."

"How do I know you're not saying this because Ari ended things and you need someone to fill a hole?"

Adam wipes his nose with the cuff of his sleeve. He gives a wet laugh; it's a sorry sound. "There is a very Josie-shaped hole in my heart. Trust me. Even if . . . even if Ari doesn't want anything to do with me, I hope you'll forgive me. I need you regardless."

Josie's not crying, there's just something in her eye. "How did you know I'd be here?"

"I just needed to see." He sniffs, then adds quietly, "Everyone else is gone."

They watch each other, Josie performing a patented Ramona Taylor visual X-ray. Adam's pale, thinner than when she last saw him. The dark circles beneath his eyes aren't new, but they're darker, starker against the lack of golden skin. She feels like all the markings are her fault.

"I'm so *mad* at you," she says. "I thought you were the one person in my life who, I dunno, thought I meant something to and you lied to me. And then you got together with the very person you lied to me about, and it felt like you didn't need me anymore, you know? And I need you. I need you so much it's not even funny. You're my best friend, and not just because you're my only friend or whatever, but because I like being around you and I like that you trust me and make me feel like I'm important or whatever and I like that you're so genuine and, and—" She's losing steam here. "—I'm *nicer* to people when I'm with you, which is—nice? Don't you dare start laughing at me, Adam Hughes; I'm trying to apologize." She pulls at the hair tie on her wrist and looks anywhere but him. "I'm sorry about what I said. Everything I said. I never meant to bully you into doing things. I shouldn't have pushed so hard. I'll work on it, okay? I'll be better."

Adam's stupid watery smile has caused her heart to grow three times its own size. Josie's only mildly annoyed about it. "You're so dumb," she says, betrayed by her tears. She pushes away from the door and meets Adam in the middle, wrapping her arms around his neck and pulling him in tight.

"I missed you so much," he eventually says, slotted back next to her where he belongs. "And your hair is suffocating me."

"Worse ways to die, dude." They part, but she keeps her hands on his shoulders. His face is still puffy, but there's a more relaxed air to him now. "Did you eat?"

"I'm not very hungry."

"What else happened? With your family?" The momentary levity wanes and she instantly backtracks. "Okay, actually, put a pin in that, but we are going to talk about it. Come upstairs. You can change and we'll watch a Hallmark movie. All the Christmas ones are up."

Adam pauses at the foot of the stairs. "Is it okay that I parked in the driveway?"

"Yeah, Ramona's gone for the weekend—and her groupies."

Adam pushes a hand through his hair, eyes flicking toward Ramona's room like he doesn't actually believe her. But he nods and follows Josie up the stairs.

Josie's determined to get more food into Adam despite his protests.

She points him to her room, telling him to borrow a shirt, and begins heating up a plate of food. She's watching the timer count down from five when a figure suddenly and silently joins her in the kitchen. It's not Adam.

Josie blinks at Silas's appearance. He looks frazzled, caught between appeasement, panic, and annoyance. "Hey."

"Uh . . . hey?" Josie says. The microwave beeps.

Silas bats the implied question away with a flick of his wrist. "Look, is Adam here? I, ah, hate to do this, but do you think he can take off?" Downstairs, there's the sound of people filling the entryway. The volume surges as they start up the stairs. Silas begins moving toward the hallway, in the direction of Josie's room. "Is he in your room? I can talk to him."

"What's going on?" Josie asks again.

"The interstate was closed, winter conditions up in Tahoe and we had to turn back." His eyes shift toward her room again and the pieces fall into place: Ari is here, Adam's car fully visible in the driveway, the two on an inevitable crash course.

Josie knows enough that Adam's not in the right state to see Ari—maybe ever, but especially now. Bodies trickle into the kitchen now, the TV room. No sign of Ari or Ramona, only those who barely spare Josie a second glance, grumbling about the lack of Tahoe in their future. Josie hopes Ramona's keeping Ari out of the picture until she can scurry Adam away.

Fate, however, has different plans. First, Adam appears in the doorway of the kitchen, wearing a t-shirt and a pair of Josie's sweats. "Jo?" he asks, eyeing Silas as he walks to stand next to Josie.

Silas and Josie both open their mouths to speak, but then Ari and Ramona are there. Ramona's expression is murderous, but Ari's gaze is only for Adam. There's the record scratch, the freeze-frame shot where everyone momentarily stares at one another, the calm before the storm—Silas defeated; Adam stunned; Josie, inexplicably, wired.

Everybody talks at once.

"Adam—" says Ari.

"Look—" says Silas.

"I thought I told you—" says Ramona.

"Don't you fucking dare," starts and finishes Josie.

Only Adam stays out of the garble. He looks at Josie, eyes wide, and she understands that even though she can't make him do anything he doesn't want to, that she needs to be better about letting him steer his own ship, she can still take the reins when he so obviously pushes the panic button.

"We'll head out," she says. It's not a retreat but a strategic lateral move—for Adam's sake.

"Wait," Ari says, stepping forward. "Stay, please. Really." He gives Ramona, then Silas a meaningful look. Back to Adam, "You're welcome here as much as I am."

Adam's looking back at him, his longing spelled out clearly, his entire body is practically leaning toward Ari; a plant starved for light.

"Are you okay?" Ari asks, gentle enough that Josie feels like an intruder.

"I miss you so much—" Adam's voice cracks. He blinks and his eyes clear of their hazy, faraway look. His face goes beet red. "I—" he says, this time to Josie, silently pleading.

"My room," she decides. She herds him toward the hall, hears Silas's suggestion that he and Ari go pick up take-out somewhere. She trusts Silas to keep Ari away for now.

In her room, door shut, Adam stands like a survivor after a hurricane. Or maybe still during one, because Josie's whirling around him, turning on her bedside lamps, moving clothes off her bed and shoes into her closet.

Adam crawls into bed where she's pulled back the comforter. Josie joins him under the covers. He's facing her, curled up on his side, hands under the pillow; pretty as a picture, as depressing as a funeral. "Tell me everything," she says.

He tells her—about the dinner with his family, the conversation with his mom. When he finishes, he adds one last thing, a non sequitur that she understands without elaboration:

"I think I love him," he whispers, his voice a small thing. And Josie's heart goes *oomph*.

Chapter 30

Adam has survived the forced separation from his family; the egg pushed from the nest. The look on his mom's face when he told her his choice will never be erased, nor the image of her breaking down, pushing him away, and telling him to leave, to "just *go*, Adam." The sight of only his grandma on the porch as he set his duffel in the trunk of his car, everyone else still inside, filled in the remaining gaps. Years of scratching at the door and windows, begging to be accepted, for nothing.

Except Josie is here, and she's the exact homecoming he needs. She's the surest part of his life at the moment, her presence beside him a lighthouse on the shore.

For the first time in a very, very long time, Adam's body wins out over his churning mind and aching heart: he sleeps.

He wakes in darkness to movement at the bedroom door. A sliver of light from the hallway disappears, the sound of loud and happy voices cut off. Faintly, he can see Josie's outline as she returns to the bed and slides in next to him. When she notices him watching her, she whispers, "I was moving your car out of the driveway. Ramona was having a conniption, making Silas text me."

"Oh, sorry. Thank you," he replies. The familiarity of her scent is a boon. "What time is it?"

"Almost midnight. They're all drunk and whining about first world problems." She's on her side, facing him. "How are you feeling? Are you hungry?"

He is a bit, but he doesn't want to leave the safety of Josie's room right now. "I'm okay." Then, because he doesn't want her to bring up what he admitted earlier, he asks, "Um, how have you been lately?"

There's a flash of her smile in the dark, like she knows he's skirting larger topics but is willing to humor him. "Oh, you know. I've had better semesters. Lots of time for introspection. Can't say I care for it."

"Did you go to any shows?" Adam finds himself suddenly concerned for her social life, disappointed that he hadn't given it a thought before.

"Some. I went to one with Silas."

Adam stills at the name, thinking of his few interactions with Ari's roommate. He'd never mentioned spending time with Josie. "Are you two . . . ?"

Josie snorts. "*No.* He's too . . ." She waves her hand, a vague gesture. "Just friends."

"Oh." They're still whispering. "And, um, Ramona?"

He senses rather than sees Josie hold her inhale for a second too long. "Funny you should ask," she says in an odd voice.

"What happened?"

She shifts next to him. "So I might've maybe ended up deciding to write a piece on her."

Adam blinks in surprise. "That's— Um, okay . . ."

"I think Ramona did some illegal stuff with her mom's political position. Like, I know she did." When Adam doesn't respond, she lays out her theory. Then, almost shyly, says, "Tilton said it's the best pitch she's ever seen as a professor."

Adam's breath catches and he reaches to grab her hand. It's the one thing Josie's ever wanted: recognition. "Jo—"

"I know." She squeezes his hand back.

"You're going to talk to Ramona?"

Josie sighs. "And her mom, and probably Andrew. Tilton says I have to, to get all sides."

Adam considers the situation. "Are you prepared for the fallout?"

"Yeah," she says after a moment. "I don't expect to be taken out by the mob. And what Ramona and Andrew are doing is crazy illegal."

"No, I know. But they could still get back at you somehow. They're both well known, and Nara's a political figure, and—"

"Adam." Josie bumps her knee against his. "I want to do this. This is a chance for me to bring attention to something that's affecting people. I'm not going to shy away from it."

"What about conflict of interest? You're her roommate—"

Josie waves that one off. "This is bigger than that. And anyway, she's making me move out." She tells him of the property management company's demand.

Adam's head spins with all the information. One thing at a time. "Does Tilton know about your connection with Ramona?" he asks, bracing himself for the answer he knows is coming.

"When I pitch the story I'll let the paper know, just to be safe, okay? This is a bigger deal than her kicking me out."

Adam remains doubtful, but says, "I think you definitely have something. That's really, really impressive you found it, Jo. Truly."

"Thanks." She emphasizes the 's' like she's a mix of cautious and proud. Then, "I missed you."

"I missed you too."

"No more secret boyfriends who are best friends with my roommate, okay?"

Adam doesn't reply. His insides collapse at the reminder. Seeing Ari today felt like a freight train to his chest, all the memories and wants back, tenfold their original impact.

"Did you mean what you said about him?"

Without a doubt. Still, he pauses first. "Yes."

Josie doesn't say anything for a long while, just rolls onto her back to look up at the ceiling. But she doesn't let go of his hand either. Finally, she breaks the silence. "You should tell him."

Adam only shakes his head. "He stopped things. I need to respect that."

"Adam, you're in love with someone for the first time in your life. Tell him how you feel. Tell him that you spoke to your mom." She rolls back over, closer now, so their faces lie only inches from one another. "It's time for you to create a life that makes *you* happy, not your family."

"*You* make me happy," he says. "I wasn't just saying that earlier. I need you in my life."

"Gee, thanks," she says drily, but he can tell she's happy about his words. "I'm going to be better, okay?" When he looks at her, confused, she continues. "I'm not gonna hitch my happiness to you telling me absolutely everything. There'll be a learning curve, but I'll work on it."

"I still should've told you. I should've trusted you more. I *do* trust you. I was wrong to not."

She rubs her thumb across his knuckles. "Deal," she says.

After a minute, Adam asks in a tentative voice, "What if he doesn't want anything to do with me? What if— I mean, we've tried twice now and I was bad at it—"

"C'mon, dude. It's time to hit the reset button and go ask the guy you love for five minutes of his time. Tell him everything; lay it all out. At the very least you'll get it off your chest. At the best, I dunno, he sweeps you off your feet. My money's on the latter, because it looked like he actually had hearts in his eyes earlier in the kitchen. Regardless, I'll be there for you after it's all done. Unless Ramona murders me in cold blood."

Adam's eyes go wide. "Do you think she'll be that mad?"

Josie snorts. "Counting on it. I don't care. This is my shot and I'm taking it. Now you need to take yours." She squeezes his hand to emphasize the next part. "I'm here. Whatever happens, I'll be here. I was wrong last time. I'm never making the mistake of ditching you again."

The distant sound of voices has died down. Adam feels his limbs grow heavy, warm under the covers and at Josie's words. He listens as her breathing begins to slow next to him. Just before he nods off, she whispers, "Adam?"

"Mmm?"

"I'm proud of you. For having that conversation with your mom."

It's quiet, the house settling around them. "Thanks, Jo."

Something warm, somewhat smooth, and delicious-smelling is plopped on his cheek, waking him the next morning. Adam blinks a few times, notices the late-morning sun shining through the bedroom window, and takes a moment to remember the heaviness of the previous day.

When more weight is added to his face, he sits up. "Jo, *gross!*"

Two pancakes fall onto the bed, leaving smears of chocolate chips on his shirt and the duvet cover. Adam wipes his face, and sure enough, melted chocolate sticks to his fingers when he pulls them away.

Josie cackles next to him, sitting cross-legged with a plate of pancakes on her lap. He reaches to wipe his hand off on her face, but she dodges him and stands. "It's almost eleven and I was bored," she says. "*And* I made you pancakes. I couldn't let them get cold."

"Then come politely shake my arm!" he says, rolling out of bed and making for the bedroom door. "I don't want a pancake facial!"

She's still laughing as he heads for the bathroom, stuttering in his steps when he considers the likelihood of Ari still being at the house. He stops, listening hard, and hears nothing.

"They're not here," Josie says, scooting by him for the kitchen. "Just you and me. Wash up and come eat."

Moving through the Valley house is a touch disconcerting to Adam. His ban from the premises has made him jittery, like he's doing something wrong by using the bathroom or sitting at the banquette next to Josie.

She seems perfectly relaxed, though. Hands him the syrup like it's no big deal.

"Sorry for sleeping so late," he tells her.

"Eh. I only woke up an hour ago," she replies through a mouthful of pancakes, waving her fork. He smiles at her with a fond shake of his head.

They eat mostly in silence. He's refamiliarizing himself with Josie's movements—the aggressive way she cuts her food, the constant rearranging of her curls so she doesn't end up eating strands of hair. She catches him watching and narrows her eyes. "What?"

He only presses his lips together, fighting another smile, and continues to eat.

When they're done, Adam washing their plates up at the sink and setting them in the dishwasher, Josie interrupts their reverie. "I'm gonna talk to Ramona today."

He looks over, hands sudsy as he turns the faucet on. She looks determined.

"I'm banking on her not being thrilled, and I don't want your conversation with Ari to be colored by it, so you should do your grand reveal beforehand."

"Oh." Adam looks back at his hands, focuses on rinsing and drying them before sitting beside Josie again. "What're you going to say to her?"

"The truth."

"How do you think she'll react?"

Josie scrunches her face. "I may need to crash at your place for a few nights."

Adam's brow is still pulled tight. He starts to say, "But what if—"

"Nope. You're cut off," Josie says. She pulls his phone out from her sweatpants' pocket and slides it across the table. "Text Ari."

Adam eyes the device, then Josie. She only raises her eyebrows and pointedly looks at the screen. When he picks it up, he sees there's already a text from Ari, sent the night before: *I miss u 2.*

Adam's heartbeat picks up in pace. He glances at Josie again, who's returning the syrup to the fridge, giving him space. Adam takes a deep breath and slowly types out, *Hi, I was wondering if you have time to talk?* He only exhales once the text is sent.

Josie grabs her laptop from the bedroom and they end up on the couch, her looking up shows at the Throne Room, crowding him to one side with her sprawl, legs atop his, the glow of the screen giving heightened attention to the frizz of tiny curls around her face, and *she's here.* Every beat of his heart is the snap of a victory banner in the wind announcing the return of his best friend.

It's not the only reason he feels lighter this morning, either. The conflict that reared its head inside him as his mom unwelcomed him home hasn't gone away, but there's a confusing tangle of loss and freedom, a weight off his shoulders. Adam feels the pain of his mom's words and her dismissal, can outline exactly what he's missing now, and will miss moving forward—dinners and game nights and drives to see Christmas lights and warm days at the lake and chatter from his siblings. He's lost in it, in the way the memories past and moments future swirl down the drain.

Maybe, though, despite the loss, he gets to place the pieces of himself around what he knows to be true—that he loves Ari. And the closest he's ever felt to the love of God that he's been taught about his entire life is what he felt with Ari's hand around his, or with Josie at his side.

His phone vibrates from the coffee table. Adam stares, his heart now pounding in his throat and ears and eyes. "Can you, um—"

Josie obliges and grabs the phone off the coffee table to read. "He's asking if you want to meet up." She looks up at him, wearing a smile packing a million emotions.

"What is it? Did he say something else?"

"No." She hands him his phone. "I'm being dumb. Go. But maybe shower first."

"Jo—"

"I have you back is all," she cuts in. "I have you back and you and Ari are gonna fix things and I won't have you anymore." She closes her laptop and leans it against the front of the couch. "And if it's not with Ari it'll be with some other guy, who'll be so lucky to have you and it won't be the same. It'll never go back to being just you and me. I know I'm being childish about it, and I know it's actually good for me, but it sucks."

Adam doesn't immediately know what to say but tries something anyway. "Um, you'll always be—"

"Don't do that. Don't say we'll be friends forever—god, how humiliating." Josie scrubs her face with both hands. "It's fine. I'm leaving after graduation anyway."

He scoots closer to curl his arms around her waist, laying his head on her stomach. "You're the most important person in my life," he says into her t-shirt. She settles a hand on his head. He doesn't give a timeline, doesn't add *forever* or *for now*, just says it like it is, because it's true.

The lookout spot in Russian Hill feels different as Adam parks. Perhaps because he's full of hope, rather than last time's forboding.

As he looks out at the view, he can feel how close the Adam of only a couple months ago remains. There hasn't been a perfect solution to bring him here, but he realizes he's reached a space that feels like peace, and he wants to hang on as long as he can.

Approaching footsteps have him turning.

The sight of Ari is a heat wave; it's sliding into a jacuzzi on a cold winter's day; it's curling up by the fire with a favorite book. If Josie's like coming home, Ari is the sunshine through the windows.

"Hi," Adam says, aiming for politeness but stumbling into helplessness.

"Hey." A bit of nerves are evident in the tremor of Ari's hand as he readjusts the baseball hat he's wearing. "Si and Ramona said I shouldn't have said yes to seeing you."

Adam's drinking in the sight of him. "They're good friends."

Ari nods, shifting his weight from one foot to the other. There's a lengthy pause before he says, "You said you wanted to talk?"

They settle on the low wall and stare out. Gray clouds hang low over the Golden Gate Bridge in the distance.

"I'm sorry about Tahoe," Adam begins. "I know you were looking forward to it."

"Hasn't been a whole lot to be happy about lately, to be honest." Ari shrugs, hands in his pockets. He looks over at Adam. "How was being with your family?"

"It was . . ." Adam recalls his mom's words to him, then firmly pushes them away. The cool breeze has him pulling his jacket tighter around him. "Um, it answered some questions."

"What kind of questions?"

Adam lets out a soft laugh. "Well. For starters, I'm—pretty sure I'm in love with you?"

Next to him, Ari goes completely still, and Adam feels fear as intensely as a physical presence. He thinks of Josie, getting ready to face Ramona, and reminds himself that she's doing the scarier thing by far.

Ari speaks: "D'you— You're not just saying that? Like—" He stops like he's waiting for a punchline.

Adam can't meet his eyes, but keeps talking. "I've had a lot of, um, realizations? Over the past few days. Like how lucky I was to, to be with you, and how amazing you are. I mean, I already— I already knew that, but the context around things changed? I've sorted some of my concerns out, and I— I know I wasn't ready last time. I was saying yes to a relationship I wasn't ready for yet, and I'm so sorry for what it did to you. What *I* did to you. I made you feel lesser than you deserve."

"Adam—"

"Wait— Please, I need to say this. I need to apologize for, for leaving you hanging so many times, and not being willing t-to explain how I was feeling in the moment." He looks over to find Ari watching him. "I spoke with my mom."

Something in Ari's eyes flickers with hope.

"She said I can't be in a relationship with someone I love and still be welcome home."

Ari exhales, and Adam can sense him pulling away, emotionally, physically. "I chose you," he says. Then, an amendment: "I mean, I chose this. My life here. Josie. Jon. The idea of you, of, of being with you." His face is warm now. "You said you didn't want to date someone who wasn't comfortable being with you. I respect that. I do. But I want you to know that I'm in love with you, and you make me feel things I never thought I'd be able or willing to feel."

"Fuck, Adam." Ari's laugh sounds wet, and he rubs at his eyes before looking over. "I've been gone for you since the moment we met. It's just that— What about all the church stuff? And hearing your mom's voice?"

Adam frowns, contemplating what that looks like now. "I want to say I don't care about that stuff anymore, but I know that's . . . not true," he says slowly. "I still need to figure out where I fit with it all.

But I know how I feel about you, so."

"I can't do this again if you're not for real."

"I am."

"Like, you can't leave if we fight and then ghost me for days. I can't handle it. I don't care if that makes me sound pathetic. I'm not good at—"

"Ari, I won't. I won't. I promise."

"And I want to be able to kiss you without feeling pervy. I mean, I want you to want it, obviously, but I'd prefer it if you didn't, like, flinch or hesitate every time I touch you."

"I'll be better. I'm, I still have some things to work through, and, and the, um, sex part isn't—" He shakes his head and takes a steadying breath. "I want this."

Ari watches as Adam moves closer, their thighs touching. "You and Josie made up?"

Adam nods, reaches out to brush his fingers against Ari's cheek. Empowerment; that's the unfamiliar current running along Adam's skin.

"Adam," Ari says, his hand wrapping around Adam's wrist. The way he's looking at Adam is something alive. "Tell me you mean it."

"I mean it." Adam settles his other hand so he's holding Ari's face. He's not thinking about his mom or his family or the weight of shame that's burdened his shoulders for years. The only sense he has is that Ari is here, and Ari equates a terrifying joy that Adam can't help but run toward. He loves him. He loves him. He loves him. "I love you."

Ari reaches out, hands mirroring Adam's, his face blasted wide open with the same want and fear coursing through Adam. "I believe you," he says.

When Adam remembers to breathe again, it's Ari he inhales.

Chapter 31

Josie envelops the expected pain as Adam leaves, hope and terror mixed across his face. It's the same sharp pain she felt when he first said he was in love, and it's there now, but a little duller. Probably because she's analyzed her reaction over the past day. She'd been pushing Adam to do exactly this for years, to find a guy to be with. Part of her must've cataloged his ongoing guilt over his sexuality and marked that as a success, cruel as it might be, in her favor. If Adam didn't date, him being gay was insurance for Josie to have him as at her side forever. She'd internalized it, and the first real fracture destroyed the foundation she'd unwittingly built their friendship atop.

It means now that Adam is back, she has to be careful. With herself and with him and with anyone who'd ever get so close.

Still, she's going to have to fake her enthusiasm over the possibility of Ari and Adam for a bit.

Anyway, with Adam safely ensconced off-site, it's time to face her own demon.

Sans Evelyn, Josie texts Silas: *I need to talk to Ramona. It's urgent.* He replies saying they're at a spa together, but he'll see what he can do. That was a few hours ago. Of course Ramona is making her wait.

When Josie finally hears movement from the stairs, it's Silas, not Ramona, who's lounging on the couch in the TV room. He's scrolling on his phone, a scarf bundled around his neck.

She feels the recognition of him consistently choosing Ramona, choosing Ari over her like a wave, and then moves forward anyway.

"It's not *that* cold," she says, falling next to him and tugging at the end of the scarf.

"Your house is freezing," Silas says.

"It's hard work to keep our frigid hearts frozen. Where's Ramona?"

"Changing in her room." Silas eyes her. "We stopped by my place on the way back. Ari said he was going to meet up with Adam. Many pieces of advice were given, but Ari looked pretty hopeful."

Josie mimes zipping her lips. "Not in the business of micromanaging my friends."

Silas rolls his eyes. "You and I both know that's not true. What do you have to talk to Ramona about?"

Josie opens her mouth to reply, and finds herself wanting to ask if he knows Ramona's trying to make her leave, yet afraid to do so. If he does know and chose not to tell her, what does that mean? "Roomie stuff," she says. "Glad to see you're back to getting quality time with your bestie. How much would I have to pay you to go pick up food for me?"

"Not enough money in the world. It's even colder outside."

"Ugh." Josie pushes off the couch. "Send Ramona my way when she's done, will you?"

"Can do."

She pauses, an unfortunate pillar of something like regret rising inside her as she glances back at him. Silas, her sole friend for a while. Even with everything that's happened since, there's an imminent loss that hurts more than she expected.

Silas, still on his phone, catches her hesitation and looks up. "Everything okay?"

"Just—thanks," she says, rocking back on her heels. "For everything you did. While Adam and I were. You know."

His expression turns lazy, cocky with a smile that she knows better than to believe. "The star-crossed friends are reunited. Shakespeare would be thrilled."

"*Ugh*," Josie says. But she's smiling. She turns, heading into the hallway and reconfiguring how the face-off will go with her roommate, but there's Ramona climbing the stairs. She reaches the top and sees Josie.

"Si said it was, like, an emergency?" Ramona says, walking past her for the couch. Josie reluctantly follows. Ramona curls up next to Silas; two raven-haired popular kids. Ramona flicks her wrist. "So?"

For a nanosecond, Josie's head goes blank, and she's on the verge of word-vomiting noise before her brain catches on at the last second. "I'm writing a story about you," she says.

Silas looks guilty. "Look, I know I—"

Ramona cuts him off. "I honestly thought college students were supposed to be smarter than this. I made it very clear I wasn't interested."

Josie's still hovering by the doorway and it feels weird, possibly looks like she's scared, and she's not. She moves farther into the room. "Yeah. Well. You're gonna want to be interested in this because it's kind of serious."

Ramona shifts from skepticism to wariness at this remark, and Josie takes that as her cue to sit—in one of the armchairs across from the couch, so at least she's got some distance.

Then, she shoots from the hip.

"I've been able to confirm that you colluded with Andrew Prosser on a recent vote of your mom's in Congress," she begins, repeating the words she'd practiced with Adam, just the right balance of research and assumption. "Can you explain to me why?"

Across from her, Ramona has a pinched mouth look. "I don't know what you're talking about."

Josie hoped she would say that. "Oh, Ramona." She clicks her tongue. "You do. And now, so do I. Evelyn told me about your deal with Andrew—"

"Evelyn quit months ago—"

"I know Andrew dumped a ton of stock right before the Innovation Zone Bill failed to pass."

"Ew, do you even hear yourself? The words you're using?"

"And the secretary of state website showed off your recent LLC revival, right after the vote. I know you did it."

Ramona's still trying to play it off: "Did *what*? I don't even— Didn't that bill fail?"

"Ramona." Josie's voice is sharp. "This is real. Stop playing dumb."

Still, Ramona doesn't give the emotional ground Josie expects. She only grows extremely still, coiled like a snake. "What would—"

Downstairs the front door opens, and Ari's voice can be heard, loud and bright. Josie stays focused on Ramona, who does likewise.

"What would it take to not write the article?" Ramona asks.

That's the confirmation Josie was hoping for. Triumph begins to take hold, but she quells it with a desperation to stay professional. She simply shakes her head. "It's happening. This is a big deal. I'm not going to not write the piece." Then, "It would look better if you answered some of my questions, I think. Better in the article. For you." A pause for semi-dramatic effect (not Adam's suggestion; Josie's decision). "And your mom."

"Josie." That's Silas, mouth pulled down as he stares at her.

Ari enters at that moment, not immediately reading the room— understandably, because he's grinning over his shoulder at Adam, who locks eyes with Josie, his face flushed.

"I didn't . . ." Ramona trails off.

"What's up?" Ari asks, smile fading.

Ramona remains in her unflappable state. Features relaxed, eyes flat, she stares back at Josie. "Andrew was the one who sold off stock, not me."

"Yes, I'm sure that'll hold up real nice in front of a judge. You two are linked. I report on Andrew, I report on you."

"I'll get a lawyer."

Josie raises her eyebrows. "I mean, you certainly have the cash to. Care to share what you want so bad you're willing to do . . . all . . ." The realization hits suddenly, a lightning strike. "Holy shit," she says. "You're buying the house. That's why you're making me move out. That's what you got from Andrew, money to buy the house."

Silas stiffens, but Ramona stays stock-still. The lack of movement looks forced.

Josie gives a hollow laugh. "Unbelievable. Really. This is absolutely insane. You are an *insane* person." She pulls her phone out. "Well, if you don't get a lawyer, I'm sure your parents will. I'm planning to call your mom next. Want me to ask her?"

"What's going on?" Ari again.

"Nobody's going to care," Ramona says. "It's not a big deal."

Josie knows she has the upper ground here, Ramona jumping around from reason to excuse to reason. "It's insider-fucking-trading. People go to *prison* for this kind of stuff. I can absolutely guarantee people are going to care."

"I'll—" Ramona's face is white, like a fear she never considered is now finally dawning. "I'll talk to my mom. I'll tell her."

"Okay? That doesn't change the situation. Where's Andrew in this, by the way? You guys got what you wanted out of each other and are both enjoying your spoils separately?"

"Can I talk to you?" Silas asks Josie.

She swats away his question, keeping her attention on Ramona. "This is happening and ignoring it or fighting me isn't going to make it go away. You've done something wrong, and I'm going to report on it. The *LA Times* plans to publish the piece next week." It doesn't even feel like a lie, considering how highly Tilton was praising her. Hell, this has to be *New York Times* level by now.

"Jo." A gentle warning from Adam.

"I don't—" Ramona says, another splinter in her demeanor. "I just wanted— This doesn't have to be a thing." So help her, there are actually tears in Ramona's eyes. "Can you just— Can I give you something else? I can find something else for you to write."

Forgo a groundbreaking article? Josie isn't impressed. "Nah."

"*Ohmigod*, why are you doing this? This won't look good for you either. I'll make sure of it."

Josie sees Adam flinch in her periphery, catches a grimace from Silas, and lets a smile spread across her face. "Are you threatening me? The reporter who's writing a story about your political bribery?"

"You're hardly a reporter," Ramona shoots back. "You're a college student doing a homework assignment. Nobody's going to publish this story knowing you're my roommate. That's, like, super biased."

Josie stands, trying not to ball her hands into fists. She's buzzing with adrenaline. "Well, it's not like I'll be living with you for much longer, huh? You're the one seeing to that. I'm not going to be intimidated into not publishing this story. Even if no one takes it, I can still put it online; it's the twenty-first century."

There's a hand at Josie's elbow, and she pulls in her arm sharply with a curse only to find Adam has moved close. "Let's go," he says.

Josie glares at Ramona. "Do you want to make a statement or not?"

Ramona's forehead is against her palm. Ari's sitting on her other side, hand on her back and whispering something. Silas's hurt has transformed to outright distaste as he watches Josie.

"Don't be pissed at me because your precious Ramona did something wrong," Josie bites out.

"Perhaps," he says coolly. "But there are ways to go about bringing it up without airing someone's dirty laundry for the entire world to see."

"Tell that to the United States' justice system."

Silas only shakes his head with profound disappointment. Josie throws off Adam's hand again, and stomps out.

In her bedroom, she begins flinging clothes into a duffel bag, still electric with the showdown. Adam stands by the closed door, twisting his hands together. "Um—"

"Don't," snaps Josie. "Just don't right now, okay? If you're going to be in here, then don't start." She puts her back to him, packing, listening hard for him to leave.

He doesn't, only walks over to the window to grab another pile of clothes to bring over to the bed. They pack in a tense silence. Josie has no idea what to expect from Ramona next, can't bring herself to have the audacity to hope for even a formal statement on the situation. Will probably end up with nothing but a line about how Ramona Taylor declined to comment. Josie wasn't trying to stoke the flame by telling Ramona it would look better for her if she said something. It will.

But there's still Nara. She can't shut Josie out, not completely, not as an elected official.

Swinging the strap of a bag over her shoulder, Josie leaves her room, striding down the hall for the stairs, scrolling to the congresswoman's contact info. Ramona and company are still in the front room, based on the murmurs. Adam remains quiet behind her.

She hits the entryway just as the phone begins to ring. Nara answers. "Josie?" She sounds concerned, and Josie wonders if she somehow knows—if Ramona has already spun the situation in her favor. But there's genuine worry in her voice as she asks, "Ramona's on the phone with Ashland. Is everything okay?"

Josie opens her mouth to reply when the phone is yanked from her hand.

She spins around, vision going red. "You motherfu—"

Silas has hung up the call. She's never seen such hatred contorting his features. Behind him, at the bottom of the stairs, Ari hangs back by Adam.

"I'd like to speak with you," Silas says.

"Get fucked," Josie spits. "And give me back my phone." She lunges for it, but Silas dodges her.

Adam steps forward; Ari grabs his arm.

Silas doesn't take his eyes off Josie as he says, "Can we have a moment alone, please?"

Josie's breathing like a bull, but after a moment, snaps *"fine"* and crosses her arms.

Ari tugs along Adam by the hand, across the entryway, Adam giving Josie a worried look as he passes.

Josie looks to the stairs in question.

"She's on the phone with her parents." Silas moves so he's barricading himself between the stairs and Josie. "Josie. I am asking you as a friend to please not do this."

"Silas."

"It will ruin her life."

"Spare me. Ramona ruined her life all by herself. This was seriously insane, what she did—and all because she was sick of her mom's nitpicking?"

"Not even a little bit of empathy? Really, Josie?" Silas says with what looks like genuine disbelief. "I thought someone who had her own struggles with her mom might be able to see the situation with a *touch* more clarity—"

"Don't you dare try to talk Ramona a way out of this. At least her mom cares in the first place!"

"Nara caring means complete control of Ramona's life. Is that what you would want? God, Josie, you don't know what it's been like—"

"And you helped her cover it up!" Josie explodes. She won't hear

272

any attempts at guilt-tripping, not now. "You found out what Ramona was doing and told me to stop!"

"So I could talk her down without turning it into a whole thing."

"Fat load of help you were. She didn't stop, did she? It's absolutely a *thing* now, Silas."

"Times a hundred, thanks to you."

Josie wants to scream. "I'm not going to feel guilty about reporting on this! You and Ramona don't get to pretend there aren't consequences to your stupid methods!"

"I know there are consequences—"

"Then fucking act like it! And give me my *phone!*"

Silas, unbelievably, is still calm, is still trying to explain it all away. "Ramona's formulating a plan with her parents—"

Josie curses, her chance at surprising Nara lost.

"Ramona said she's willing to allow you to continue living here in exchange for not doing the piece. I didn't know she was trying to force you out. I'm sorry about that." One of his hands twitches for his pocket, where she's sure a pack of cigarettes is tucked away. "I know Ramona hasn't been kind to you. But it's more to do with her parents than anything. You shouldn't take it personally—"

"I'm not doing this because I have a chip on my shoulder." Josie blows a stray curl out of her face with a huff. "I don't even care that she's kicking me out. I'm doing this because it's *news*, even if it is the most privileged, whiny-baby tantrum I've honestly ever heard of. Her preferred day job for the rest of her life is posting selfies and she's pouting that her mom wants a little more merit out of her daughter?"

"Not everyone has dreams of higher education or writing world-changing news articles, but everyone acts like if you're not doing something worth winning the Nobel Peace Prize over, it's worth nothing. I wish people would stop shitting on her for doing something she likes."

"She's a victim," Josie snorts. "Right, sorry, must've missed that part."

"Fuck off, Josie," he snarls. Finally, a tell. "Just because someone doesn't fit your standards doesn't mean you get to be a dick about it. You think Ramona doesn't know what people say about her? It's all there, right in the comments for the world to see. These anonymous assholes who criticize every fucking thing about her, and she takes it. From them, from her mom. She hears it all and still shares extremely personal content—"

"—taking a picture of a kale smoothie isn't *extremely personal*—"

"—and she still puts her life in front of others because she knows that a lot of people actually really value her posts and insight, and she's found good friends through it all, and it makes her *happy*. And yeah, she fucked up, but remember Andrew is an older guy with a lot more power and money who guided her along in it. I don't blame Ramona looking for a bit of control in her life for once, and I know she's going to learn from all this. She knows now that she went about it the wrong way."

"Holy shit, dude," Josie says, voice rising again. "You're seriously complimenting Ramona for being a martyr because she posts on social media? She took a bribe to make a vote happen, and when it didn't, she did something illegal anyway. Now she's buying a house with the money. People have a right to know. I would do the same thing if it were you, or if it were—"

"Don't insult my intelligence and say you would still do it if it were Adam. Me? I thought I meant a little more to you, but okay." He takes a step forward. Josie doesn't budge. "Don't pretend the Taylors won't push back on this, that Andrew won't. Everyone will pull out all the stops to make sure you suffer consequences."

"Gee, is that part on the record? If they try to ruin my life, I'll fucking write about it."

"Why do you have to be this way? Is it really just because you want some breaking news story? Is it worth destroying friendships over?"

"I'm not *friends* with Ramona—"

"Damnit, Josie, you're *my* friend!" Silas yells. He visibly forces himself to relax, closing his eyes as he rolls his shoulders. When he opens his eyes again, he hisses, "Do you really not care about your relationships with people? I would never do something like this to you—if it were you involved, or if someone close to you was. Ramona didn't have any ill intent; she got a little too eager and ended up shaking hands with people she shouldn't have. But she's going to fix it. All you'll be doing is drawing attention to a fumble and losing someone who genuinely cares about you."

Silas moves his hand suddenly toward her, and Josie rears back like it's a punch. Then she sees her phone. "Please, Josie," he says as she swipes it from him. "Just—please. You don't have to be cruel."

Josie watches as he moves away and turns sharply for the hallway leading out to the garage.

Outside, the trunk of Adam's car is popped, both Adam and Ari sitting in the back and not speaking. They're close, though, Ari holding Adam's hand between both of his, clutched in his lap.

She tosses her bag next to Adam and unsuccessfully avoids Ari's glare. "Ready?" she asks Adam, not meeting his eyes—assuming he's even trying to meet hers—and heads for the passenger-side door before he answers.

The door slams closed harder than she means, but it seems appropriate: Everyone thinks Josie's being harder, more difficult, more *cruel* than she should be. She shoves her feet against the dashboard and closes her eyes, trying to ignore the ever-growing voices in her head telling her to stop.

Adam doesn't say anything on the drive back to his house. Josie's a thunderstorm in the seat next to him. Nara's texted: *Please call me asap.*

275

"Would you do it?" she finally grinds out as he turns onto his street. "This story. If you were in my shoes."

Adam, as is his way, waits until he's pulled in the driveway and shifted into park before he answers. "Jo," he says softly, looking over at her. "You know I wouldn't."

"But I'm not you," she says. Her gaze is sullenly fixed on the garage door in front of them. "Would you do it if it were me? Knowing what it could mean?"

Adam turns the car off. "Maybe . . . maybe if it were cleaner?" he says. "I— The conflict of interest is suspect, I think. I don't believe a well-established newspaper would run the story, to be completely honest. Not from you."

She doesn't reply, only kneads her forehead. "This is stupid," she mutters, voice scratchy. "This was supposed to be my shot."

"There's still time. You could— *We* could find another topic, Jo. You know I'll help you."

She scoffs, but it's without malice, and as she turns her head away from him, a tear falls. "This was supposed to be *my own*. I found it out. I did it by myself. Tilton—" She has to stop.

"It's still your own, I think," Adam says. "You're the one who ultimately decides what'll happen. Others might not . . . agree? But it's still your shot to take."

Josie roughly swipes at her cheek, still turned away from him.

"I think you should consider what you're willing to live with," he says. "To write the story."

They end up inside after a while—long enough for darkness to fall completely outside. Josie pulls a pair of ear buds out of one of her bags and lies on Adam's bed, back to him, to listen to music.

It's utterly unfair, the situation. Unfair, unjust, unethical. That Ramona is in the wrong and nobody seems to care except for Josie.

That Josie has this opportunity to uncover such an act, launch her career forward when it's most important. That those closest to her are crying foul; Adam in ethics and Silas in friendship.

Adam's asleep when Josie slides out of bed and tiptoes for the door. The house is dark as she moves through it, down two sets of stairs for the front door, and out to sit on the front step.

Her mom doesn't answer when Josie calls, which—fair. But within seconds Josie's phone vibrates with a return call.

"Josephine?"

"Hey, Mom."

They're both quiet, and it's the first time in a long while Josie allows her mind to settle. Five years without talking; what's a little bit longer? Above, the city's glow hides all but a few stars.

Josie intended some sort of showdown, a circling back to the information that set her on her journey to matter—*something* she can claim definitive power over. Instead, she finds herself saying, because no one can break tension like her former plumage, "Did you know I spent two years living with a woman named Feather?"

The reply is all Hicks, the perfect amount of disdain. No projecting of Nara's appreciation or Lois's devotion, and no acknowledgement of how they last left things. "I'm sorry, did you say '*Feather*'?"

Josie recounts the most memorable scenes from her apartment in Bernal Heights, Tarot card readings, nude book club, a shrunken cat head experiment. Her cheeks hurt from grinning, despite the painful thump of her heart as she listens to a sound she rarely heard growing up: her mom's laughter.

Notwithstanding everything they're not saying to each other, there's a sense of equal footing between them. A first. The immensity of what's at hand knocks Josie clean over.

Adam took his chance at combining who he is and who he wants and lost. Ramona is obviously still figuring out how to walk that tightrope, desperate for independence on her own terms, separate from the structured life of a politician's daughter.

Silas's earlier comparison now feels truer than Josie wants it to be: both she and Ramona find their maternal relationships, seemingly opposite on the surface, lacking. It wouldn't be a surprise if Ramona readily volunteered to hear her mom admit regret for having a child in the first place.

Josie has spent her own life fighting to stand out—with no strings attached. She's never needed other people's permission for what she liked or didn't like. She's never needed to rely on others to rubber-stamp her choices. Maybe it's because they've been unextraordinary. Or maybe it's because she hasn't ever had to keep her dreams separate from one another, contingent upon an approving smile and pat on the back. Or, maybe, Josie's only direction was up.

She hangs up the call with reciprocated well wishes. There's no mention of her mom's admission, nothing of their severed ties. In fact, there's no mention of anything with substance. Josie's glad of that.

Crawling back into Adam's bed, she carries a sense of unexpected clarity. The decision here remains without an easy route; it's a blend of TV-static black and white, morphing and scratchy and growing louder as it demands a course. Josie's chance at something versus lost friendship, a trickle-down of justice that leaves bloody footprints in its wake. Silas—gone. The Valley house—gone. Adam—split between two warring parties. But that's not what she needs to base this decision on. If Josie's going to be her own hero, this decision is fully on her shoulders. It's not about how others see her, as the victor or the monster; it's like Adam said: *You should consider what you're willing to live with.*

That is where her thoughts lie as the hours stretch. Shadows deepen as she recalls the sound of Silas's laugh next to Ramona on the couch, Adam in a car-wrinkled shirt on her doorstep, and how different everything will be no matter what she decides.

When she pokes Adam awake, his return to consciousness is a slow thing until it's not and he's simply watching her and waiting.

"Okay," she tells him. "Okay."

Epilogue

Awhining noise fills the car, high-pitched and worrisome. Josie's already made one joke about Adam being so miserable that he can't stop keening, but that only got her as dirty a look as he could muster while sitting ramrod straight in the driver's seat, verbally coaxing his car across the Bay Bridge.

"Even your Subaru is pouting," Josie says, patting the dashboard. It's a sunny afternoon in May, skies clear, wind nipping, and Adam wretched. The traffic is minimal, like the Bay Area has paved the way for Josie's departure. He sighs—*again*, Josie will say, and sure enough, she gives him a wry smile as if she didn't spend all last night wrapped up in a list of lasts alongside him. One last open flirtation with Jon, one last argument with Ari, one last night at the Throne Room, one last carton of Ben & Jerry's, one last of everything.

This ride is only the two of them, the home stretch. It's mostly silent, Adam latching onto his worries about his car so he doesn't have to sit there and think about how his best friend is flying across the country to start the next chapter of her life. She's merely fulfilling a promise she'd made back when he first met her, but he never believed it until this moment.

"Ski trip this winter?" Josie suggests as they cross the entrance to the

280

Oakland airport. "Or you could fly out during the fall, and we could do a New England tour, see all the leaves?" Her voice is uneven now.

Adam swallows. "Yeah."

It's quiet again, the kind that hurts, as Adam pulls up to passenger drop-off. Josie doesn't even comment on Adam not walking her in; this moment feels too personal.

"We've done this before, you know," she says. "It'll be like last summer, FaceTiming every day."

He doesn't point out that there's no timeframe to work toward, no deadline, no stretch of months to get through. This is forever. He only offers another "yeah" as he reaches for her. They hug fiercely.

"I love you," Josie says.

"Love you," Adam says. "You're going to be the best arts and culture reporter Harrisburg, Pennsylvania's ever seen."

Josie snorts wetly, still clinging to him. "Bet your ass I am." Her final story for the capstone: a profile on a local band that often plays at the Throne Room; Tilton said it was fine. Josie pulls back, wipes her face. "Help me with my bags?"

Two large suitcases that barely squeak under the fifty-pound limit are all she has to show for her life in California. It'd been a day of packing and boxes and trips to a donation center, Adam taking time off from his job as a staff reporter with the *Chronicle*, Josie solemnly shaking Feather's hand as she said goodbye—returning to her room in Bernal Heights after all. But not because she was kicked out.

Upon learning about Ramona's under-the-table deal, Nara and Ashland almost immediately sold the Valley house as punishment. According to Ari, Ramona now lives in a much smaller apartment, though still spacious by San Francisco standards, on her own dime and with two roommates.

As one final middle finger, Josie sent an anonymous email to the money-obsessed editor at the *Business Times*, noting that VYBE board member Andrew Prosser had suspiciously sold off a bulk of shares leading up to the high-profile Innovation Zone Bill in mid-November. She let them take it from there, and while no one else was aware of a connection to the Taylors, the optics weren't great; Andrew stepped down.

"Think your car'll be okay?" Josie asks, squinting against the glare off the rear windshield.

Adam shrugs, not really caring at the moment. "Thank you," he says. "For everything."

Josie gives him her feline grin, freckles starting to really gain momentum amid warm, sunny weather. "You have a good life here. I'm glad I got to be part of it." She hugs him again, then maneuvers the suitcases into a better position to pull. "I'll spit on your parents' house as I'm flying over Utah, 'kay?"

Adam gives her a weak smile. "Text me when you land?"

Josie begins walking toward the sliding doors but keeps her attention on him over her shoulder. "I'll FaceTime you, no matter the hour."

"Bye, Jo."

"Love you. Go give Jon and Ari big smooches for me."

With that, she flips her hair over her shoulder, curls wild in the California sun one last time, before strolling into the airport.

Adam settles behind the wheel, crossing his fingers that his car will get him back home. As he pulls out into the lanes of traffic leaving the airport, he has a brief urge to call his mom, find the confusing comfort in her rattling off scriptures about love and friendship, trials everyone goes through to gain wisdom, and tell her how he's been since he last saw her.

Josie's loss isn't the same severing he's still trying to cope with. He may be absent a family but he's wealthy in friendship, even if she's going to be thousands of miles away and three hours ahead. He still has her.

He still has Cal, too. A mentor in book-loving and treat-baking and religion-recovering. Cal, who's become a conduit between Adam and the Mormon church, representative of members who believe in some but not all doctrines. There's a chance there, for Adam to reconcile his lingering beliefs and enduring attraction. Cal has Ari and Adam over for dinner regularly now.

And speaking of which, Adam is wealthy in love. Ari's at a baseball game with Jon, and sure enough, Adam stopped at a red light, he finds a text from him—Ari, who won't offer biblical passages or condemn Adam for his sins but is someone Adam wants to be the best version of himself for; through whom Adam has found his own religion. The text shows a picture of Ari and Jon in the stands, matching hats. *wish u were here. hope ur ok*, Ari adds. *lets go to ur bookstore tonite to help u feel better. luv u.*

Adam replies with a heart emoji and an *I love you, too* just as an incoming text arrives from Josie, not even five minutes after he's dropped her off.

It's a picture of a shelf of books on display, hardback copies found in the same stores in airports everywhere. *reading rec for the road?* she asks.

He calls her. "Jo," he says with a frown. "I offered you some and you didn't want any."

"I know, I know," she says with a laugh. "But I already miss you, and I just realized a book is the closest physically I'll be able to get to you for a while. So. Hit me."

He laughs, too, then sniffs. "Okay," he says, and takes a moment to think. "See if they have *The Hobbit*."

Acknowledgments

The original concept for *Who We Thought We Were* was completely different from what it ended up being, and I have many, many people who helped me get to this iteration.

To those on Reddit (r/BetaReaders) and Scribophile (especially Steve and Amanda), each of you taught me how to make this story that much better.

My writing group: Becca, Cindy, Kristin, and Stephanie. What an honor to work with each of you. I feel so lucky to read your words and receive your feedback—same goes for Susan.

To Chelsey and Tanner, you saw versions of this story many drafts before it was even close to being ready. Thank you for encouraging me. Tanner especially, sharing your experience as a gay man growing up in the Mormon church grounded the work. You and the other anonymous queer people who beta read this book helped solidify Adam.

To my family: Tallahassee, my dog, who happily joined me on numerous walks as I noodled over plot points; to my daughter, oblivious to me writing a book but giving of an unconditional love I hope everyone experiences at least once; and to Alex, my husband and the final checkpoint—thank you for keeping me honest about pizza slice counts (and so much more).

Lastly, to Adam, who was easy to love, and Josie, who wasn't. You will both be part of me forever.

Want to read more
from the characters of
Who We Thought We Were?

Enjoy bonus short stories from Silas, Ari, Ramona, Josie, and Adam. This content will be made available on a review-based system for *Who We Thought We Were* (x amount of reviews across Amazon and Goodreads equals a new point-of-view story being dropped).

Visit **www.ahoeft.com/book** for the review tier and access the first released perspective, from Silas, for free!

www.ahoeft.com/book

or scan the QR code below

Alex Hoeft works as a news reporter covering the Truckee/North Tahoe region in California and Nevada. She has both her bachelor's and Master's in journalism and her reporting has appeared in the *New York Times*. Her short story fiction work has been published in numerous literary journals and she is an editor for *Creation Magazine*. When she's not writing for work or fun, she's wrangling her toddler or reading a book — or doing both at the same time.

Visit www.ahoeft.com to learn more.

 @alexhoeftwrites

substack.com/@alexhoeft